ISBN 978-1-332-25381-4
PIBN 10304843

1 MONTH OF
FREE
READING

at

www.ForgottenBooks.com

By purchasing this book you are eligible for one month membership to ForgottenBooks.com, giving you unlimited access to our entire collection of over 1,000,000 titles via our web site and mobile apps.

To claim your free month visit:

www.forgottenbooks.com/free304843

English
Français
Deutsche
Italiano
Español
Português

www.forgottenbooks.com

Mythology Photography **Fiction**
Fishing Christianity **Art** Cooking
Essays Buddhism Freemasonry
Medicine **Biology** Music **Ancient**
Egypt Evolution Carpentry Physics
Dance Geology **Mathematics** Fitness
Shakespeare **Folklore** Yoga Marketing
Confidence Immortality Biographies
Poetry **Psychology** Witchcraft
Electronics Chemistry History **Law**
Accounting **Philosophy** Anthropology
Alchemy Drama Quantum Mechanics
Atheism Sexual Health **Ancient History**
Entrepreneurship Languages Sport
Paleontology Needlework Islam
Metaphysics Investment Archaeology
Parenting Statistics Criminology
Motivational

BY-WAYS ON SERVICE

NOTES FROM
AN AUSTRALIAN JOURNAL

BY

HECTOR DINNING

LONDON
CONSTABLE AND COMPANY, LTD.
1918

PRINTED IN GREAT BRITAIN

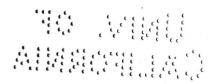

To

AUSTRALIA

NOTE BY THE AUTHOR

THESE sketches were not originally written for publication in the form of a book; and there has been little opportunity of revising them with that object. The idea of collection and publication came late, after they (most of them) had appeared in the daily press or in some other journal; and it came rather by suggestion from friends than on the writer's initiative.

The collection is rough and inconsecutive. It does not attempt to give a complete picture of what was to be seen by an Australian at any stage after embarkation from Australia. It is a series of impressions gained from an outlook necessarily limited. I wrote about the things that impressed me most, chiefly for the reason that they impressed me; there was also the motive of conveying to a small circle of friends some notion of what I saw.

In the light of the offensive fighting of 1917 in Western Europe, a great deal of this book will appear feeble, and even flippant. Descriptions of Egyptian cities and of the Canal-Zone will seem a kind of impertinence, in a book from the War-area, after tales of the fighting in Picardy. But they are published with the belief that after Peace has broken out som soldiers may find an interest in awakening the memory of their first-love in the world outside Australia. For most of them Egypt was that; and though in the desert they often declared themselves " fed-up " with Egypt, it was a transient and liverish judgment, and their relationship with this first-love was never stodgy. For the East of the sort they stumbled across in Cairo and on the Canal, Australians discovered in themselves a liveliness of interest that was almost an affinity.

But no apology for reminiscences of Anzac is called for, let the fighting at Pozieres be never so fierce. It is certain that Gallipoli is overshadowed by the fierce intensity and ceaselessness of the struggle in France. But it is only the intensity of the Turkish fighting that is overshadowed. No intensity of the struggle on the Somme will ever eclipse the intense pathos of that ill-starred adventure on the ridges of Anzac.

These sketches were written hurriedly and in the midst of a good deal of distraction. There has been no time to attend to considerations of style or arrangement of the matter within the limits of single articles. Often I was stuck for leisure, and sometimes for paper. Most of the Anzac sketches were written in the dug-out at nights in circumstances that would have contented transitorily the most Bohemian scribbler. Those from Egypt were mostly scrawled in a desert camp. In either case there was the Censor to reckon with. That is seized as another excuse for inconsecutiveness.

My acknowledgments are due to Messrs. Cassell and Company for their permission to include in this volume the sketch of Anzac which appeared in the *Anzac-Book*.

HECTOR DINNING.

SOMME,
December, 1917.

CONTENTS

BOOK I.—WAITING

SECTION A.—ON THE WAY

CHAPTER   PAGE
I. TRANSPORT - - - 1
II. UP THE CANAL - 13
III. ABBÁSSIEH .. 24

SECTION B.—CAIRO

I. ON LEAVE IN CAIRO - - - 33
II. THE MOOSKI - - 42

BOOK II.—GALLIPOLI

I. THE JOURNEY - 55
II. GLIMPSES OF ANZAC.—I. - 67
III. GLIMPSES OF ANZAC.—II. - 82
IV. SIGNALS - - 92
V. THE DESPATCH-RIDERS - - - 96
VI. THE BLIZZARD - - 98
VII. EVACUATION - - - - - 103

BOOK III.—BACK TO EGYPT

I. LEMNOS - - - - - 111
II. MAHSAMAH - - 118
III. CANAL-ZONE - - - - 127
IV. ALEXANDRIA THE THIRD TIME - - -. 138
V. THE LAST OF EGYPT - - 152

CONTENTS

BOOK IV.—FRANCE

SECTION A.—A BASE

CHAPTER   PAGE

I. ENTRÉE -   163

II. BILLETED -   -   169

III. THE SEINE AT ROUEN   175

IV. ROUEN *REVUE* -   -   180

V. LA BOUILLE -   184

SECTION B.—PICARDY AND THE SOMME

I. BEHIND THE LINES.—I.   -   -   -   188

II. BEHIND THE LINES.—II.   -   196

III. C.C.S. -   -   -   200

IV. THE FOUGHTEN-FIELD   213

V. AN ADVANCED RAILHEAD   -   219

VI. ARRAS AFTER THE PUSH   -   232

SECTION C.—FRENCH PROVINCIAL LIFE

I. A MORNING IN PICARDY   -   242

II. THÉRÈSE -   -   -   251

III. LEAVES FROM A VILLAGE DIARY -   260

IV. THE CAFE DU PROGRÈS   -   270

V. L'HÔTEL DES BONS ENFANTS   -   275

VI. PROVINCIAL SHOPS -   -   278

BOOK I

WAITING

BY-WAYS ON SERVICE

CHAPTER I

TRANSPORT

THERE is something high-sounding in the name Australian Imperial Expeditionary Force. The expedition with which our troopship cast loose justified, so far, our part in that name. The false alarms relating to the date of embarkation, raised whilst we were still in camp, had bred in us a kind of scepticism as to all such pronouncements. When it was told that we would go aboard on Tuesday, most of us emitted a sarcastic "te-hee!" And it was not until on Monday morning our black kit-bags were piled meaningly on the parade ground for transport that we began to rein-in our humour and visualise the method of voyaging and believe there must have been some fragment of truth in what we called the Tuesday fable. We believed it all when the unit marched in column of route on Tuesday to the ship, and the quartermaster brought up the odds and ends on a lorry in the rear. But even so, we were prepared to lie a few hours, at least (and some said a few days), before casting-off. Some of us had even devised visits to and from the homes of our friends,

3

in our mongrel-civilian fashion, to sit once more—
or twice—and say good-bye. Quite the majority of us
saw ourselves swaggering about the port, slaking thirst,
and being pointed at as "the Boys." By two o'clock
the last baggage came over the side, and we sat a
moment to breathe. Some didn't wait to breathe. As
soon as they got well off the pier, the gangways
were raised. By 2.20 we were in motion. The hope
of embarkation, deferred so long, was realised with a
suddenness that almost forbade the saying good-bye.
Many a friend, expecting the hand-clasp, watched the
transport steam relentlessly away; many a man,
bracing himself to the final show of a light heart, saw
the gangway rudely raised as he innocently rested after
the labour of embarkation; and all his show of bravery
ended in an unwonted glistening of the eye and a
silent turning away from those who would have turned
homewards from the shore, but could not. Many
smothered what they felt in the wild hilarity of jin-
goistic dialogue with the shore and with civilian craft
flitting about the transport. Two belated members
of the column tore along the pier towards the ship in
motion, embarked in a launch, and were received; and
three months of irksome sitting in a preparatory camp
were well-nigh gone for nothing. Two others, who had
"gone up the street for an hour" to make merry finally
with their friends, were left lamenting.

It was a Leviathan we found ourselves upon; the
largest boat—as they say—that ever has come to us.
And certainly she carries more men than one ever expected to find afloat (in these waters) on one vessel—
a kind of city full. So huge is she that you wonder,
in the half-logical excitement of the first few hours,

whether she will pitch on the open sea. " Sweet delusion !" smiles the quizzical reader; " you'll soon see." Well, we haven't seen. She has pitched hardly enough to upset the gentlest sucking-dove. That, however, is, perhaps, not all by virtue of our tonnage; so smooth a sea, and so consistently smooth, the tenderest liver could hardly hope for. There have, perhaps, a dozen men been ill; and what are they among so many ? With a smooth start, such as we are blest with, notoriously weak sailors may even hope to get through without a spasm. At least there are those aboard amazed at their own heartiness.

Is there any call to relate the daily routine on a troopship ? Everyone at home, you say, knows it; it's all there is in most letters from the fleet. But all kind and patient readers of these notes may not have friends in the fleet.

Well, then, *réveille* blows providentially later than on shore—six o'clock; providentially and paradoxically, for who wants " a little more folding of the hands to sleep " at sea ? Who, on land, does not, save the few fanatical or deranged ? As many as can find ground-room there, sleep on deck, and have been peeping at the Day's-Eye for half an hour before the strident note crashes along the decks. He is *blasé* and weary indeed who can lie insensible to the dawn here. There is one glory of the hills at sunrise; the sea hath another glory. On land you see the dawn in part, here the whole stately procession lies to your eye, and you see all the detail of the lengthening march defined by the gently heaving sea. He who sees it not has got well to the Devil ! But whether you are of the Devil or not, you obey the summons to get up, and cut short your contemplation of the pageant.   There is no before-breakfast duty, except for a casual swabbing-fatigue. The men mess at seven on their troop-decks; th' sergeants and officers at 8.30.   Thereby hang tw' digressions.

The troop-decks have been installed in the holds, or located where old passenger cabins have been knocked out.   Much refitting of a liner, indeed, had been necessary to make of her a troopship.   The troops have been quartered thus: the sergeants mess and sleep in the old dining-saloon; the officers' mess is the old music-room; both the smoke-room and gymnasium have been transferred into hospitals.   The sergeants and the men sleep in hammocks slung above their mess-tables.   The officers sleep in such cabins as are left standing.

The other digression ought to show why the sergeants and officers (apart from the distinctions which the superiority of those creatures demands) mess an-hour-and-a-half later than the men.   Each unit must appoint, as ashore, an orderly-officer and orderly-sergeant for the day, and part of their duty is to super-vise the issue and distribution of rations.   Each sergeant is given, beside, the supervision of the quarters of a section of the unit, and this includes overlooking the complete setting-in-order after messing.   Each unit in rotation supplies a ship's orderly-officer and ship's troop-deck sergeant, whose duties are general and at the dictation of the ship's commandant.

After breakfast we massage ourselves internally and open up our chests with an hour's exercise, much as ashore; but we must drill in small sections, for want of space.   Most parades, apart from this last, which is universal, are for lectures; in which the officers endeavour to put the theoretical side—appropriately enough, for the practice must precede the theory in any matter whatsoever, but especially in the game of war. We were men before we became philosophers; we digested our food before we thought of physiological research; and we can put a bullet through a vulnerable part before we know much about the chemical combustion preceding the discharge. Lectures are, naturally, more or less directly on the topic of mechanical-transport, in some aspect of it, but some are on topics of generally military importance.

Curious is the variety in the method of receiving lecture; the rank and file do not readily adjust themselves to the academic outlook. "Another b——y lecture, Bill!" "That's all right; 'e'll take a tumble ——" (*The Censor did not pass the rest of this conversation.*) But these are extreme comments, and rather a form of playfulness than serious utterances. Of the rest, some sit it through in a bovine complacency, some take the risks of dozing, some crack furtive jokes; most listen attentively enough. There are many intelligent, well-trained men who prick up their ears here and there and carry on a muffled discussion, in a sort of unauthorised *semina*. There is, on an average, one hour's lecture in the day.

Perhaps half the day is the men's own—clear. It is spent largely in lounging and smoking, partly in sleeping, a little in reading. There are well-worn magazines —such as Mr. Ruskin would disapprove—and little else, except sixpenny editions of the limelight authors. But in reading and such effeminate arts what good soldier will languish long ?

There are sports, of a sort—very sporadic and very confined. They commonly take the form of passing-the-ball and leap-frog.

The Censor has an *ipse dixit* way, and is his own court of appeal. These notes could otherwise be made a little less inconsecutive.

We steamed out of —— a little after dawn in column of half sections, artistically out of step and with the alignment nautically groggy. Our ship took the head of one column; the flagship led the other. That procession is a sight unique, which you are defied to parallel in the annals of passenger shipping. The files come heaving along, like a school of marine monsters disporting themselves. . . .

(Censor at work again.)

In preparation for the European winter in store for us, about which so much has been written and spoken at home, and by which so much Red Cross knitting and tea-drinking have been inspired—as a preparation for this, the weather is becoming intolerably hot. As we approach the line the best traditions of that vicinity are being maintained. We wake in the morning with that sense of lassitude you read of as the regular matutinal sensation of the Anglo-Indian in Calcutta. At six o'clock the sun beats down—or beats along—with as much effect as he achieves high in the heavens in the early Australian summer. No sluggard sleeping on deck but would rather get up and under cover than remain stewing in the oblique, biting rays. At the breakfast-mess, situated in as cool and strategic a position as the brazen sergeants could get chosen, you perspire as though violently exercising. In a few

isolated cases this is justified; but as the day wears
on you perspire without provocation of any sort. The
men on their improvised troop-decks are in hell—and
use a language and attitude appropriate in the circumstances. Not unnaturally, you see the most
grotesque attires designed to make life tolerable. To
the devil with uniformity! Men must first live. The
general effect is motley. Leggings and breeches and
regimental boots are not to be seen—except on the unhappy sentry. A following wind blows upon us, and
just keeps our pace; there is not a breath; the sea is
unruffled; the men lie limp off parade (for parade
persists); one begins to recall an ancient mariner and
the tricks the sultry main played upon him. And dis-
cussions arise, as animated as the heat will allow, as to
whether you'd rather fight in the burning Sahara or
the frozen trenches of Northern Europe.

A change in the manner of life on a troop-ship has
been effected almost as complete as *Oliver Twist* shows
to have taken place in the administration of public
charity, or as Charles Reade shows in the conduct of
His Majesty's prisons. Trooping in the 'seventies
and 'eighties resembled pretty closely transport on an
old slaver—in respect of rations, ventilation, dirt, and
space for exercise. By comparison this is luxurious.
Perhaps the most notable difference is that there is
no beer. The traditional regimental issue of one pint
per man *per diem* (and three pints for sergeants) has
been abolished. It is chiefly in a kind of Hogarth
theory that this is deplorable; most of the romance of
beer-drinking is confined to the art of such delineators
as Hogarth and Thackeray. But amongst a section
of the men the regret is genuine. Especially hard was

a beerless Christmas for many who had been accustomed to charge themselves up with goodwill towards men at that season.

There is a dry canteen, the most violent beverage, obtainable at which is Schweppes's Dry, and hot coffee. Besides, it drives an incessant trade in tobacco, groceries, clothing, and chocolate. We are a people whose god is their belly. During canteen hours an endless queue moves up the promenade-deck to either window of the store, and men purchase, at the most prodigal rate, creature comforts they would despise on land. With many of them it is part of the day's routine.

The leisure and associations of Christmas Day here brought home to the bosoms of most men, more clearly than anything had done previously, what they had departed from. There was hilarity spontaneous; there was some forced to exaggeration, probably with the motive of smothering all the feelings raised by the associations of the festival. You may see, in your " mind's eye, Horatio," the troop-decks festooned above the mess-tables, and all beneath softened with coloured sheaths about the electric bulbs. There is strange and wonderful masquerading amongst the diners, and much song. A good deal of the singing is facetiously woven about the defective theme of " No Beer."

But beside, the old home-songs were given, and here and there a Christmas hymn. It was a strangely mingled scene, but not all tomfooling—not by a great deal.

The Chaplain-Colonel celebrated Holy Communion in the officers' mess at 7 and 8 a.m., and afterwards at Divine-Service on deck addressed the men. Chiefly he was concerned with an attempted reconciliation of

the War with the teaching of Christianity. The rest
of the day went *ad lib.*

. The night is the unsullied property of the men—
in a manner of speaking; but in a manner only. The
same could not be said of the officers, as a body. The
officers, it is true, fare sumptuously every night, and
dress elaborately to dine. The ill-starred private,
his simple meal long since consumed, perambulates,
and looks on at this good feasting from the promenade
deck. " Gawd ! I'd like them blokes' job. Givin'.
b——y orders all day, an' feedin' like that—dressin' up,
too ! 'Struth !. Nothin' better t' do !" Now, that
is the everlasting cry of the rank-and-file against those
in authority. It's in the business house, where the
artificer glares after the managing director—" 'Olds all
the brass, an' never done a day's work in 'is loife !"
It's not so common in military as in civil experience.
But as the artisan overlooks the brooding of the managing director in the night watches, whilst he sleeps
dreamless, filled with bread, so the private tends to
forget that when the Major's dinner is over and his
cigar well through, he may work like the deuce until
midnight, and be up at *réveille* with the most private
of them. The officers are a picturesque group of diners,
and they promenade impressively for an hour thereafter; but they have their night cares, which persist long
after the rank and file is well hammocked and snoring.

But before any snoring is engaged in there is a
couple of hours of yarning and repartee and horse-
play and mirth of all orders. The band plays; the
name of the band is legion aboard, and often several
members of the legion are in action simultaneously,
blaring out their brazen hearts in some imperial noise

about (say) Britannia and the waves and the way she rules them; and if you're one of the dozen ill, you cast up a prayer that she will see fit, in her own time, to rule them rather more straight.

Hardly a night but there is a concert, from which the downright song—as such—is rigidly excluded, and nothing but burlesque will be listened to.

As the sun sets, you may lie and wait the lift of the long southern swell of the Indian Ocean. The sunsets are already coloured with the rich ultra-tropical warmth that caught the imagination of so many who looked on that " Sunset at Agra." " Yet but a little while," you say fondly, " and we shall glide south of that fabled Indian land of spice "; and you shudder at the vileness of contending man. There is danger in the distracting fascination of a voyage of discovery, embraced by this transporting to the land of war. For the old soldier—of whom the fleet carries more than a few —it is hardly possible to realise the utter glow of the imagination in the tyro, seeing for the first time those spaces of the earth he has visualised for twenty years. You, therefore, like a good soldier, put on the breast-plate of common sense, and look up on the fore-mast-head at the tiny mouth of fire, delicately gaping and closing, uttering the Morse lingo (St. Elmo's fire, caught and harnessed to human uses, by some collective Prospero) and make an attempt to construe in your clumsy, 'prentice way.

Almost you will always fall asleep at this, and lie there a couple of hours. And when you wake you go on lying there; and it is of little consequence whether you lie there all night, or not, in the delicate tropic air. And often you do so, and dream of all things but war.

UP THE CANAL

WE put into the outer harbour at Aden for some hours to wait for the main fleet, from which we had been parted mysteriously off Colombo. They came in the early morning, handed us a heavy home-mail, and by sundown we were all in motion, steaming up into the heat of the Red Sea. If this is the Red Sea in midwinter, the Lord deliver us from its summer! The heat is beguiled by heavy betting as to the port of disembarkation. But as we get up towards Suez the hand of the war-lords begins to show itself in cryptic paragraphs of troop-ship orders—and the like. Marseilles is our desired haven, and next to that Southampton. But—

> It sounds like stories from the land of spirits
> If any man get that which he desires,
> Or any merit that which he obtains.

Before lunch on the —th the African coast loomed up on the port-bow. About midday we were steaming over the traditionally located Israelitish crossing. Curious! the entirely unquestioning attitude of the most blasphemous trooper afloat towards the literal authenticity of Old Testament history. The Higher Criticism has, at any rate, no part with the devil-may-care soldier full of strange oaths. Apparently to a man the troops speak in quite an accepted fashion of the miraculous Israelitish triumph over the Egyptian army : the inference from which is, perhaps, that blasphemy is rather an habitual mannerism in such men than anything deliberate. But after a month's living in their midst it requires no such occasion as this discussion of Mosaic geography to tell you that.

After lunch the Arabian coast also was to be seen. The contrast between the coasts is memorable. It was a warm, grey day, and Arabia showed more delicate than we had yet seen it. The immense mountains were almost beyond sight. All the foreground was opalescent sand shot with tiny cones and ridges of rock, themselves streaked with colour as though sprinkled with the same sand. The effect of opalescence must be purely atmospheric—but it is very beautiful.

But the African coast is rugged to the water's edge. The mountains tower out of the sea; and the grey day, which drew out the iridescence of Arabia, only blackened deeper the gigantic mountains of Africa. The one is delicate pearl and amber, the other is ebony. Well justified by sight and feeling were the judgments of books upon the perfumes and delicate-bred steeds and philosophy of Arabia as over against the grimness of " Darkest Africa."

All gazing was distracted by a death on board at sunset. The body was buried under the moon at eight o'clock. Every soldier stands to attention; the engines are stopped; in the sudden silence the solemn service is read; the body is slid from the plank; the massed buglers sound the Last Post. . . . The engines begin again to throb and grind, and the routine, broken rudely but momentarily, resumes.

Next morning we wakened in the harbour of Suez. We lay here a day. There appeared to have been some guerilla sniping from the banks of the Canal. The troopship bridges were barricaded with sandbags, and all ranks warned against exposing themselves unnecessarily. A shot in the back out of the desert would be a more or less ignominious beginning, and, as an ending, unutterable !

At ten in the morning we started into the Canal. Much valuable Egyptian shore was missed by our being obliged to cross to starboard and salute a French cruiser lying in the mouth. But before we had well passed her the Arabian bank became thick with Ghurkas. War—or the rumour of war—was brought home to our bosoms by their deep and elaborate. entrenchments, barbed-wire entanglements, and outworks. The Ghurkas justify, seen in the flesh, all that has been said of their physique: short, deep-chested fellows, with a grin that suggests war is their sport indeed.

On the Egyptian side the Suez suburbs stretched away in a thin strip of fertile country bearing crops and palm-groves and following the rail to Cairo—easily visible, running neck-and-neck with a half-dozen telegraph-lines. Later on, the line draws still nearer to the Canal, making a halt at each of the Canal stations. The stations, with their neat courtyards and neat French offices, and the neat and handsome red-roofed villa, break the monotony of sand-ridge. And the monotony of ejaculation from the deck is broken by a robust French voice shouting a greeting through the megaphone from the station pontoon.

The Egyptian bank is still more strongly fortified;

for in addition to the entrenchments and entanglements of the other shore, the place bristles with masked-batteries. The troops here were chiefly Australian, with a sprinkling of Ghurka and of Sikh cavalry. Here and there an Indian trooper would indicate by pantomime that firing and bayoneting were in progress in the interior. But how much was histrionic fervour and how much the truth remains to be known.

The Canal is embanked with limestone as far as the Bitter Lakes, and at intervals thereafter. The Egyptian shore from the Lakes almost to Ismailia is planted with a graceful grove of fir. The controllers of the Canal evidently intend it shall be more than a commercial channel—in some sense, a place to be seen. This is essentially French.

It was evident that trouble from the Turk was expected. The strongest fortifications yet seen had been erected on the Arabian bank: much artillery, thousands of men, searchlight, and frequent outpost. Our own stern-chasers were unmasked and charged, ready in the event of game showing. Almost every hour the troops were called to attention to pass a British or French gunboat. All the warships had their guns run out and their sandbags piled.

We steamed steadily to Port Said, at a pace which, if made habitual by shipping here, would prove bad for the Canal shore and channel.

The towns of this route increase in size as we progress. Port Said spreads herself out to prodigal limits. . . . On a nearer approach you may see the wharves of the Arabian side lined with coaltramps, backed in like so many vans and disgorging into barges. There is the flash of a grin, the white of an eye. The Port-side is the more interesting. The finest buildings of the city would seem to be standing along the water's edge. The business advertisements of the most cosmopolitan city in the world are emphatically English; the signs for Kodak, and Lipton's, and King George the Fourth Whisky, and the rest of them, look familiarly out.

The touch of war is to be seen at any interval along the Canal; here it is laid on with a trowel. Ghurkas are encamped in the suburb; reclining at the foot of the Admiralty steps is a submarine rusted and disfigured; ten minutes after, you pass the seaplane station; and before the ship is at rest a hydroplane has buzzed over our masthead and taken the water for a half-mile at the stern. Before dark three monoplanes and a biplane have swept in out of the southern distance and gone to roost after their scouting flight.

We were anchored within fifty yards of the heart of the city. One knew not whether to be galled by the proximity of our prison-house to the blandishments of such a city or grateful for a proximity which let us see so much of it from deck. Seen through a glass, Arab, Frenchmen, Italian, British, Yankee, Jap, and Jew justified the cosmopolitan reputation of a city mid-set on the trade-route between the East and West. The Canal here is gay as a Venetian highway and busy with flying official cutters and pleasure craft and native boats. These last swarmed to the side and drove a trade that was fierce; for the night was coming, when no man could work at that. This was the degenerate East indeed—not a cigar to be had, nothing to smoke but cheap and foul Turkish and Egyptian cigarettes,

fit food for eunuchs and such effeminate rascals—for
their vendors (for example) dressed in a most ambiguous
skirt: you never know whether, beneath skirt and
turban, you have a man or a woman!

The money-getters over the side included, here, a
boat-load of serenaders and one of jugglers. The first
rung the changes on their orchestra and their throats
until we were as tired as they; and in consequence their
gorgeous parasol, gaping for coin in the hands of the
boy, gathered in some missiles whose purchasing
power was not high. The jugglers were more deserving.

The same unhallowed load of black bargees as at
Aden came alongside to coal and make night hideous.
But they worked harder—time was short and the boss
used a rope's-end, and actually " laid-out " more than
one who dared to stop for scraps thrown. They eked
out their industry with an alleged chant, echoed in
derision by the troops all over the ship. About midnight firing—or its equivalent—began to the south.
At the sound of guns the Mohammedan bargees forgot
their labours and the rope's-end—as did the boss,
together with his authority—cast aside their baskets,
and incontinently fell on their faces in the coal-dust
and called in terror upon Allah.

Soon after dawn we stood out for Alexandria, and
were there early the following morning. The sun rising
behind the city cast into flat black Pompey's Pillar
and the Port. It was hard to see, in the first blush,
in this city—when the sun had risen above it—a centre
of action of Pompey and of Alexander and of Cæsar.
There is a curious blending of age and of what is intensely modern; and so it is more easy to conceive
Sir Charles Beresford bombarding from the *Condor*,

with Admiral Seymour pounding from behind; or Napoleon storming the citadel. From our anchorage it was with ease we saw the scene of bombardment and the converging-point from which the Egyptians fled helter-skelter to the hinterland.

Anchored in the harbour, we supposed by habit we should have to be content with externals and with conjecture as to what was to be seen in the midst of the city. But we loitered some days to disembark infantry, and leave was granted freely. One would have easily given a month's pay for a day ashore—apart from the month's pay he could spend there—had that been necessary.

Your first business after leaving the gangway is to stave-off the horde of beggars and gharry-drivers (an Australian cab-rank is put to shame here) and choose one of the latter's vehicles approximately respectable. It takes ten minutes' brisk driving to get you well out of the labyrinth of wharves, docks, and dhows. You emerge by one of seven dock-gates, vigilated by native police, into the Arab quarter, by which alone approach to the city proper is possible. Cook's tourists drive hurriedly through this region, and protect their eyes and noses with the daily newspaper. The wise man knows that if he is to see Alexandria he will dismiss the gharry and walk—and walk slowly—through the native-quarter. In fact, he will care not a damn whether he ever gets to imposing French and English residential quarters or not. . . .

So, in your wonder at the utter strangeness of everything you overpay the driver some five piastres and begin to thread your way over the cobbles. All building is of stone, with a facing of cement, which once was bright-coloured, but has faded into faint blues and browns and greys; and if you look up and along the street of crumbling, flat-faced upper storeys broken by tiny balconies, you feel intensely the gentle irregularity and the mass of mellow colour. The one and the other is never seen in Australia, with our new shining-painted angularities of hardwood and bright nails and eaves and gables and sharp-sloping roofs. A gentle irregularity, in a street where boards thrust out and planks give way and vulgarly project themselves, where neither roofs nor fronts are flat, is unknown in our country.

What Mr. Wells calls " the inundating flood of babies " ebbs and flows in the streets. The Arab women, bare-legged, slovenly of gait, broad of person, with swaying, unstable bust, move up and down or sit in the doorways, or lounge and haggle over a purchase. Every hovel in the bazaars, with its low door and dark recesses, sells or makes something, and the Arab quarter is a succession of bazaars. The artificers squat at their work in brass or clay or fabric or gold; the greybeards sit at the doors with hubble-bubble and dream through the day in a state of coma. Fruits and dates, sweets and pastry, and Eastern culinary products that defy nomenclature by the Australian, are piled in an Eastern profusion. Sweets and pastry abound in excess and are curiously cheap. Toffee is sold from stands at every street-corner, and the quantity you might carry off for sixpence would be embarrassing. Pastry is made here of a flavour and lightness unexcelled by any Enghsh housewife. Sit at an open restaurant, call for a light lunch, and you will have a plate heaped with the most delicious meat and spice pastry and sugared fruits, for something less than the price of a street-stall pie in Australia, and with a glass of sherbet thrown in. The fineness of the fabrics sold (amongst bales of Manchester rubbish) will draw the better class of Egyptian woman into the bazaars of this east-end; they are beautiful in rich black silk from head to toe, with a delicate white yashmak; they have a regularity of feature and a complexion and a beauty of eye and of gait to make you look again. Nothing is lost to them by the setting through which they glide: the ragged bargainers, the sluttishness of the women, the unmitigated dirt of earth and asses and children and tethered goats, and water-carriers with their greasy swine-skins filled and shining. They offer an analogy to the stately mosque and minaret which lifts its graceful head above the squalid erections of the poor. And as futilely might the stranger pry into those features with his free curiosity as attempt an entrance to the Mosque unattended.

Progress is slow towards the Square. Not the interest of the scene alone invites you to linger: the whole atmosphere is one of lounge. Everyone moves at a lounging pace; those not in motion lounge; there are periodical cafés where the men lounge in the fumes of smoke and native spirits by the half-day together. No one hurries. Business seems rather a hobby and an incident than the earnest, insistent thing it is in England. The advantage surely lies with the Arab; he finds time to live and contemplate and get to know something of himself. God help the American! Better, perhaps, to spend the evening of your life with your chin on your knees and your hubble-bubble adjacent, looking out on the life before you, and within upon your own, than boast yourself still keen in the steel trade; that your features are " mobile and alert," though your head is grey, whereas your contemporaries are " failing." . . .

At the end of a half-day you'll know your proximity to the Centre by the uprising of " respectable " cafés and imposing cigarette-manufactories and of hotels. And you come into the Square overlooked by the noble statue of the noble Mahomet Aly—every ounce a soldier.

Wide and well-built streets lead away into the regions of high-class trade and residence. You had best take a gharry here. There are two extreme classes amongst tourists—the thoroughgoing Cook's sight-seer who works exclusively by the vehicle and the book, and the tourist who steadily refuses to " do " the stock places. Each is at fault if he is inflexible: the former in the Arab quarter, the latter when he emerges from it. For in a city such as Alexandria the visitor who declines to see the spots relict of the ancient history of this world is clearly an obdurate fool with a strange topsy-turvey-dom of values. Let him take a gharry and a book in his hand when the time is ripe; let him be free with his piastres when Pompey's Pillar stands over the cata-combs of the city. The Forts of Cæsar and of Napoleon watch over the sea. He may stand upon the ground where was the library of Alexandria and where Euclid reasoned over his geometrical figures in the sand. Here Hypatia suffered martyrdom and Cleopatra held her court and died in her palace. On the northern horn of the harbour stood the great Beacon of Pharos, one of the Seven Wonders.

So you get your vehicle and a chattering guide. . . .

On the way back to ship the Park and the Nouzha Gardens are a delicious sight after the aridity of the desert. . . . The gharry is dismissed on re-entering the Arab quarter; it would be a sad waste of opportunity to drive. . . .

We climbed the gangway bearing much fruit and dirt, and very much late for dinner. And after mess the boat-deck and the pipes and our purchases in tobacco and our ventures in cigars—and the day all over again.

CHAPTER III

ABBASSIEH

WE left the ship's side in a barge that might have carried twice our number without crowding. Every man of us had chafed at the confinement of the voyage, but not one did not now regret the dissociation from our unit, with all the chances it carried of never rejoining, and even, possibly, of never getting to Europe at all. Private friendships do not fall within the consideration of motives in the issue of military orders. Men were calling a farewell from the deck with whom we would have given much to go through the campaign. There was nothing for it but to cultivate the philosophy of the grin and simulate an elation at being free, at last, from the prison-house, and chaff the others about the bitter English winter they were sailing into, and claim we had the best of it. But in our hearts we coveted their chances of moving into Europe first. No part in the Egyptian army of occupation, with the off-chance of a fitful brawl with the Turk, compensated for that.

Baggage required but brief handling. We had little more than our rifles and equipment and kit-bags. By sunset we were entrained, and flying between the back-yards of Alexandria. A five hours' run was before us. There was nothing to be seen except each other, and we had had enough of that in the last five weeks.

We cast about for something to eat (the ship's cooks' fatigue had bagged a sack of cold fowl before making their exit from the bowels of the transport), and composed ourselves to sleep. The cessation of motion at Cairo, at 2 a.m., awakened us. Half an hour afterwards we were at Abbassieh, tumbling out into the cold and "falling-in." A guide was waiting. The baggage was piled on the platform under a guard until the morning. A pair of blankets per man was issued, and we marched through a mile of barracks to the camp. The fuddled brains of those still half asleep had conceived a picture of tents and the soft, warm sand and the immediate resumption of slumber. This was ill-founded. We poked about for a place in which to sleep. Ultimately we stumbled upon a line of block-houses erected for messing, wherein we crept, posted a couple of sentries, and disposed ourselves about the tables. It was very cold; had we been less tired, we should have been about before seven the next morning.

Abbassieh, except for its mosque, is nothing but a barrack-settlement. Barracks almost encircle the camp. Indeed, it would appear that the Regular Cairene troops are mostly quartered in this suburb. The eastern and northern barracks are for the Egyptian Regulars; the Territorials occupy those on the west. We see much of either. The Egyptians are impressive—very lithe and strongly built, but not tall. Alertness is the badge of all their tribe. The first impression they give is that everything in their training is done "at the double." As you turn in your bed at 5.30, you hear their *réveille* trumpeted forth from the whole barrack settlement; and that is significant. To a man, they bear about the mouth those lines seen

upon the face of the thoroughgoing athlete. They love
to fraternise with the Australians. The Turks they
hate with a perfect hatred; more than one has lost a
brother " down the Canal." If this is the type of
man Kitchener had with his British, the consistent
victories of his Egyptian campaign are quite in the
order of nature. They show an individual strength,
efficiency, and alertfulness which probably is to be
seen nowhere else—except, perhaps, among the
Ghurkas—in all the British forces now under arms.
The best Australian or Territorial unit will have its
weeds and its blear-eyed and its round-shouldered and
its slouchers. Here you look for them in vain.

The Camp is busy enough at any time of the day,
and the Army Service Corps which supplies it is almost
as busy as any unit on active service. The difference
is that it is not feverishly busy, and that it has a convenient and resourceful base from which to work—
the city of Cairo, as well and variously stocked as the
most fastidious army could wish. And an army which
is merely sitting in occupation is in danger of growing
fastidious—with shops of Parisian splendour and
Turkish baths and cafés of the standard of the *Fran-
catelli* within two miles, and opportunity of generous
leave. In the first half of the day the camp supply
depôt is animated with men of more than one race
and beasts of many breeds. Long trains of camels
and donkeys move in from the irrigation with their
loads of green fodder and vegetables, and the high
and narrow Arab carts, decorated fore and aft in
quasi-hieroglyphic, bring in the chaff and grain.
General service waggons, manned by Australians, are
there too. The unloading and distribution is done

chiefly by hired Arabs working under the superintendence of our men. The din is terrific; no Arab can work without much talk and shout. If he has no companion to be voluble with, he talks with and at his beast. But here is a crowd of a hundred of them, and it is with difficulty the superintendents make themselves audible, much less intelligible. All the heavy fatigue work is done by natives attached—splitting wood, digging drains and soakage-pits, erection of out-houses, removal of refuse of all sorts. Native labour is extremely cheap, and beside its official employment the men use it for such purposes as private washing; a native takes your week's soiled clothes and returns them next day, snow white, for a couple of piastres. During certain hours the camp swarms with Arab vendors of newspapers, fruit, sweets, cakes, postcards, Arab-English phrase-books, rifle-covers (invaluable, almost indispensable, here to the right preservation of arms), clothing, tobacco and cigarettes. They easily become a bane if encouraged in any degree. Native police patrol the place day and night for the sole purpose of keeping them in check. This is no easy matter. They are slippery as eels, cunning as foxes, and impudent as they make 'em. They fight incessantly; bloody coxcombs are to be seen daily, and the men rarely hesitate to fan an embryonic fight into a serious combat as a relief from the lassitude of the midday; for the noon is as hot as the night is cold. To incite is the soldier's delight: " Go it, Snowball ! "—" Well hit, Pompey ! "—" Get after him ! " . . . until a couple of native police break in and carry off the combatants by the lug. Even then, they often break away and resume, or clear off into the desert. And a policeman in thick blue serge, with leggings and bayonet, is no match in a chase for a bare-footed Arab in his cotton skirt.

The Arab is intelligent, and in many cases has picked up decent English and speaks with fluency. Between the early parade and breakfast we often engage them in talk, partly for amusement, partly to improve our mongrel Arabic. They are good subjects for interrogation, with a nice sense of humour—indulged often at your expense—and a knack of getting behind the mind of the questioner. They excel, too, in the furnishing of examples in illustration of answers to questions about custom and usage in Egypt. The best conversationalists, by far, are the native police sergeants, who are chosen a good deal for their intelligence and mental alertfulness. Get a police sergeant into your tent after tea, and you have a fruitful evening before you. He readily discusses Mohammedanism, and Egyptian history and peoples, and local geography and customs, and is as pleased to discuss as you to start him. The intelligent Arab in British employ is a revelation in intellectual freshness and open-mindedness. He never speaks in formula, and is clearly astonished at the want of intellectual curiosity in many of his interlocutors.

The men sleep in bell-tents—some in the sand; others, more flush of piastres, on a species of matting supplied by the native weavers. Sand may be warm and comfortable enough in itself, but it breeds vermin prolifically, specialising in fleas. And at midnight you will see an unhappy infested fellow squatting, roused from sleep because of their importunity, conducting a search by candle-light, engaged in much the same business as his Simian ancestors; the difference is that whereas they were too strong-minded to be disturbed in their sleep by any such trifle, his search is mostly nocturnal—though not exclusively so; and, moreover, in place of their merely impatient gibbering, he speaks with eloquence and consecutiveness, often in quite sustained periods, logically constructed and glowing with purple patches. . . . The Medical Officer has got a paragraph inserted in camp routine orders about a bathing parade on Fridays, compelling a complete ablution. But what avails cold water, once a week ? Most men, however, have been known to bathe more often.

The military Medical Officer in this country is as considerable a personage as the medicine-man amongst the American Indians. In a land where the rainfall is not worth mentioning, and the sun is hot, and the natural drainage poor, and sanitation little considered by the natives, he is a man whose word in camp is law. He speaks almost daily, through camp orders or through pamphlets of his own compiling, imperative words of warning, and in the daily camp inspection the Commandant is his mere satellite. " Avoid," says he (in effect) in his fifth philippic against dirt, " the incontinent consumption of fruit unpeeled and raw or unwashed vegetables. Therefrom proceed dysentery, enteritis, Mediterranean fever, parasitic diseases, and all manner of Egyptian scourges. Would you fly the plagues of Egypt, abhor the Arab hawker and the native beer-shop." Certain quarters are hygienically declared " out of bounds." They include " all liquorshops and cafés, except those specified hereafter . . ."; the village of Abbassieh; the village adjoining the Tombs of the Caliphs (the most squalid in Cairo). It is for other reasons than hygienic that the gardens of the Sultan's palace at Koubbeh and the Egyptian State-railways are placed out of bounds too.

Men scarcely need go to Cairo for the satisfaction of their most fastidious wants. The regimental institute receives camp-rent from grocer, haberdasher, keeper of restaurants, vendor of rifle-covers, barber, boot-repairer, tailor, and proprietor of the wet-canteen.

We get precious and intermittent mails from Australia. Their delivery is somewhat irregular. That is no fault of our friends. What may be the fault of our friends is an ultimate scarcity of letters. One has read of the ecstasies of satisfied longing with which the exile in Labrador reads his half-yearly home mail. If friends in Australia knew fully the elation their gentle missives inspire here, they would write with what might become for them a monotonous regularity. The man who gets a fair budget on mail-day hankers after no leave that night.

Sabbath morning in the Egyptian desert breaks calm; there is no before-breakfast parade. The sergeants set the example of lying a little after waking, as at home. Through the tent door, as you lie, you can see the sun rise over the undulating field of sand. The long stone Arab prison, standing away towards the sun in sombre isolation, is sharply defined against the ruddy east. The sand billows redden, easily taking the glow of the dawn; and the hills of rock in the south, which look down over Cairo, catch the level rays until their rich brown burns. A fresh breeze from the heart of the desert, pure as the morning wind of the ocean, rustles the fly and invites you out, until you can lie no longer. Throwing on your greatcoat, you saunter with a towel, professedly making for the shower-baths, but careless of the time you take to get there, so gentle is the morning and so mysteriously rich the glory of Heliopolis, glittering like the morning star, and so spacious the rosy heaven reflecting the sun-laved sand.

You dawdle over dressing in a way that is civilian. By the time these unregimental preliminaries to breakfast are over, the mess is calling; and thereafter is basking in the sun beneath the wall of the mess-hut with the pipes gently steaming, reading over the morning war-news. The news is cried about the camp on Sunday more clamorously than on any other day: Friday is the Mohammedan Sabbath. Sunday brings forth special editions of the dailies, and all the weeklies beside. The soldier is the slave of habit, and the Sunday morning is instinctively unsullied. Even horse-play is more or less disused. The men are content to bask and smoke.

. At 9.15 the " Fall-in " sounds for parade for Divine service. Columns from all quarters converge quietly on a point where the Chaplain's desk and tiny organ rest in the sand. By 9.30 the units have massed in a square surrounding them and are standing silently at ease. The Chaplain-Colonel whirrs up in his car. He salutes the Commandant and announces the Psalm. Thousands of throats burst into harmonious praise, and the voice of the little organ, its leading chord once given, is lost in the lusty concert. The lesson is read; the solemn prayers for men on the Field of Battle are offered: no less solemn is the petition for Homes left behind; the full-throated responses are offered. The Commandant resumes momentary authority. He commands them to sit down; they are in number about five thousand. The Chaplain bares his head, steps upon his dais, and reclining upon the sands of Egypt the men listen to the Gospel, much as the Israelites may have heard the Word of God from the bearded patriarch—even upon these very sands.

At no stage in the worship of the God of Battles is the authority of military rank suppressed. The parade which is assembled to worship Him that maketh wars to cease is never permitted to be unmindful of a Major. One despises proverbial philosophy in general, but herein the reader may see, if he will, a kind of comment on the truism that Heaven helps those that help themselves. Colonels and Majors are part of the means whereby we hope to win. The persistence of military rank throughout Divine worship is the implicit registering of a pledge to do our part. There is nothing in us of the unthinking optimist who says it will all come out well and that we cannot choose but win. . . .

As the Chaplain offers prayer a regiment of Egyptian Lancers gallops past with polished accoutrements and glittering lance-heads for a field-day in the desert. Bowed heads are raised, and suppressed comments of admiration go round, and the parson says *Amen* alone.

SECTION B.—CAIRO

CHAPTER I

ON LEAVE IN CAIRO

It is not so long ago as to render it untrue now that Dean Stanley said, looking down from the Citadel: "Cairo is not the ghost of the dead Egyptian Empire, nor anything like it."

The interval elapsed since that reflection was uttered has, indeed, only deepened its truth. Cairo is becoming more modern every season. The "booming" of Cairo as a winter resort for Europeans was begun at the opening of the Canal by the Khedive Ismail. His ambition was the transforming of Cairo into a kind of Paris of Africa. The effort has not died with him. It has persisted with the official-set and their visitors. The result now is that in half an hour's ride you may pass from those monuments of antiquity, the Sphinx and the Pyramid of Cheops, in a modern tram-car, along a route which is neither ancient nor modern, into a city which blends in a most amazing fashion Europe of to-day with Egypt of a very long time past. There are wheels within wheels: at the foot of the Great Pyramid are crowded shanties and taverns such as you might enter in a poorer Melbourne Street or on a new-found gold-field; and the intensity of the contradiction in Cairo itself baffles description.

Cairo has been so accurately portrayed in every aspect with the pen that it seems presumptuous to attempt to reproduce even impressions, much less relate facts. One prefers, of course, if he does attempt to do either, to give impressions rather than facts. Any guide-book will give you facts. And the reader who demands a sort of Foster-Frazer tabulation of facts is analogous to those unhappy readers of romance who rank incident above characterisation.

What one feels he must say, chiefly, is that it is the living rather than the dead in Cairo that attract most strongly. You go to the Museum or stand beside the sarcophagus of the King's Chamber in the Great Pyramid once, and again; not because it is conventionally fitting, but because that conventional appropriateness rests upon a broad and deep psychology: these places have their hold upon you. But incomparably stronger is that which draws you times without number to the bazaars. "Fool!" says Teufelsdröckh. "Why journeyest thou wearisomely, in thy antiquarian fervour, to gaze on the stone Pyramids of Geeza, or the clay ones of Sacchara? These stand there, as I can tell thee, idle and inert, looking over the desert, foolishly enough, for the last three thousand years. . . ."

A half-day in the bazaars I would not exchange for a whole wilderness of Sphinxes. You may go twice and thrice before the Sphinx, but there comes a time when there is no place for you but the ebb and flow of the human tide in the narrow streets; when you spend all your leave there, and are content to commend the venerable dead and their mausolea to the Keeper of Personality for ever.

I dare not enter on the multiplicity of the charm of
the bazaars: more accurately, I cannot. The dazzling
incongruity of vendors and of wares under the over-
meeting structures multiplies multiplicity. They move
and cry up and down classified bazaars. A vociferous
Arab hawks a cow for sale through the boot-bazaar;
the delicious Arabian perfumes of the picturesque
scent bazaar are fouled by a crier of insanitary food;
Jews, French, Italians, Tunisians, Greeks, and
Spaniards jostle each other through the alleys of the
tent bazaar, braziers' bazaar, bazaar of the weavers,
book bazaar—bazaar of any commodity or industry
you care to name; and the proprietors and artificers
squat on their tiny floors, maybe four feet square.
In the busy forenoon, looking up the Mooski, it is as
though the wizard had been there: almost you look
for the djin to materialise. Rich colour is splashed
over the stalls and the throng; there is music in the
jingle of wares and the hum of voices; and the sober
and graceful mosque, its rich colour gently mellowed
by centuries of exposure, lifts a minaret above the
animation. If this is the complexity of the broad
view, what contrasts are thrust at you from the detail
of men and things, as you saunter through !

Here in the Mooski is the micro-Cairo—Cairo bodied
forth in little, except for the intruding official set and
the unrestrained quarter of the brothels. But less
truthfully might you set out to picture the real Cairo
with the former than without the latter. Any account
which passes without note the incessant trade—in the
high-noon as under the garish night-lights—driven by
the women of Cairo will altogether misrepresent the
city. It is with a hideous propriety that she should

stand partly on the site of Old Babylon. She is a city which, in perhaps her most representative quarter, lives in and for lasciviousness. The details of that trade in its thoroughgoing haunts are no more to be described than looked upon. There is no shame; sexual transactions are conducted as openly and on as regular and well-established a footing of bargaining and market values as the sale of food and drink. Meat and drink, indeed, they must furnish to much of the population, and its alimentary properties are to be seen at every corner and in every gutter in hideousness of feature and disease unutterable. Not Paris, nor Constantinople, approaches in shamelessness the conduct of venereal industry in Cairo. All the pollution of the East would seem to drain into their foul pool. That which is nameless is not viewless. I speak that I do know and testify that I have seen. The phrase, the act, every imagination of the heart of man (and of woman), is impregnated with the filth of hell.

The official set you will see disporting itself on the piazza at Shepheard's or the Continental every afternoon. The official set is also the fashionable set, and it or its sojourning friends—or both—make up the monied set. I had no opportunity of going to a race-meeting at Gezireh; but it should come near to holding its own in " tone " with the great race-day at Caulfield.

Shepheard's is an habitual rendezvous of British officers at any time. The officers of the permanent army at Cairo assemble there, and the general orders are posted in the entrance-hall as regularly as at the Kasr-el-Nil Barracks. It is at Shepheard's that officers most do congregate. According to a sort of tacit agreement—extended later into an inescapable routine order—none lower in rank than a Subaltern enters there.

Otherwise, everywhere is the soldier; there is nothing he does not see. Everything is so utterly new that a day in Cairo is a continual voyage of discovery; and if he does no more than perambulate without an objective, it is doubtful if he has not the best of it. Fools and blind there are who look on everything from a gharry, fast-trotting. God help them! How can such a visitor hope to know the full charm of manner and voice and attire of the vendor of sherbet or sweet Nile-water if he move behind a pair of fast-trotting greys? How may he hope to know the inner beauties of a thoroughgoing bargaining-bout between two Arabs, when he catches only a fragment of dialogue and gesture in whisking past? What does he know of the beggars at the city gate in the old wall?—except how to evade them. Little he sees of the delicate tracery of the mosque; no time to wander over ancient Arab houses with their deserted harems, floor and walls in choice mosaic, rich stained windows, with all the symbolism of the manner of living disposed about the apartment. It is denied to him to poke about the native bakeries, to converse with salesmen, to look in on the Schools chanting *Al Koran*, to watch the manual weavers, tent-makers, and artificers of garments and ornaments. One cannot too much insist that it is a sad waste of opportunity to go otherwise than slowly and afoot, and innocent of " programmes," " schemes," *agenda*—even of set routes.

The alleged romance of Cairo is alleged only. Cairo is intensely matter-of-fact. In Carlyle's study of

Mahomet you read: "This night the watchman on the streets of Cairo, when he cries 'Who goes?' will hear from the passenger, along with his answer, 'There is no God but *God.*'—'*Allah akbar, Islam,*' sounds through the souls, and whole daily existence, of these dusky millions."

This is romance read into Cairo by Carlyle. The watchman gets far other rejoinders to his cry this night—answers the more hideous for Carlyle's other-worldly supposition. Romance is gone out of Cairo, except in a distorted mental construction of the city. Cairo is not romantic; it is picturesque, and picturesque beyond description.

Alfresco cafés are ubiquitous. Their frequency and pleasantness suggest that the heat of Australia would justify their establishment there in very large numbers. Chairs and tables extend on to the footpaths. The people of all nations lounge there in their fez caps, drinking much, talking more, gambling most of all. Young men from the University abound; much resemble, in their speech and manner, the young men of any other University. They deal in witty criticism of the passengers, but show a readiness in repartee with them of which only an Arab undergraduate is capable.

The gambling of the cafés is merely symbolic of the spirit of gambling which pervades the city. It is incipient in the Arab salesman's love of bargaining for its own sake. The commercial dealings of Egypt, wholesale and retail alike, are said to want fixity in a marked degree. Downright British merchants go so far as to call it by harder names than the "spirit of gambling." The guides are willing to bet you anything on the smallest provocation. Lottery tickets are hawked about the streets like sweetmeats; there are stalls which sell nothing but lottery tickets, and thrive upon the sale.

You will see much, sitting in these cafés at your ease. Absinthe and coffee are the drinks. Coffee prevails, served black in tiny china cups, with a glass of cold water. It is a delicious beverage: the coffee fiend is not uncommon. Cigarettes are the habitual smoke in the streets. At the cafés you call for a hubble-bubble. They stand by the score in long racks. The more genteel (and hygienic) customers carry their own mouth-pieces, but it is not reckoned a sporting practice.

You cannot sit five minutes before the vendors beset you with edibles, curios, prawns, oranges, sheep's trotters, cakes, and postcards. The boys who would polish your boots are the most noisome. The military camps in the dusty desert have created an industry amongst them. A dozen will follow you a mile through the streets. If you stop, your leg is pulled in all directions,.and nothing but the half-playful exercise of your cane upon the sea of ragged backs saves you from falling in.

The streets swarm with guides, who apparently believe either that you are inevitably bound for the Pyramids or incapable of walking through the bazaars unpiloted. And a guide would spoil any bazaar, though at the Pyramids he may be useful. If you suggest you are your own guide, the dog suggests an assistant. They are subtle and hard to be rid of, and frequently abusive when you are frank. The hawkers and solicitors of the streets of Cairo have acquired English oaths, parrot-wise. The smallest boy has got

this parasitic obscenity with a facility that beats any
Australian newsboy in a canter.

There is a frequent electric tramway service in Cairo.
It is very convenient and very dirty, and moderately
slow, and most informally conducted. The spirit of
bargaining has infected even the collector of fares.
Journeying is informal in other ways; only in theory
is it forbidden (in French, Arabic, Greek, and English)
to ride on the footboard. You ride where you can.
Many soldiers you will see squatting on the roofs.
And if the regulations about riding on footboards were
enforced the hawkers of meats and drinks and curios
would not plague you with their constant solicitation.
The boot-boys carry on their trade furtively between
the seats: often they ride a mile, working hard at a
half-dozen boots. The conductor objects only to the
extent of a facetious cuff, which he is the last to expect
to take effect. Both motorman and conductor raise
the voice in song: an incongruous practice to the earnest-
working Briton. But the Cairene Arab who takes life
seriously is far to seek. There is nothing here of the
struggling earnestness of spirit of the old Bedouin Arabs
to whom Mahomet preached. The Cairene is a carnal
creature, flippant and voluptuous, with more than a
touch of the Parisian. You'll find him asleep at his
shop-door at ten in the morning, and gambling earlier
still. Well-defined articulation is unknown amongst
the Arabs here, except in anger and in fight. They
do not open their teeth either to speak or to sing. The
sense of effort is everywhere wanting—in their slouching
gait, their intonation; their very writing drags and
trails itself along. But what are you due to expect in
a country where the heat blisters most of the year;

where change of temperature and of physical outlook
are foreign—a country of perennially wrinkled skins,
where a rousing thunder-storm is unknown, and where
the physical outlook varies only between the limits of
sand and rock ? The call for comment would arise if
physical inertia were other than the rule. And of the
Anglo-Egyptian, what may you expect ? . . .

One has not seen Cairo unless he has wandered both
by day and by night. So, he knows at least two different
worlds. To analyse the contrast would take long.
It is hard to know which part of a day charms you the
most. The afternoon is not as the morning; the night
is far removed from either. Go deeper, and you may
get more subtle divisions of twelve hours' wandering
than these; with accuracy of discrimination you may
even raise seven Dantean circles in your day's progress.
The safe course, then, is to " make a day of it." Tramp
it, after an early breakfast, over the desert to the car,
and plod back past the guard after midnight. You'll
turn in exhausted, but the richer in your experience
(at the expense of a few piastres) by far more than any
gold can buy.

CHAPTER II

THE MOOSKI

THE camp at Tel-el-Kebir is a good camp, as camp sites go. None the less exhilarating for that is the prospect of leave in Cairo. After retiring, you spend most of the night before you go in planning the most judicious economy of the few hours you will have in the great city. And so you wake up short of sleep—for the train leaves soon after sunrise—and curse yourself for an incontinent fool, no better than some mercurial youngster who cannot sleep for thinking of the party on the next day.

But the journey revives you. How deliciously it revives you !—and how generously ! as you skim across that green delta, sleeping under the dew, with the mist-wreaths winding about the quiet palm-fronds. The sweet-water canal runs silently beside you all the way between its clover-grown tow-paths, without a ripple. The buffalo stand motionless in the lush berseem. The Egyptian State railways are the smoothest in the world. Two hours' swift gliding through these early-morning haunts of quietness retrieves your loss of sleep, and would reinforce you for a day in any city.

As you approach Cairo you find the delta has wakened. The mists have departed, disclosing the acres of colour in the blossom of the crops. The road beside the Canal is peopled. The fellaheen and his family are moving along to work on donkey and buffalo and camel. The women in their black robes and yashmaks are moving to the dipping-places in the Canal, pitcher on head, walking with a grace and erectness that does you good to look on. Some are already drawing, knee-deep in the cool water; or emerging, and showing to the world, below the freely raised robe, that of whose outline they have no call to be ashamed. Some of the labourers are already at work, hoeing in squads under an overseer or guiding the primitive Vergilian plough behind its yoke of oxen. The blindfold yak has started his weary, interminable round at the water-wheel. The camels are looping along with their burdens of fruit and berseem, and the tiny donkeys amble under their disproportionate loads, sweeping the ground; they are hardly to be seen; in the distance they show merely a jogging hillock of green. By nine o'clock, as you race through the outskirts of Cairo, you see an occasional waiting man asleep full-stretch on the sod; the hour is early for sleeping. On the suburban roads are moving towards the centre venerable sheikhs, squat on the haunches of their well-groomed donkeys; merchants lying back in their elaborate gharries; gabbling peasants driving their little company of beasts; English and French officials, carefully dressed, smoking the morning cigarette.

Shortly the Pyramids emerge on the eastern skyline, and over the thickening house-tops rises the splendid relief of the Makattam Hills, with the stately citadel perched on the fringe, looking down on the City under its soaring minarets.

You had formed plans for the economy of the day;

they are all dissipated when you step from the train and realise yourself within a mile of the bazaars. Their call is irresistible. The Pyramids, the mosques, the museum—all can wait, to be visited if there is time for it. You enter a gharry and alight at the mouth of the Mooski. It is palpably a mouth to that seething network, as plainly defined (as you gaze up Mooski Street from the Square) as the entrance to an industrial exhibition.

There is a crowd of men in the early stages of Mooski Street, whose business, day and night, is to conduct. They lurk privily for the innocent, like the wicked men in the Book of Psalms. The guides have come so much into disrepute that they mostly hasten to tell you they are not guides. " What are you, then ?"—" I am student, sair "; or " I am agent, sair "; or " I am your friend; I do not wish for money." You'll meet such self-abnegation nowhere on earth as in the Mooski. Those who do own to being guides will never name a price. " How much do you want ?"—" I leave that to you, sair. If you are pleased, you give me what you think." . . . This is all very subtle: the man who is agent will get his commission and tender for baksheesh for having put you in the way of purchase (whereas he is in league with the rogue who fleeces you in the sale). The student shows no sort of ideal scholastic contempt for lucre; it's of degrees of gullibility that he's chiefly a student—and an astute one, gathering where he has not strawed. The man who is your friend and wouldn't think of money turns out a mere liar, downright—who does care, greatly. These are the subtlest ways of approaching you and broaching the subject of a tour. The rascal may simply fall into step and ask the time of day and proceed to talk of the weather—merely glad of your company—and abruptly close the half-mile walk with a demand for cash, like any guide requisitioned. In short, it's to be doubted whether in any city men live on their wits more artfully and unscrupulously than in the Cairene bazaars.

As a practice, it's wise to decline all offers to accompany—as a practice; but first time through it's wise to accept. No one can hope to unravel the tangle of the Mooski geography unaided or by chance. The labyrinth of overshadowed alleys is as confusing as the network of saps near the firing-line. Take a guide at your first going. If he does no more than show "the bright points" in an experience of the bazaars, he has earned his exorbitant fee. After that, refuse him, which you will never do without harsh discourtesy. A mere "No, thank you," is as nothing. "Yallah minhenna"—or its equivalent—uttered in your most quarrelsome manner, is the least of which he will begin to take notice.

The best beginning is through the narrow doorway off Mooski Street into the spice bazaar. Of so unpretentious a doorway you never would suspect the purpose without a guide, and that's the first argument for tolerating him. Can such a needle's-eye lead to anything worth entering? You arrive in an area where the air is voluptuous with the scent of all the spices of the East—something more delicious than even the scent bazaar, and less enervating. All the purchasers are women, moving round behind their yashmaks. They boil and beat the spices to grow fat, and to be fat is a national feminine aspiration. The boys are pounding the wares in large stone mortars, crushing out the sweetness, which pervades like an incense.

Appropriately enough, it is but a step into the scent bazaar proper, and many of the purchasers there are (inappropriately) men. That the men should wear and hanker after perfumes to this degree is one phase of Egyptian degeneracy. The vendors squat in their narrow cubicles lined with shelf upon shelf of gaily-coloured phials. They invite you to sit down. Coffee is called for, and whilst that is preparing you must taste the sweets of their wares on your tunic-sleeve. Bottle by bottle comes down; he shakes them and rubs the stopper across your forearm: attar of roses, jasmine, violet, orange-blossom, banana, and the rest of them, until you are fairly stupid with the medley of sweet fumes. You saunter off rubbing your sleeve upon your breeches, and wondering what your comrades in arms will say if they catch you wearing the odours of the lord of the harem. You have a tiny flask of attar of roses upon you to send home to its appropriate wearer.

You move on to the tarbush bazaar; Tunis bazaar, where the fine Tunisian scarves of the guides are sold; slipper bazaar, showing piles of the red canoe-shoe of the Soudanese hotel-waiter, and of the yellow heelless slipper of the lounging Egyptian; blue bazaar, where the women buy their dress-stuffs—their gaudy prints and silks, all the rough material for their garments. No Australian flapper can hold a candle to them in their excited keenness of selection; and there is the added excitement of bargaining. The feminine vanities of adornment are deep and confirmed in Cairo. To see the Cairene aristocrats purchasing dress-material, go to Stein's or Roberts's, Hughes's or Philips's or Senouadi's, or to any of the other big houses, in the middle afternoon. It's there, and not at any vulgar promenading (for they all drive), that you see the fine women of Cairo. Mostly French they are, and beautiful indeed, dressed as aptly and with as much artistry as in Alexandria; and that is saying the last word. There you will see a galaxy of beauty—not in any facetious or popular sense, but actually. It's a privilege to stand an hour in any such house and watch the procession: a privilege that does you good. The Frenchwomen of Cairo perform very naturally and capably the duty of matching their beauty. They have an unerring æsthetic sense, and evidently realise well enough that to dress well and harmoniously is a form of art almost as pure as the painting of pictures.

But we were in the Mooski, where the art is not so purely practised. The Egyptian women do not dress beautifully nor harmoniously. They dress with extreme ugliness; their colours outrage the sense at every turn. Only the extreme beauty of their features and clarity of complexion save them from repulsiveness. The glaring fabrics of the blue bazaar express well the Egyptian feminine taste in colour.

The book bazaar leads up towards the Mosque al Azhar. The books are all hand-made. Here is the paradise of the librarian who wails for the elimination of machine-made rubbish of the modern Press. At any such work the Egyptian mechanic excels in patience and thoroughness. Making books by hand is, in fact, an ideal form of labour for him, as is hand-weaving, which still prevails, and the designing and chiselling of the silver and brass work. *Al Koran* is here in all stages of production; and with propriety there is a lecture-hall in the midst of the book bazaar, which is, so to speak, " within " the Al Azhar University close by. A lecture is being delivered. The speaker squats on a tall stool and delivers himself with vigour to the audience seated on the mat-strewn floor. Well dressed and well featured they are, jotting notes rather more industriously than in most Colonial halls of learning, or listening with an intensity that is almost pained.

The Moslem University in the Mosque al Azhar has a fine old front designed with a grace and finished in a mellowness of colour that any Oxonian College might respect. You show a proper respect—whether you will or no—by donning the capacious slippers over your boots, as in visiting any other mosque, and enter the outer court, filled with the junior students. The hum and clatter rises to a mild róar. All are seated in circular groups, usually about a loud and gesticulating teacher; and where there is no teacher the students are swaying gently in a rhythmic accompaniment to the drone with which *Al Koran* is being got by heart. There is no concerted recitation or repetition : every man for himself. That, perhaps, helps to visualise the swaying mass of students and to conceive the babel of sound. There is no roof above that tarbushed throng. This is the preparatory school. The University proper, beyond the partition, containing the adult students, alone is roofed. Here they are all conning in the winter sunshine. Little attention is given to visitors; most students are droning with closed eyes, presumably to avert distraction. Few are aware of your presence. That consciousness is betrayed chiefly by a furtively whispered " Baksheesh !"—the national watchword of Egypt—uttered with a strange incongruity in a temple of learning—a temple literally.

Beyond, in the adult schools, you will hear no mention of baksheesh, except from the high-priest of the Temple, the sheikh of the University, who demands it with dignity, as due in the nature of a temple-offering, but appropriated (you know) by himself and for his own purposes. Any knowledge of a British University renders this place interesting indeed by sheer virtue of comparison. The Koran is the only textbook—of literature, of history, of ethics, and philosophy in general: a wonderful book, indeed, and a reverend. What English book will submit successfully to such a test ? . . .

Here is the same droning by heart and the same rhythmic, absorbed accompaniment, but in a less degree. The lecturer is more frequent and more animated in gesture and more loud and dogmatic in utterance. Declamation of the most vigorous kind is the method with him, and rapt attention with the undergraduates. The lecturers are invariably past middle age, and with flowing beards, and as venerable in feature as the Jerusalem doctors. The groups of students are small —as a rule, four or five. Yet the teachers speak as loud as to an audience of two hundred. The method here is that of the University *semina :* that is to say, small, and seemingly select, groups of students; frequent, almost incessant, interrogation by the student; and discussion that is very free and well sustained. The class-rooms, defined by low partitions, go by race, each with its national lecturers.

Within the building are the tombs of former sheikhs, enclosed and looked upon with reverence. These

approximate to tablets to pious founders.   The sheikh
will tell you that, as he puts it, the Sultan pays for
the education of all students: he is their patron.
That is to say, in plain English, the University
is State-controlled and State-supported.   Moreover,
the students sleep there.   You may see their bedding
piled on rafters.   It is laid in the floor of the lecture-
room at night.   .

When you have delivered over baksheesh to the sheikh
and to the conductor and to the attendants who re-
move your slippers at exit, you move down to the
brass and silver bazaar.   Here is some of the most
characteristic work you'll see in Egypt.   Every vessel,
every bowl and tray and pot, is Egyptian in shape or
chiselled design, or both.   As soon as you enter you
are offered tea, and the bargaining begins, although
Prix Fixé is the ubiquitous sign.   It is in the fixed-
price shops that the best bargains are struck, which is
at one with the prevailing Egyptian disregard for truth.
The best brass bazaars have their own workshops
attached.   Labour is obviously cheap—cheap in any
case, but especially cheap when you consider that at
least half the workers in brass and silver are the
merest boys.   Whatever may be the Egyptian judgment in colour, the Egyptian instinct for form is sound;
for these boys of eight and ten execute elaborate and
responsible work in design.   They are entrusted with
" big jobs," and they do them well.   There is almost
no sketching-out of the design for chisel work; the
youngster takes his tool and eats-out the design without preliminaries.   And much of it makes exacting
demands upon the sense of symmetry.   This is one of
the most striking evidences of the popular artistic

sense. The national handwriting is full of grace; the national music is of highly developed rhythm; and the national feeling for form and symmetry is unimpeachable.

You need more self-control in these enchanting places than the confirmed drinker in the neighbourhood of a *pub*. Unless you restrain yourself with an iron self-discipline, you'll exhaust all your *feloose*. The event rarely shows you to emerge with more than your railway-fare back to camp. But under your arm are treasures that are priceless—except in the eyes of the salesman. You trek to the post office and send off to Australia wares that are a joy for ever. And there you find on the same errand officers and privates and Sisters. There is a satisfied air about them, as of a good deed done and money well spent, as who should say: " I may squander time, and sometimes I squander money and energy in this Land; but in this box is that which will endure when peace has descended, and purses are tattered, and Egypt is a memory at the Antipodes."

BOOK II

GALLIPOLI

CHAPTER I

THE JOURNEY

WE were given twelve hours to collect bag and baggage and clear out from Abbassieh. It was a night of alarms and excursions. In the midst of it all came a home-mail. That was one of many occasions on which one in His Majesty's service is forced to postpone the luxury of perusal. Sometimes a mail will come in and be distributed just before the "Fall-in" is blown. This means carrying about the budget unopened and burning a hole in the pocket for a half-day—and more. In this case the mail was read in the train next morning. We were out of camp at sunrise, with the waggons ahead. By eight o'clock we had taken leave of this fair-foul, repulsive yet fascinating city, and were sweeping across the waving rice-fields of the delta towards the city of Alexandria

We arrived about midday. The urgency of the summons had justified the inference that we should embark directly. Not so. We entered what was technically known as a rest camp at Gabbari. Rest camps had been established at various points about the city to accommodate temporarily the British and French expeditions then arriving daily *en route* to the Dardanelles. The time was not yet ripe for a landing. Here was the opportunity to stretch the legs—of both men and horses, and of the mules from Spain.

At no stage even of the classical occupation of Egypt—or thereafter—could the inner harbour of Alexandria have given more vividly the impression of the imminence of war. It was crammed with transports, ranged in long lines, with here and there a battle-cruiser between. As many as could come alongside the Quay at one time were busily disembarking troops (mostly French), which streamed down the gangways in their picturesque uniforms and moved off in column through the city to the camps on the outskirts. The moral effect of such processions upon the Egyptians could hardly be over-estimated. Long queues of Arab scows ranged along the railway wharf, taking ammunition and moving off to the troopships. Day and night the harbour was dotted with launches tearing from transport to transport bearing officers of the General Staff. As for the city—the streets, the restaurants, the theatres and music-halls, fairly teemed with soldiers; and civilian traffic constantly gave way before the gharries of officers—and of men.

Many French were in our camp. There was something admirable in them, hard to define. There was a sober, almost pathetic, restraint amongst them— beside the Australians, which was as much as to suggest that what they had seen and known through their proximity to the War in Europe had had its effect. It could hardly be temperamental in the vivacious French. They were not maudlin; and on rare occasions, infected by the effervescing spirits of the Australians, would come into the mess-hut at night and dance or chant the *Marseillaise* in unison with the melody of a French accordion. But in general they seemed too much impressed with the nature and the possibilities of their mission for jollification. They showed a simple and honest affection amongst themselves. The Australians may—and do—have it, but it is concealed under their knack of mutual banter and of argument. The French love each other and do not shame to show it. Riding in the car a man would fling his arm about his friend; in the streets they would link arms to stroll. Very pathetic and very sincere and affectionate are the French fighters.

The evenings off duty were precious and well earned and well spent. Little can be seen of the city at night, except its people. The best way of seeing them as they are is to take two boon companions from the camp, ride to town, and instal yourselves in an Egyptian café for the night, containing none but Egyptians, except yourselves; invite three neighbours to join you in coffee and a hubble-bubble. They'll talk English and are glad of your company. At the cost of a few piastres (a pipe costs one, and lasts two hours, and a cup of coffee a half) you have their conversation and the finest of smokes and cup after cup of the best Mocha. This is no mean entertainment.

This kind of thing developed into a nocturnal habit, until the Italian opera-season opened at the Alhambra. We sat with the gods for five piastres ("a bob"). The gods were worth that in themselves to sit amongst. The gallery is always interesting, even in Australia; but where the gods are French, Russian, Italian, English, Jewish, Greek, and Egyptian, the intervals become almost as interesting as the acts, and there is little temptation to saunter out between them. . . .

But all theatres and all cafés were for us cut short abruptly by the order to embark.

The refugee camp at Alexandria made its contribution. One had been galled daily by the sight of strong men trapesing to and from the city or lounging in the quarters provided by a benevolent Government. This resentment was in a sense illogical: they had their wives and their babies, and were no more due to fight than many strong Britishers bound to remain at home. But the notion of refugee-men constantly got dissociated from that of their dependents. It was chiefly the thought of virile idleness under Government almsgiving that troubled you. Eventually it troubled them too; for they enlisted almost in a body and went to Cairo for training. The Government undertook to look after the women.

We found them fellow-passengers on our trooper. They were mostly young, all from Jaffa, in Palestine. Seemingly they marry young and are fathers at twenty. They brought three hundred mules with them, and were called the Zion Mule Transport Company. It is a curious name. They were there to carry water and food to the firing-line.

Their wives and mothers incontinently came to the wharf to see them leave. Poor fellows ! Poor women ! They wailed as the women of Israel wail in Scripture, as only Israelitish women *can* wail. The Egyptian police kept them back with a simulated harshness, and supported them from falling. Many were physically helpless. Their men broke into a melancholy chant as we moved off, and sustained it, as the ship passed out over the laughing water, until we reached the outer-harbour. They got frolicsome soon, and forgot their women's weeping. We stood steadily out into the rich blue Mediterranean. The Zionites fell to the care of their beasts. By the time the level western rays burned on the blue we had the geography of the ship, and had ceased speculation as to the geography of our destination—except in its detail. We knew we should run up through the Sporades: it was enough for us that we were about to enter the Eastern theatre of war. That was an absorbing prospect. To enter the field of this War at any point was a prospect to set you aglow. But the East had become the cynosure of all eyes. No one thought much about the sporadic duelling in the frozen West. The world's interest in the game was centred about the Black Sea entrance. It was the Sick Man of Europe in his stronghold that should be watched: is he to persist in his noisome existence, or is the community of Europe to be cleansed of him for ever ?

But before reaching the zone in which an attempt was being made to decide that we were to thread a course through the magical Archipelago. All the next day we looked out on the beauty of the water, unbroken to the horizon. The men of Zion did their work and we took charge of their fatigues. They cleaned the ship, fed and watered their mules, and resumed their military training on the boat-deck. The initiative of the Australian soldier is amazing. Abstractly it is so; but put him beside a mob from Jaffa (or, better, put him over them) and he is a masterful fellow. The Jews leap to his command. Our fellows found a zest in providing that not one unit in the mass should by strategy succeed in loafing. Diamond cut diamond in every corner of the holds

and the alley-ways. The language of the Australian
soldier in repose is vigorous; put him in charge of
fatigue and his lips are touched as with a live-coal—
but from elsewhere than off the altar. He is commonly
charged with poverty in his range of oaths. Never
believe it. The boss and his fatigue were mutually
unintelligible—verbally, that is. But actually, there
was no shadow of misunderstanding. Oaths aptly
ripped out are universally intelligible, and oaths here
were supplemented with gesture. There was no injustice done. The Australian is no bully.

The Jerusalem brigade, though young men, were
adults, but adults strangely childish in their play and
conversation. It was with the eagerness of a child
rather than with the earnestness of a man that they
attacked their drill. They knew nothing of military
discipline, even less of military drill. Their sergeant-
major made one son of Israel a prisoner for insubor-
dination. He blubbered like a child. Great tears
coursed down as he was led off to the "clink." The
door closed after him protesting and entreating.
This is at one with the abandoned wailing of their
women.

Drill must be difficult for them. The instruction
was administered in English. The men, who speak
nothing but an admixture of Russian, Hebrew, German,
and Arabic, understood not a word of command or
explanation. They learned by association purely.
They made feverish and exaggerated efforts, and really
did well. But of the stability and deliberative coolness
of a learning-man they had not a trace. This childish
method of attack never will make fighters. But they
are not to fight. They are to draw food and water.

As a matter of form they are issued with rifles—Mausers taken from the Turks on the Canal.

At evening of the second day out we got abreast of Rhodes, with Karpathos on the port-bow. Rhodes stood afar off: would we had come nearer! The long darkening streak of Karpathos was our real introduction to the Archipelago. All night we ploughed through the maze of islands. " Not bad for the old man," said the second-mate next day; " he's never been here before, and kept going through a muddy night." The night had been starless. And when morning broke we lay off Chios, with a horrible tempest brewing in the north.

A storm was gathering up in the black bosom of Chios. Here were no smiling wine-clad slopes, no fair Horatian landscape. All that seemed somehow past. A battle-cruiser lay half a mile ahead. She had been expecting us, together with two other transports and a hospital-ship in our wake. A black and snaky destroyer bore down from far ahead, belched past us, turned in her own length abreast of the transports, flashed a Morse message to the cruiser across the darkening water, and we gathered round her. She called up each in turn by semaphore: " Destroyer will escort you westward "; and left us.

The journey began again. There was not a breath of wind; no beam of sunlight. The water was sullen: The islands were black masses, ill-defined and forbidding. This introduction to the theatre of war was apt. We were bearing up into the heart of the Sporades in an atmosphere surcharged and menacing. No storm came. It was the worse for that. Gone were the golden " isles that crown the Ægean deep " beloved of Byron. Long strata of smoke from the ships of war lay low over the water, transecting their shapes.

After lunch the sun shone out. In the middle afternoon we came west of Skyros, and left our transports there. They were French: Skyros is the French base. At the end of the lovely island we turned east and set our course for Lemnos. It was ten before the lights of Lemnos twinkled through the blackness. At 10.30 we dropped anchor in the outer harbour of Mudros Bay. The light on the northern horn turned and flashed—turned and flashed upon us. Inside the boom a cruiser played her searchlight, sweeping the zone of entrance. A French submarine stole under our bows and cried "All's well," and we turned in to sleep.

We were up before the dawn to verify the conjectures as to land and water hazarded in the darkness and the cruiser's pencil of light. At sunrise we moved in through the boom. Here were the signs of war indeed: a hundred and fifty transports lying at their moorings; a dozen cruisers before; the tents of the Allies clothing the green slopes.

Lemnos is beautiful. The harbour is long and winds amongst the uplands. We were anchored beside an islet, flecked with the colour of wild-flowers blooming as prodigally as the Greeks said they did when they sailed these seas. The slopes about the shore were clothed with crops and vines. Behind were grey hills of granite.

In Mudros we lay a week, waiting, waiting. Let the spot be lovely as you will, waiting is not good with the sound of the guns coming down on the wind day and night. Our fifth morning on Lemnos was the

Sabbath. We woke to the soft boom of naval guns. Lemnos is a goodish sail from the straits. The " boom, boom," was a low, soft growl, felt rather than heard. The day before, at sundown, the first trooper of the fleet had gone out, with band playing, to the cheering of the cruisers. The Army and Navy have always in this campaign, shown themselves happily complementary. A seaplane escorted them out aloft, two cruisers below. Great was the rejoicing at the beginning of the exodus.

Next morning we left the mules of Zion and transferred to a store-ship. She lay two days. We solaced ourselves with bathing in the clear bay from the ship's side, and basking nude, with our pipes, afterwards in the pleasant heat of the spring sun; with visits to the shore, where we wandered into the Greek Church, in size and magnificence of decoration out of all consonance with its neighbouring villages, and where the wine of Lemnos might be drunk for a penny a glass; with bargaining at the boats that drew alongside from the shore, as at Aden, filled with nuts, figs, dates, Egyptian delight—all the old stock, except Greeks, who manned them here. The dwellers on Lemnos are all Greeks. . . . Would we never move ?

On the seventh day at noon the naval cutter ran alongside. In half an hour we were moving through the boom. As soon as we had cleared the south-east corner of the island, Imbros stood out to port, and Tenedos, our destination, lay dead ahead, under the mountains of Turkey in Asia. A fresh breeze blew out of the Dardanelles, thunder-laden with the roar of the guns, and every heave of our bow brought it down more clear. Before sundown we were abreast of

Tenedos and had sighted the aeroplane station and had seen five of the great amphibious planes come to earth. As we swung round to a view of the straits' mouth, every eye was strained for the visible signs of what we had been hearing so long. The straits lay murky under the smoke of three days' firing. The first flash was sighted—with what a quickening of the pulse! In three minutes we had the lay of the discharges and the bursts. An attempt was made to muster a fall-in aft for the first issue of tobacco ration. Not a man moved! The attempt was postponed until we should have seen enough of these epoch-making flashes. "We can get tobacco at home—without paying for it; you don't see cruisers spitting shrapnel every day at Port Philip!" At length two ranks got formed-up—one for cigarettes (appropriately, the rear), the front rank for those who smoked pipes. Oh, degenerates!—the rear was half as long again! Two ounces of medium-Capstan per man—in tins; four packets of cigarettes: that was our momentous first issue.

The bombardment went on, ten miles off. No one wanted tea. At 7.30 the Major half-ordered a concert aft. Everyone went. It was really a good concert, almost free of martial songs. But here and there you'd find a man sneak off to the bows to watch the line of spurting flame in the north; and many an auditor, looking absently at the singer, knew as little of the theme as of the havoc those shells were working in the night.

We lay three days at Tenedos: so near and yet so far from the forts of the Dardanelles. We could see two in ruins on the toe of Gallipoli, and one tottering down the heights of the Asiatic shore at the entrance to the straits. But the straits ran at a right-angle with the shore under which we lay. We could see the bombarding fleet lying off the mouth. We could see them fire, but no result. What more tantalising ?

We lay alongside Headquarters ship, loaded with the Directing Staff. H.Q. moved up and down, at safe distances, between us and the firing-line. We were one of an enormously large waiting fleet of transports and storeships. The impression of war was vivid: here was this waiting fleet, and tearing up and down the coast were destroyers and cruisers without number, and aloft, the whirring seaplanes.

Our moving-in orders came at three on an afternoon. This was the heart-shaking move; for we were to sail up, beyond the mouth, to an anchorage off the Anzac position. We were to see in detail everything that we had, for the last three days, seen as an indistinct whole. We were to pass immediately behind the firing-line, to test the speculations we had been making day and night upon what was in progress, upon the geography of the fighting zone, upon the operations within the mouth. Every yard was a step farther in our voyage of discovery.

The demolitions became plain. The ports on the water's edge had toppled over " in a confused welter of ruin." Such wall as still stood gaped with ghastly vents. These had been the first to come under fire, and the cruisers had done their work with a thoroughness that agreed well with the traditional deliberation of the British Navy. And thorough work was in progress.

Far up the straits' entrance lay the black lines of gunboats. We moved up the coast past an ill-starred village: the guns were at her from the open sea. By sundown we had passed from this scene of action to another, at —— Beach, where the Australians had landed. The heights above —— Beach were the scene of an engagement far more fierce than any we had seen below. The Turks were strongly posted in the shrubs of the Crest. Our batteries were hardly advanced beyond the beach, and were getting it hot. Night was coming on. A biting wind was blowing off the land, bringing down a bitter rain from the hills of the interior. It was almost too cold to stand in our bows and watch: what for those poor devils juggling shell at the batteries and falling under the rain of fire ? After dark there was an hour's lull. At nine o'clock began a two hours' engagement hot enough to make any fighter on shore oblivious of the temperature. Towards midnight the firing ceased and the rain and the wind abated.

CHAPTER II
GLIMPSES OF ANZAC
I.

IT's the monotony that kills; not hard work, nor hard fare. We have now been disembarked on the Peninsula rather longer than three months. But there has been little change in our way of living. Every day there is the same work on the same beach, shelled by the same guns, manned by the same Turks—presumably the same; for we never seem to knock-out those furtive and deadly batteries that enfilade the Cove Beach and maim or kill—or both—almost daily. Every morning we look out on the same stretch of the lovely Ægean, with the same two islands standing over in the west.

Yet neither the islands nor the sea are the same any two successive days. The temper of the Ægean, at this time, changes more suddenly and frequently than ever does the Pacific. That delicious Mediterranean colour, of which we used to read sceptically, and which we half disbelieved in J. M. Turner's pictures, changes in the quality of its hue almost hourly. And every morning the islands of the west take on fresh colour and are trailed by fresh shapes of mist. The atmosphere deludes, in the matter of distance, as though pranking for the love of deception. To-day Imbros stands right over-against you; you see the detail of the fleet in the harbour, and the striated heights of rocky Samothrace reveal the small ravines; to-morrow in the early-morning light—but more often towards evening —Imbros lies mysteriously afar off like an isle of the blest, a delicate vapour-shape reposing on the placid sea.

Nor is there monotony in either weather or temperature. This is the late October. Late October synchronises with late autumn. Yet it is a halting and irregular advance the late autumn is making. Changes in temperature are as incalculable as at Melbourne, in certain seasons. Fierce, biting, raw days alternate with the comfortableness of the mild late-summer. To-day to bathe is as much as your life is worth (shrapnel disregarded); to-morrow, in the gentle air, you may splash and gloat an hour, and desire more. And you prolong the joy by washing many garments.

The Ægean autumn has yet shown little bitterness. Here on Anzac we have suffered the tail-end of one or two autumn storms, and have had two fierce and downright gales blow up. The wind came in the night with a suddenness that found most unprepared. There was little rain; insufficient to allay the maelstroms of choking dust that whirled over our ploughed and powdered ridges. In half an hour many of us were homeless, crouching about with our bundled bed-clothes, trespassing tyrannically upon the confined space of the more stout dug-outs of our friends: a sore tax upon true friendship. Men lay on their backs and held down their roofs by mere weight of body, until overpowered. Spectral figures in the driving atmosphere collided and wrangled and swore and blasphemed. The sea roared over the shingle with a violence that made even revilings inaudible. It was a night for Lear to be out. Men had, for weeks, in spare time, been formally preparing dug-outs against the approach of winter, but they were unprepared for weather of such violence. And if this is a taste of the quality of winter storms, the warning comes timely.

For the morning showed a sorry beach. Barges had been torn adrift from moorings and trawlers, and hurled ashore. Some were empty; some were filled with supplies; all were battered; some disabled; some utterly broken. One was filled with rum. Never before, on active service, had such a chance of unlimited spirits offered. Many jars had been spirited away when the time of unlading came. There were riotous faces and super-merriment on the beach that morning; and by mid-day the " clink " was overflowing. Far more serious was the state of the landing-piers. There were—there had been—three. One stood intact; the landward half of the second was clean gone; of the third there was no trace, except in a few splintered spars ashore. A collective grin overlooked the beach that morning at the time of rising. The General grinned too—a sort of dogged grin. The remedying began forthwith; so did the bursting of shrapnel over the workmen. This stroke of Allah upon the Unfaithful was not to go unsupplemented. But it was as with the unhappy Armada: the winds of heaven wrought more havoc than the enemy guns. By nightfall the abridged pier was re-united to the shore—and this in spite of a sea that made it impossible for barges to come alongside. For two days the after-wind of the gale kept bread and meat and mails tossing on the face of the waters off Anzac; and we fed on bully-beef and biscuit, and eyed wistfully the mail-trawler pitching there with her precious burden.

The arrival of mails eclipses considerations of life and death—of fighting and the landing of rations. The mail-barge coming in somehow looms larger than a barge of supplies. Mails have been arriving weekly for six months, yet no one is callous to them. Sometimes they come twice in a week; for a fresh mail is despatched from the base post-office in instalments which may spread over three or four landings. The Army Corps Post Office never rests. Most mails are landed between sunset and dawn—generally after midnight. Post-office officials must be there to supervise and check. It's little sleep they get on " mail nights." Incoming mails do not constitute all their cares. Mails outgoing from the firing-line are heavy. And there are the pathetic " returns " to be dealt with, the letters of men who will never read them— letters written before the heavy news had got home. It is a huge bulk of correspondence marked *Killed* and re-addressed to the place of origin of the fallen. Their comrades keep their newspapers. Usually the parcels of comforts directed to them bring melancholy cheer to their still fighting comrades in arms. What else is to be done with them ?

Of incoming mails letters stand inevitably first. They put a man at home for a couple of hours. But so does his local newspaper. Perusing that, he is back at the old matutinal habit of picking at the news over his eggs-and-coffee, racing against the suburban business-train. Intimate associations hang about the reading of the local sheet—domestic and parochial associations almost as powerful as are brought to him by letters. Relatives at home, did they know this fully, would despatch newspapers with a stricter regularity.

And what shall be said of parcels from home ? The boarding-school home-hamper is at last superseded. No son away at grammar-school ever pursued his voyage of discovery through tarts, cakes and preserves, sweets, pies and fruit, with the intensity of gloating expectation in which a man on Gallipoli discloses the contents of his " parcel ": " 'Struth ! a noo pipe, Bill ! —an' some er the ole terbaccer. Blimey ! cigars; too ! 'Ave one, before the crowd smells 'em. D——d if there ain't choclut ! look 'ere ! An' 'ere's some er the dinkum coc'nut ice the tart uster make. Hullo ! more socks ! Never mind: winter's comin'.—'Ere ! 'ow er yer orf fer socks, cobber ? Take these—bonzer 'and-knitted. Sling them issue-things inter the sea. . . I'm b——d !—soap fer the voy'ge 'ome. . . . 'Angker-ch'fs !—orl right when the —— blizzerds come, an' a chap's snifflin' fer a ——in' week on end. . . . Writin' paper !—well, that's the straight —— tip ! The ——s er bin puttin' it in me letters lately, too. Well, I'll write ter night, on the stren'th of it. . . . Gawd ! 'ere's a shavin'-stick !—'andy, that; I wuz clean run out—usin' carbolic soap, —— it ! . . . Aw, that's a dinkum —— parcel, that is !"

" Bonzer tarts " (and others) may infer that a parcel is as a gift from the gods, and carries more than " its intrinsic worth." Such treasures as the 'and-knitted socks and coc'nut ice bring home rather more near than it ever comes to the man who has no part in the parcel mail.

Mails deserve all the organised care the War-Office can bestow; they make for efficiency.

There is no morning delivery of the daily newspaper at Anzac. But we get the news. At the foot of Head-quarters gully is the notice-board. The wireless messages are posted daily. At any hour men are elbowing a way into the perusing circle. There is news of the operations along our own Front and copious messages from the Eiffel Tower of the Russian and Western Fronts. The Melbourne Cup finish was cabled through immediately. The sports foregathered and collected or "shelled out"; there were few men indeed who did not handle their purses round the board that evening. No war news, for months, had been so momentous as this. The associations called up by the news from the Australian Mecca at Flemington, whither the whole continent makes annual pilgrimage, were strong, and homely as well as national. All the detail of the little annual domestic sweeps at the breakfast-table came back with a pathetic nearness. Men were recalled for a while from the land of blood to the office, the bank, the warehouse, the country pub., the shearing-shed, where the Cup bets were wont to be made. Squatters' sons were back at the homestead making the sweeps. The myriad-sided sporting spirit is per-haps stronger than any other Australian national trait. The Defence-Department knew it when they made provision for a cabled despatch of the running.

Three weeks ago began the flight of birds before the Russian winter. They came over thick, in wedge formation, swallowing up, in their hoarse cries, the crack of rifles over the ridges, from which, otherwise, only the roar of a half-gale delivers us, day or night.

Over Anzac—which seemed to mark a definite stage in the journey—they showed a curious indecision as to direction. Possibly they were interested in the bird's-eye view of the disposal of forces. They wheeled and re-formed into grotesque figures; men would stop in their work and try to decipher the pattern. " That's a W."—" Yes; and what's that ?"—" Oh, that ?" (after a crafty pause)—" that's one er them Turkish figgers—'member them in Cairo ?"

The flight of birds south is surely the most reliable of all forecasts as to what we may expect in temperatures. Yet the official account, published for the information of troops, of the traditional weather between October and March shows we need expect nothing unreasonably severe before the middle of January; but that then will come heavy snow-storms and thoroughgoing blizzards.   Furthermore, men are advised to instruct their sisters to send Cardigans, sweets in plenty, and much tobacco. *Amen* to this; we shall instruct them faithfully.

Meanwhile the systematic fortification of dug-outs against damp and cold goes on.

We foresee, unhappily, the winter robbing us of the boon of daily bathing. This is a serious matter. The morning splash has come to be indispensable. Daily at 6.30 you have been used to see the bald pate of General Birdwood bobbing beyond the sunken barge in shore, and a host of nudes lining the beach. The host is diminishing to a few isolated fellows who either are fanatics or are come down from the trenches and must clear up a vermin- and dust-infested skin at all costs. Naturally we prefer to bathe at mid-day, rather than at 6.30, when the sun has not got above the precipitous ridges of Sari Bair. But the early-morning dip is almost the only safe one. The beach is still enfiladed by Turkish artillery from the right flank. But times are better; formerly both flanks commanded us. The gun on the right continues to harass. He is familiarly known as Beachy Bill. That on the left went by a name intended for the ears of soldiers only. Beachy Bill is, in fact, merely the collective name for a whole battery, capable of throwing over five shell simultaneously. Not infrequently Beachy Bill catches a mid-morning bathing squad. There is ducking and splashing shorewards, and scurrying over the beach to cover by men clad only in the garments Nature gave them. Shrapnel bursting above the water in which you are disporting yourself raises chiefly the question: Will it ever stop? By this you, of course, mean: Will the pellets ever cease to whip the water? The interval between the murderous lightning-burst aloft and the last pellet-swish seems, to the potential victim, everlasting. The suspense always is trying.

The times and the seasons of Beachy Bill are inscrutable. Earlier on, the six o'clock bather was not safe. Now he is almost prepared to bet upon his chances. Possibly an enemy gun is by this time aware that there goes on now less than heretofore of that stealthy night discharge of lighters which used to persist beyond the dawn—until the job was finished.

Wonderful is the march of organisation. It appreciably improves daily, under your eyes—organisation in mule transport to the flanks, in the landing of sup-

plies, in the local distribution of rations; the last phase
perhaps most obvious, because it comes home close to
the business and bosoms of the troops. Where, a
month ago, we languished on tinned beef and biscuit,
we now rejoice daily in fresh meat, bread, milk, and
(less frequently) fresh vegetables. It all becomes
better than one dared to expect: a beef-steak and toast
for breakfast, soup for dinner, boiled mutton for tea.
This is all incredibly good. Yet the sickness diminishes
little. Colic, enteric, dysentery, jaundice, are still
painfully prevalent, and our sick are far-flung and
thick over Lemnos, Egypt, Malta, and England. So
long as flies and the unburied persist, we cannot
well be delivered. But the wastage in sick men
deported is near to being alarming.

A regimental canteen on Imbros does much to
compensate. Unit representatives proceed thence
weekly by trawler for stores. One feels almost in the
land of the living when, within fifteen miles, he tinned
fruit, butter, coffee, cocoa, tinned sausages, sauces,
chutneys, pipes, " Craven " mixture and chocolate.
Such a *répertoire*, combined with a monthly visit
from the Paymaster, removes one far from the com-
missariat hardships of the Crimea.

The visualising of unstinted civilian meals is a prevalent pastime here. Men sit at the mouths of their
dug-outs and relate the *minutiæ* of the first dinner at
home. Some men excel in this. They do it with a
carnal power of graphic description which makes one
fairly pine. I have heard a Colonel-Chaplain talk
for two hours of nothing but grub, and at the end
convincingly exempt himself from the charge of carnal-

mindedness. Truly we are a people whose god is their belly. One never realised, until this period of enforced deprivation, the whole meaning of the classical fable of the Belly and the Members.

Yet in the last analysis (all this talk is largely so much artistry) one is amazingly free from the hankering after creature-comforts. There is a sort of rough philosophy abroad to scorn delights and live laborious days. Those delights embraced by the use of good tobacco and deliverance from vermin at nights are the most desired; both hard to procure. There is somehow a great gulf fixed between the civilian quality of any tobacco and the make-up of the same brand for the Army. (The Arcadia mixture is unvarying, but cannot always be had.) This ought not to be. Once in six months a friend in Australia despatches a parcel of cigars. Therein lies the entrance to a fleeting paradise —fleeting indeed when one's comrades have sniffed or ferreted out the key. After all, the pipe, with reasonably good tobacco, gives the *entrée* to the paradise farthest removed from that of the fool. One harks back to the words of Lytton: "He who does not smoke tobacco either has never known any great sorrow or has rejected the sweetest consolation under heaven."

Of the plague of nocturnal vermin little needs be said explicitly. The locomotion of the day almost dissipates the evil. It makes night hideous. One needs but think of the ravages open to one boarding-house imp amongst the sheets, to form some crude notion of what havoc may be wrought at night by a vermin whose name is legion. Keating's powder is *not* " sold by all chemists and storekeepers" on the Peninsula. One would give a week's pay for an effective dose of insectibane.

The tendency is to retire late, and thus abridge the period of persecution. There is the balm of weariness, too, against which no louse is altogether proof. One's friends "drop in" for a yarn and a smoke after tea, and the dreaded hour of turning in is postponed by reminiscent chit-chat and the late preparation of supper. One renews here a surprising bulk of old acquaintance, and the changes are nightly rung upon its personnel. All this makes against the plagues of vermin; and against the monotony that kills, too. Old college chums are dug out, and one talks back and lives a couple of hours in the glory of days that have passed and in the brighter glory of a potential re-entry to the old life. Believe it not that there is no deliverance possible from the hardness of active service, even in its midst. The retrospect, and the prospect, and the ever-present faculty of visualisation, are ministering angels sent to minister.

Rude interruptions come in upon such attempts at self-deliverance. Enemy air-craft make nocturnal bomb-dropping raids and rudely dissipate prospect and retrospect. One harbours a sneaking regard for the pluckily low elevation at which these night flights are made. Happily, they have yet made few casualties. . . . On a ridge above us stands a factory for the manufacture of bombs and hand grenades. Every night mules are laden there for the trenches. One evening a restive mule, ramping about, thrust his heel through a case of bombs adjacent. They responded with a roar that shook the hill-side. Three other cases were set going. At once the slopes and gullies were peopled by thinly clad figures from the dug-outs rushing to and fro in astonishment. The immediate inference was of enemy missiles: no one suspected our own bomb factory. The most curious conjectures were abroad. One fellow bawled that the Turks had broken our line and were bombing us from the ridge above; another shouted that Zeppelins had crept over; one man cried that the cruiser, at that moment working under her searchlight on enemy positions, had "messed up" the angle of elevation and was pouring high-explosive into us. Shouting and lanterns and the call for stretcher-bearers about the bomb factory soon disclosed the truth. The festive mule, with three companions, had been literally blown to pieces; next morning chunks of mule were lying about our depôt. The worst was that our own men were killed and shattered. This was ghastly. Is it not enough to be laid low by enemy shell?

Yet the work of enemy shell on this beach is peculiarly horrible. Men are struck down suddenly and unmercifully where there is no heat of battle. A man dies more easily in the charge; here he is wounded mortally unloading a barge, mending a pier, drawing water for his unit, directing a mule-convoy. He may even lose a limb or his life off duty—merely returning from a bathe or washing a shirt on the shingle.

One of our men was struck by shrapnel pellet retiring to his dug-out to read his just-delivered mail. He was off duty—was, in fact, far up the ridge above the beach. The wound gaped in his back. There was

no stanching it.   Every thump of the aorta pumped
out his life.   Practically he was a dead man when
struck; he lived but a few minutes, with his pipe, still
steaming, clenched in his teeth.   They laid him aside
in the hospital.   That night we stood about the grave
in which he lay beneath his ground-sheet.   Over that
wind-swept headland the moon shone fitfully through
driving cloud.   A monitor bombarded offshore.   Under
her friendly-screaming shell and the singing bullets of
the Turk the worn, big-hearted Padré intoned the
beautiful Catholic intercession for the soul of the dead,
in his cracked voice.   At the burial of Sir John Moore
was heard the distant and random gun.   Here the
shell do sometimes burst in the midst of the burial-
party. Bearers are laid low.   There is indecent
running for cover.   The grave is hastily filled in by a
couple of shovelmen; the hideous desecration is over;
and fresh graves are to be dug immediately for stricken
members of the party.   To die violently and be laid
in this shell-swept area is to die lonely indeed.   The
day is far off (but it will come) when splendid mausolea
will be raised over these heroic dead.   And one foresees
the time when steamers will bear up the Ægean pilgrims
come to do honour at the resting-places of friends and
kindred, and to move over the charred battle-grounds
of Turkey.

There is more than shrapnel to be contended with
on the beach, though shrapnel takes far the heaviest
toll.   Taube flights over the position are frequent by
day, and bombs are dropped.   The intermittent
sobbing shriek of a descending bomb is unmistakable
and heart-shaking.   You know the direction of shrap-

nel; you know in which direction the hellish shower will spread; there is time for lightning calculation and action. But a bomb gives little indication of its degree of proximity, and with it there is no " direction " of burst; a circle of death hurtles forth from the missile. No calculation is possible as to a way of escape.

Taube bombs and machine-gun bullets are not the only missiles from above of which it behoves Anzac denizens to beware. Men are struck by pellets and shell-case from the shrapnel discharged at our 'planes from Turkish anti-aircraft guns. Our aircraft is fired at very consistently. There is a temptation to stand gaping there, face to the sky, watching their fortunes. Such temptation comes from below, and should not be yielded to—unless our 'planes are vertically overhead or on our west. If they are circling over the Turkish position, take cover; for " what goes up must come down," according to the formula accompanying a schoolboy trick; and shrapnel discharged at 'planes on your eastern elevation may as well come down on your altruistically-inquisitive head as bury in the earth beside you.

To all such onslaughts from aloft and around most men show an indifference that is fairly consistent. The impression is left with you that there is quite a large number of them who have " come to terms with themselves " on the subject of an eventuality of whatever nature, and this is abundantly clear when you see them after their tragedy has eventuated. There is little visible panic in the victims in any dressing station, little evidence of astonishment, little restlessness. Men lie there quiet under the thrusts and turns of the sword of pain, steadfast in the attitude of no-compromise with suffering. To this exceptions will be found; all men have not reckoned up squarely and accurately beforehand the cost of all emergencies that are possible. But most of them have.

CHAPTER III

GLIMPSES OF ANZAC

II

A WHOLE legion of Gallipoli maps has been published in the Press. They show the landing-places. All Australians know the Anzac positions where their sons and brothers scrambled from the boats, splashed to the fatal sand, and fell forthwith or fixed the steel and charged to conquer or fall above. This spot, where Australians showed the world what manner of man is nurtured beneath the Southern Cross, is fair to look on. We saw it first from the sea, in the full burst of the spring. Literature, ancient and Byronic, glows with the beauties of the Ægean spring. It's all true. Anzac is reckoned a true type of that loveliness. The charge was made up a steep ridged hill opening upon an irregular tableland. Either flank of that hill is gently undulating low country. The thin belt of light sand fronts all. The deep wild-flower colour flung in broad splashes upon the low country of the flanks is foiled by the delicious blue that bathes the sand-strip. When the ancients gave us a picture of all this we questioned it, as perhaps painted inaccurately in the elation of literary composition. That is not a right inference. One attempts to describe it as it appears in 1915; but there is the danger of being disbelieved, because the prodigal flinging of spring colour over the shores of Gallipoli utterly surpasses in richness the colour of Australia. England doubtless shows something far more like it in spring. The colour ashore is a glowing red—acres of poppy waving there upon the green plains. Neither do we know the Ægean blue in Australian waters, somehow. The reader, harassed by the war news from this smiling land, may conceive the incongruity of this fair land-scape splashed with colour of another sort—the red dust of a moving troop, the hideous discolour of bursting lyddite, and the grey smudge of shrapnel. A grand range of chalk hills runs south behind the pasture of the right flank. The low shore plain of the left flank is backed by a group of green pinnacles moving north towards the glittering salt-lake. The coast, northerly, sweeps out to the southern horn of Saros Bay—a rough, sheer-rising headland, southern sentinel of the great Saros Cliffs.

Moving inshore to the foot of the Anzac plateau, one gets a delusive impression of Anzac smoothness. Anzac in detail is rough: small gulches, ravines—Arabian *wadys*—which at once hindered and assisted the aggressors at landing. Leaving behind the beach, with its feverish busyness, the climb up to the trenches begins forthwith. You follow a well-engineered road levelled in the bed of the ravine. In the sides the dug-outs are as thick as dwellings in a Cairene alley—which is saying much. Beaten side-tracks branch off like rivulets which join a mountain torrent. The only haven for mules and horses is the shelter of the banks, which have been half dug out at intervals into an extensive sort of stable. It is the height of the after-

noon. There is no wind stirring under the hill. The
men off duty are sleeping heavily—have flung themselves down, worn-out, and lie in the thick dust of their
shelters, where the flies swarm and the heat reeks
But all are not sleeping. Periodically a regimental
office is dug in; the typewriters are noisy: they make
a strange dissonance with the hum of bullets above,
which does not cease. The post-office lies in a bend of
the path. This is dug deep, with sandbag bulwarks.
There's no sleeping here. A khaki staff sorts and
stamps, in this curious subterranean chamber, amidst
a disorder of mail-bags and the fumes of sealing-wax.
One hopes, in passing, the shrapnel will spare this
sanctuary. . . . Half a mile up, the road peters out
into a rough and dusty track under the hill-crest. It
is heavy climbing. One realises fully for the first time
what a scaling was here at the first charge. It has
been hard work up a beaten road: what for those
hampered infantrymen, with their steel-laden rifles
and their equipment, and the Turks raining death from
their entrenchments aloft ? It was seventeen minutes'
work for them; we have been panting and scrambling
for forty, and are not up yet. Five minutes more
brings us to the sentry guarding the entrance to the
communication-trench. He sets us on our stooping
way. You dare not walk erect. Here the bullets are
not " spent," though " spent " bullets can do damage
enough. The labour of trench-making must have
been enormous. Here is a picked trench five feet deep,
and half as wide again as your body, cut out of a soft
rock—hundreds of yards of it, half-miles of it. Fifteen
minutes looping along brings us to an exit opening on
a battery, where two guns are speaking from their

pits. In a dug-out beside the pit lies the presiding genius with his ear to a telephone. His lingo is almost unintelligible, except to the initiated. From the observers on our flanks he is transmitting the corrections and directions to his gunners. One man is jugghng shell from the rear of the pit; one is laying the gun; the rest are understrappers. The roar of discharge, heard from behind, is not excessive. What comes uppermost is the prolonged whizz and scream of the shell. Artillery work must be far the most interesting. The infantryman, a good deal, aims " in a direction," and hopes for the best. The man at the gun watches each shot, the error is gauged, and he acts accordingly at the next. His is a sort of triumphal progress upon his mark. . . . Re-entering the trench, we crept to our second line. There were a few scattered marksmen. There is a kind of comfort, even in trenches. The sleeping-places hollowed out under the lee of the wall, a foot from the floor, will keep one more or less dry in rain. There are carnal symbols of creature comfort scattered up and down—blankets, newspapers, tobacco-tins, egg-shells, orange-peel, and the wrappings of Mexican chocolate. But it's harsh enough. From the crackle of musketry and the song of the bullet and the intimate scream of the shell there's little respite.

The labyrinth of trenches becomes very intricate as you approach the front line: saps, communication trenches, tunnels, and galleries, make a maze that requires some initiation to negotiate successfully. In the rear lines the men off duty are resting, as well as may be, plagued as they are with flies, heat and dust. In general they are too far exhausted to care much, so long as they can get their tobacco and a place to lie. They try to lie comfortable in the squalor; try to cook a trifle at their pathetic little hole-in-the-wall fires. The most impressive thing near the first line (there are things more impressive when you get there) is the elaborateness and permanency of the trenches and dug-outs and overhead cover. One might think the beggars are here for a year: which God forbid! The impression of keenness and alertness here is in striking contrast with the easy-going aspect of the "reservists." The men work at frequent intervals, in pairs, one observing with the periscope, the other missing no chances with the rifle. We looked long and earnestly through a periscope. Two things arrest you. The first is the ghastly spectacle of our dead lying beyond the parapet. They have been there since the last charge; that is three weeks ago, and they are black and swollen. They lie in so exposed a place that they dare not be approached. The stink is revolting; putrefying human flesh emits an odour without a parallel. An hour's inhalation was almost overpowering. One asks how our men have breathed it for three and five months. The flies swarm in hosts.

The second thing that arrests you is the amazing proximity of the enemy trenches. You put down the periscope and look furtively through a loophole to verify. The average distance is about fifteen yards. Our conductor smiled at the expression of amazement. "Come along here; they're a bit closer." He took us to a point at which the neutral ground was no more than five yards in width; rifle and bayonet extended from either trench could have met across it. We well believed our men could hear the Turks snore. This is an uncanny proximity. One result is that the bomb is the chief weapon of offence. To shy a bomb effectively over five yards is as good a deed as drink. Bomb wounds are much to be dreaded. The missile does not pierce, it shatters, and there is no choosing where you will have your wound. We laid well to heart the admonition to be momentarily on the look out for bombs.

We worked slowly back along a tortuous route. These are old Turkish trenches. They had been so constructed as to fight in the direction of the sea. When our men took them they had immediately to turn round and build a parapet on the side more remote. They were choked with Turkish dead. To bury them in the open was unthinkable; they had to be thrown into pits excavated in the trench wall, or flung aloft. and buried beneath the new inland parapet. The consequence is that as you make your way along the trench floor you occasionally come into contact with a protruding boot encasing the foot of a Turk. We had more than one such unsavoury encounter. The odour arising from our own dead is not all with which our infantry have to contend. War isn't fun. A good deal of drivel is spoken and written about the ennobling effects of warfare in the field.

The men who have had four months of this are, in great part, pasty-faced ghosts, with nerves on raw edge. What may one expect ? Inadequate rest, and that rudely and habitually broken; almost an entire want of exercise—except in the charge; food that is necessarily scanty and ill-nourishing ; a perpetual and overpowering stink of the most revolting kind; black swarms of flies that make quiescence impossible—even if enemy shelling and enemy bomb-slinging did not; a nervous strain of suspense or known peril (or both) that never is lifted. Australians have done their part with unequalled magnificence. But they are not gods. Flesh and blood and spirit cannot go on at this indefinitely. God help the Australian infantryman with less than a frame of steel wire, muscles of whipcord, and a heart of fire. The cases are rare, but men have been driven demented in our firing-line, and men who in civil-life were modest, gentle, tender-hearted, and self-effacing, have become bloody-minded, lusting to kill. War is *not* fun; neither is it ennobling.

It was fighting of another sort when Greeks and Persians traversed this ground. For the Narrows was, more than possibly, the crossing-place of the Hellespont for either host. Anzac or Gaba Tepe would be, almost inevitably, right in the track. Australian trenches perhaps cut across the classic line of march. Who is to say that the site of Xerxes' Headquarters-camp is not at this moment serried with Australian dug-outs ? Where he stood to embark, the wireless operator may now be squatting in his sandpit receiving from our cruisers. Certainly every mile over which we are fighting is charged with classical associations.

The new geographical nomenclature stands contrasted with the classical, as do methods of transport and fighting. What does the dust of Persian Generals know of Quinn's Post, Walker's Ridge, or Pope's Hill ? Even the Turkish names are despised. We are "naming" our own map as we go on. Pope's Hill is a feature in the lansdcape considerable enough to have justified a Turkish name before we came here. The map of Gallipoli, as well as that of Western

Europe, is in a state of flux. Should Gallipoli be garrisoned, Australian terms, not to be found in the dictionary, will stick; scrubs, creeks, and gullies, dignified with the names of heroes who commanded there, will abound.

It is by way of Shrapnel Gully we regain the beach. The Australian hospital stands on the right extremity— by no means out of danger. A sparse line of stretchers is moving down almost continuously. This is a hospital for mere hasty dressing to enable wounded to go aboard the pinnace to the Hospital ship standing out. Collins Street doctors who have left behind surgeries " replete with every convenience " find themselves in others that are mere hastily run up *marquées.* Half the attendants hop or limp. They have been peppered. The dentist's outfit is elaborate, and plagued men may have teeth " stopped " or extracted. There is a mechanical department, too, where artificial teeth are repaired—teeth that have been wrecked on the Army biscuit, which is not just angels'-food. Dentists' kit is almost complete; lacks little, in fact, but an electric current.

The beach is animated. There are A.S.C. depôts almost innumerable, wireless stations, ordnance stores, medical supply stores, and what-not. This is not the pride, pomp, and circumstance of glorious war, but the hard facts and hard graft and dirt, sweat and peril, of righteous war. It is by these mundane means the clash of ideals is proceeding, and by which a decision will come. . . .

Only when the masked enemy batteries of the flanks are firing (which is many times in the day) is the beach cleared and quiet. At one stage a couple of Lieutenants-Colonel limited the adminitory patrolling to themselves during fire. They walked up and down unconcernedly with an heroic and nonchalant self-possession, swearing hard at the men who showed themselves. The hidden battery cannot be located. The cruisers are doing their best with searching fire; their bluejackets are climbing the masts to observe; the balloon is aloft; the seaplanes are vigilant; our own outposts never relax. There is no clue. It is concealed with devilish ingenuity. Every day it is costing us dearly.

All's fair in war. Their sniping is awfully successful. They have picked off our officers at a deadly rate. Lance-corporals have become Lieutenants in a single night. Transport of supplies to the flanks is done by mule-carts manned by Sikhs. The route is sniped at close intervals, by night as well as by day, and by machine-gun as well as by the rifle; beside, it is swept by shrapnel. Only under the most urgent necessity are supplies taken to the flanks by day. Then the loss in men and mules is heavier than we can bear. The Turkish sniper is almost unequalled—certainly un-excelled—as an unerring shot. At night the rattle of the mule-carts directs the fire. At certain more exposed intervals of the route the carts move at the gallop, the drivers lying full-stretch in the bottom of the carts and flogging on to safety. Is not this worse than trench-fighting ? The Sikhs are doing a deadly dangerous work unflinchingly well.

It was reported unofficially that two Turkish women were captured sniping. Rumours are persistent enough as to the presence of women in and behind the Turkish lines. Our outposts claim to have seen them, and victorious attacking parties that have captured Turkish camps have been said to declare they have found hanging there garments of the most significant lace-frilled sort. The unbelieving diagnose these as the highly-embellished pyjamas of Turkish officers. The whole thing is probably to be disbelieved. The Turk is too seriously busy to be distracted by the blandishments of his women. Harems doubtless are left · well at home, to be revelled in when the British have ultimately been driven into the sea.

The men bathe, but often pay too dearly for the bath. The bathing beach is a place notorious for good-humoured but successful "lifting." In the early stages there was mixed bathing of Colonels and lance-corporals, Majors and full privates. The Colonel leaves his boots on the sand; a private is sneaking off— " Hey ! those —— boots are mine !". . . All ranks go about ashore dressed alike, with the rank shown symbolically; distinguishing marks of rank become distinguishing marks for sharp-shooters too: you must know a Captain by his bearing rather than his clothes. Curious dialogues arise. The officers are in a garb which differs in many ways from their dress of the promenade at Shepheard's Hotel.

There is little damping of spirits. Most men are happy. Pettiness is snubbed. All are bound by the common danger into the spirit of amity. There is growling day and night—the legitimate growling of the overwrought man, which means nothing. Little outbursts of the liver there are, but of a different quality from those civilian ventings of the spleen.

CHAPTER IV

SIGNALS

THE step is a far one from the signal-office of the first month in Anzac to that of December. The first crude centre of intelligence was like a Euclidean point— without magnitude, with position only. It was a mere location from which signals could be despatched, without any of the show of a compartment, and without apparatus. And the wireless station was a hastily scratched hole in the sand, where the operator supported himself on an elbow and received.

Now in December this is all changed. The Army Corps Signal Office is a building, of sandbags and timber and galvanised iron, standing four-square, solid as a blockhouse, protected alike from wind and the entrance of rain and (by its branch-thatched roof) from the hawk-glance of the aircraft observer.

Within there is an incongruous sense of civilisation. The staff is clean, neatly dressed, shaven—in a word, civilianised. The spirit of order presides. Except that the denizens wear a uniform, and that the walls are of sandbag, you might be in a metropolitan telegraphic office. They sit there tap-tap-tapping in their absorbed fashion. The shrapnel screams overhead and bursts to their north. They are too intent to hear it, mostly. All that has disturbed them, in the last month, is the cry of " *Taube !*" (colloquial *Torb !*).

Anti-aircraft bring them trooping out to squint up at the swift, black, forbidding craft humming raucously across the position. They laugh at shrapnel, under the lee of the protecting ridge: no ridge makes immune from that whirring dove of peace up there!

As you stumble up the Gully at night the illumination of the signal-office gives a touch of the arclight and of city brilliance to the place. The operators, sitting there, as you peer in from the outer darkness, are a part of another world. Those not transmitting or under call sit reading sixpenny editions and smoking cigarettes. They are tapping out no orders from Headquarters. Neither in the words before them nor in the placid *tap* of the instruments is there any hint of war. They're in London. But that sudden roar as of a locomotive is of no London street traffic; London streets do not roar in a *crescendo*. This is as of a rushing, mighty wind, rising to the scream of a tornado. Comes the blast of explosion which unsettles them in their seats. The walls of their house quake about them, and the shower of earth and *débris* descends; the foul stink drives through the dust, and the well-ordered city room is hurried back, in the twinkling of an eye, into the midst of war in the troublous land of Turkey. A six-inch howitzer shell has exploded in the bank over against them—so close that the unuttered thought flies to the possibility of a nearer ultimate burst. The howitzer; searcher out of the protected sites in ravines, under looming hill-crests, is a searcher of hearts too—a disturber of the placid sense of security.

The *débris* is cleared and the fumes pass, and order returns. The operator goes back to his dot-and-dash monotone, and his neighbour resumes his novel and lights another cigarette. The quiet undertone of conversation revives.

Money is the sinews of war: where, in the anthropomorphic figure, will you place these men of the Army Corps Signal Office? Analytical reader, you may place them at your leisure—if you can. They make vocal (or scriptural) the will of Headquarters. A general order they tap out to the utmost post on the flanks. The flanks flash into them the hourly report of progress. The watch in the trenches is realised, through them, by Headquarters. If the Turk is quiescent, it is the telegraphist here who knows it; if a move is made in the enemy lines—a Turkish mule convoy sighted from the outpost, an enemy bombardment set up—it is flashed through incontinently. These men, who see so little of war—apart from searching howitzer—may, if they choose, visualise the whole outlook along our line. They are to Army Headquarters what the sergeant is to the Captain of infantry: the one may scribble or bawl orders until weary; if the other is not there to distribute and enforce the given word, all will perhaps be in vain.

And Army Corps Signal Office is the link between the Peninsula and General Headquarters stationed in that island lying on the west. Divisions flash in their reports from the flanks to Army Corps; all is transmitted by cable to Imbros. And this is the medium through which G.H.Q. orders materialise. Helles reports here also, by cable, for transmission by cable. Here is the hub of all intelligence relating to the Turkish campaign. For the network of cables centres here: cable from Alexandria to Lemnos, Lemnos to Tenedos, Lemnos to Anzac, Helles to Anzac, Anzac to G.H.Q. on

Imbros. Thus there is direct communication between G.H.Q. and the intermediate base in Egypt; cabled dialogues are practicable regarding reinforcements of troops and supplies of equipment and of food. The storeships that dodge submarines from Alexandria lie at Lemnos waiting to disgorge; Anzac requirements are cabled down to them, and they off-load accordingly into the small transports that the Turks shell daily off Anzac. News of mail is flashed up from Alexandria and from Mudros, and the mail despatch from the Peninsula cabled down. No progress in operations is possible apart from this wizard's hut where the signallers sit and tap and smoke and read.

CHAPTER V

THE DESPATCH-RIDERS

BUT though Army Corps Headquarters is in touch with the flanks by both telephone and telegraph, that is not enough. Either or both may fail. But apart from that, there are some communications which no officer will trust to a wire. And until that is premised one wonders vaguely what is the use for despatch-riders. Almost it would seem that in these days, when so much of the romance of war has departed, telephone and telegraph would do all; indeed, the despatch-rider and his steed would seem among the first of the old usages to vanish before the march of science in the field. But here they are, these lithe, brown fellows with their furrowed bushmen's features —lined, not with years (they average twenty-five) nor with care (they're of a flinging, happy frame), but with the sparse, clear lines of the athlete about the mouth, and about the eyes of the man who has peered into long distances over the interminable plains of Western Queensland. They're horsemen down to the tendons of their heels. You may see them tending their horses at sundown, any day, in mule gully, slinging their saddles across the bar outside their dug-out; and, after, boiling the billy. They're modest, too, like many another good horseman, and will relate the experience of their rides from Suvla only if you press for it. But there is no need for a relation; you may see them ride and sniped most days of the week, if you'll be at the pains to climb the ridge overlooking the level country of the left flank. Before the saps were made their work was no game at horsemanship. But there are intervals where the sap avails them nothing; and here they gallop at the stretch; you may trace their route by the cloud of dust in the wake; and you see them slow suddenly as they get into protected territory. The sniping (they will tell you) is, curiously enough, worst at night; the Turk creeps forth into advanced sniping-positions, and even brings up his machine-gun within striking distance, and directs his aim by the horse's clatter. Despatch-riding, day or night, is known as " the dinkum thing."

CHAPTER VI

THE BLIZZARD

ONE knows little of the times and the seasons at which the early Gallipoli winter plays its pranks. It is fairly gymnastic in its turns of temperature. Still, we never expected a snow-blizzard in November. For thus spoke the official weather-god (through the *Peninsula Press*) regarding that fair month: "November generally comes in fine, with a lovely first ten-days or so. It, however, becomes rather sharp at night, and there may be expected a cold snap in the second or third week of the month. This lasts a few days, after which the weather gets fine and warm until the end of the month. November is, in fact, considered by many to be the most glorious month of the year.". . . .

Thus had it been a month to mark with a white stone. Instead, it marked itself with white stones that were many. The halting autumn was full of vagaries, but there was a persistent bitterness creeping in the wake of the fitful November gales:

And all around me ev'ry bush and tree
Says autumn's here, and winter soon will be—
That snows his soft white silence over all.

We had foreseen the snow-drift no nearer than that. But on the Sabbath morning of the 28th of November we woke to find a Peninsula of snow, with snow-men

98

bearing snow-rifles walking over the snow-ridges. This was the introduction of most of us to a fall. The nearest we had yet come to the meeting was at the " movies " which had shown Cossacks ploughing through their native drifts for the Front. Here was our first touch with reality in utter cold.

The Australian has a reputation for adaptability of which not even cold can rob him. He moved about like any Esquimau. This was true, literally; for the first time he donned his rabbit-skin jacket and his Balaclava cap and peaked field-service. The resemblance to an Esquimau in his bear-skin coat and hood was remarkable. His curiosity worked complementarily to his adaptability. This was like seeing a new country for the first time. The snow made a new world, and no excess of cold was to keep him from examining and wandering. He sloshed about the gullies scrutinising the flakes as they lodged on his clothes; he climbed the ridges to see something more of the general effect. The Englishman regarded him from the stronghold of his snowy tradition with superior commiseration, as who should say: " This'll make the beggar hop !" The ill-starred Egyptians, never previously out of Lower-Egypt, literally and piteously wailed with the cold. The Australians mostly grinned and sky-larked.

By eight o'clock he was pasting all passers-by from his store of ammunition; and after breakfast was conducting a sort of trench-warfare in the gullies, bombing out the glowing enemy with a new brand of hand-grenade, pure-white.

The wind blew a gale, driving the snow like thick smoke over the turbid Ægean. Like rain it was not:

far too thick and cloudy. The towering ridges on our east happily saved us the extreme bitterness of the blast. But it whistled down our sheltered ravines in a gusty fashion.

The trenches had another tale to unfold. For them was no grateful ridge shelter. The freezing gale cut like a frosty knife across the parapet, and drove a jet of ice through the loophole, and whistled ruthlessly down any trench it could enfilade. The " Stand-to " at 5.30 that morning was an experience of Arctic rigour.

No sun relieved the grey, relentless day. The men slopped on through the slush. Never had they conceived anything so cold underfoot. But next morning the ground was frozen hard. Every footprint was filled with ice. Where yesterday we had bogged, we progressed to-day like windmills, with arms spread to keep a balance on the glassy and steep inclining surface. Buckets and pans were frozen over. The bristles of shaving-brushes were congealed into a frozen extension of the handle. It was a valiant man who, having pounded them out into a sort of individuality, ventured to use a razor: the blade seared like a knife of fire.

The sun shone bravely, but could not touch the stubborn ice of the ground. That night was, to denizens of tropical Australia, incredibly frosty. There was no breath of air. The cold bit through six thicknesses of blanket and lay like an encasement of ice about your limbs beneath the covers. Few in Turkey slept two hours that night, and those by no means consecutively.

Next morning the slush oozed out to the sun, and the whole position was as an Australian cow-yard in the winter rains. And that's how the glorious month of November made its *adieux* to Gallipoli.

Yet it's an ill blizzard that blows nobody good. Recent storms had played Old Harry with the landing of supplies at Anzac. In especial, the water-barge had been cast high and dry on Imbros. Warfare is not easy in a country where every pint of water consumed must be landed under fire. Though summer was past, men must drink; salt bacon, salt " bully," dry biscuit, are thirst-provoking; and beside that " insensible perspiration " of which De Quincey was wont to make so much, there is activity on the Anzac Beach, if not in the trenches: a normal activity intermittently stimulated by the murderous shriek of shell from the flanks.

The reserve-supply of water had been already tapped. For a week we had been on a quarter-ration. This eked out at about half a mug of tea per man *per diem*. You ate salt beef for the evening meal without tea; went to bed thirsty, dreaming of the rivers of water, woke to a breakfast of salt bacon unmitigated by tea; and entered on a burning day—though it was winter— a day relieved only by the half-pint at lunch, at which you crunched biscuit and jam.

Men were foregoing their precious nightly issue of rum because it wrought a pleasant fire in the veins, and they had already had enough of fire in the veins. Not only were you drought-stricken, but frozen too, and that to a degree from which heating food would have saved you in part. But there was no water for cooking the heating oatmeal waiting to be issued, nor for the heating rice, which could not be boiled in sea-water.

Though the blizzard came in the midst of this drought it changed all that. Rum-jars, buckets, biscuit-tins, water-cans—yea, the very jam-tins—were filled with snow and there was the precious potential water. Parched and frozen throats were slaked, beards shaven, porridge boiled, bacon and beef defied to do their worst. Removed from the fire, it had a dusty smack. But it was water !

CHAPTER VII

EVACUATION

THERE will be a leavening of Egyptian in the Australian vernacular after peace has broken out. It will persist, and perhaps have a weighty etymological influence— at any rate on the colloquial vocabulary. " Baksheesh " will be a universal term, not confined to sketches of Oriental travel. " Baksheesh " is merely one of the many grafted Arabic terms, but it will be predominant. " Sae 'eda " will be the street greeting (varied by the Sikh " Salaam, sahib "). " Feloose kiteer," " mafish," " min fadlak," " taali hina," " etla," and the rest of them, will be household words. Other phrases, not remarkable for delicacy, will prevail in pot-houses and stable talk. Forcible ejection from a company and polite leave-taking will both be covered by an " imshee "; there will be " classy " " imshees " and " imshees " that are undignified.

Such an evacuation as was effected at Anzac was distinctly " classy." When first the notion of evacuation was mooted there was misgiving. We were with our back (so to speak) to the sea, hemmed in in a narrow sector of coast, with no ground whatever to fall back upon. There was no one who did not expect disaster in evacuating a position such as that; the only debate was as to degree. What would it cost us in lives and money ? And there was a greater fear unspoken—

the hideous reflection that an evacuation would make almost vain the heavy losses of eight months' fighting. Everyone hoped against a giving-up. But soon there was no mistaking the signs of the times—the easing off in the landing of supplies, the preliminary and experimental three days' restraint from fire all along the line, the added restriction upon correspondence—in especial the order to refrain from any reference to the movements of troops either present or prophetic, and either known or surmised; the detailing of inordinately large fatigues to set in order once more the last line of defence.

The most obtuse soon saw his worst fears realised. Notice to quit was, in general, short. On Sunday afternoon, the 12th, the O.C. came panting up the gully. "Fall in the unit at once." They were given an hour and a half's notice to have all ready for transport to the pier. Notice was in many cases far shorter, resolving itself into minutes. But an hour and a half is brief enough. Then there was bustle and feverish stuffing of kit-bags. The dug-out which had been as a home for four months was dismantled and left in dishevelment in a half-hour. It's hard to leave a dug-out—your shelter from shrapnel and the snowy blast and the bitter Turkish frost. It's here that you have smoked the consolatory pipe for so many months—consumed the baksheesh steak and marmalade, read the home letters and the local sheet of home from Australia, played nocturnal poker, yarned with a fellow-townsman, and spread the frugal late supper. It has been home in a sense other than that you ate and slept there; it was home indirectly—by virtue of home mails, home talk, home memories, visualisations nurtured under its shelter in the night watches. Home because it was in Turkey, and that way duty lay.

Now, in a few desecratory minutes, it was rudely stripped, bunks overturned, the larder ratted, the favourite prints brushed from the hessian in the bustle. The vultures from neighbouring dug-outs flocked round for the spoil; the men who yet had no notice to evacuate came for baksheesh. With a swelling heart you disgorged your little stock of luxuries, that you would have taken but had no room for. It breaks your heart to give over to the hands of strangers your meagre library amassed during a quarter's residence, your little table, your baksheesh butter and strawberry jam, potatoes and oatmeal, surplus luxuries in clothing, the vital parts of your bunk, the odds and ends of private cooking utensils that have endeared themselves by long and frequent service at the rising of the sun and at the going down of the same, and late at night. Though the life of a soldier is checkered, without any abiding city, shot with hurried moves by flood and field, yet we had had so many months in Anzac, in the one spot, that we had broken with tradition and had made a sort of home in a sort of settled community. And this was the rude end of all.

We took a hurried snack as the mule-carts were loaded. The cooks made merry (cooks, somehow, always contrive to have a convivial spirit at hand), calling on all and sundry to drink a farewell with them while they scraped and packed their half-cold dixies. Nevertheless—for reasons explicit and subconscious— it was a melancholy toast. We followed the transport to Walker's Pier—taking the sap, though, without exception. This thought was uppermost: "What if

Beachy Bill should get us now?" To a man we took all the cover there was. No one, at such close prospect of deliverance for ever from that shell-swept beach, neglected precautions.

Round at Walker's the beach was thickly peopled with units awaiting embarkation. The bustle and shouting were almost stupefying. The unit " pack up " had been this in a small degree. That was bad enough. Here our own little preparation was both magnified and intensified. It was growing dusk. A whole brigade was waiting with all its Cæsarian *impedimenta*. Impromptu piers had been run out, and were lighted by smoking flares. Pinnaces and barges moved noisily between them. Military landing-officers and naval transport-officers, and middies and skippers of trawlers, bawled orders and queries and responses. On the beach the men lay about on their baggage. Non-commissioned officers marshalled and moved them off. Mule transports threaded a way amongst the litter of men and kit-bags. Officers who knew their time was not yet stood in groups chatting and joking. The men, always free from responsibility, played cards and formed schools of two-up, dipped into their haversacks, and munched and raised to their lips vessels which were not always mess-tins, and did not always contain cold tea only—or even cold tea at all.

We waited. The hour of embarkation was postponed from six to nine. At nine most of the excitement had subsided, and the men lay quiet—except where they revived themselves with a dark issue-liquid. There was melancholy abroad—more than that of weariness in physical exertion. As the hour of embarkation drew on (it was now postponed to ten) its significance came home to their bosoms. The rifles cracked on the ridges, the howitzers spoke, the din of bombs came down the ravine. There were those fellows in the trenches being left to see the last of it, and to get off if they could. Not the most resolute optimist could look towards the bloodless evacuation which the event has shown to an astonished world. Every flash of the guns in the half-moonlight, every rifle fusillade, called up the vision of a last party attempting to leave, and perhaps failing fatally to its last number. "If I could get drunk," said a man wearing his equipment, "I would—blue-blind paralytic. I never felt so like it in my life."

We lay about another hour and a half. Then the order came suddenly to go aboard—so suddenly that the half of the equipment had to be left. The first load was got down; a return was being made for another. "Can't wait," roared the N.T.O.; "leave your stuff or get left. The barge is leaving now. Cast off, for'ard. Go ahead, cox'n." This was not bluff. There was a scramble for the barge. There up in the sap lay the cooks' gear, and half the private kit, to be despoiled (so we said) by some barbarous Turk. "Put that match out. No talking." We puffed out otherwise in silence, into the Ægean darkness. Liberty to talk, to smoke, would have been a boon. There was talking in whispers—worse than nothing. Cigarettes were quenched—and the spirits of that unhappy, close-packed, silent load of silent men. The spent bullets sang overhead in a kind of derision, getting lower and more intimate as we moved on. Soon they were spitting about us and tapping the barge, coming unreasonably near to tapping skulls and chests.

But we got to the side of the darkened transport untouched, after long wandering and hailing of many ships in the darkness. There was complete exhaustion at the end. The men dropped down against their kits and slept fitfully (it was bitterly cold) till the dawn. This was the last look on Gallipoli; it had been a penultimate sight we had of it in the dusk of the previous Sabbath evening, though we knew it not. For a time we could only see the great grey mass flecked with an occasional spurt of flame, where the guns were still belching. Then the glorious sun slowly uprose, and threw up the detail. There were the old and well-remembered and well-trodden heights of Anzac, and lower down we came abreast of all the positions we had known, afar off, and now saw more clearly than ever before. We looked along the deadly Olive Grove. There lay the Beachy Bill battery, which every day had rained screaming hell over the Anzac Beach, and was even now speaking sullenly in the early morning glow.

Achi Baba rose up to the south in a sort of soft splendour; how different from the reality ! That rosy tipped mountain, could we have seen its detail, would show looming bastions, high forbidding ridges, and galleries of guns, and rugged ravines that had well-nigh flowed with the blood of our storming parties. Now it stood there, sloping gently down towards Helles, behind the high, quiet headlands and the bays of the coast. Soon we were abreast of Helles, then of the multitude of shipping in the Straits mouth, and so on down behind Imbros and under Tenedos, and away over the freshening sea to Lemnos, a pale cloud, bigger than a man's hand on the starboard bow. And by mid-day we lay in the quiet waters of Mudros Bay, looking over the canvas-clad slopes.

BOOK III
BACK TO EGYPT

CHAPTER I

LEMNOS

AFTER many delays we landed, and after many wanderings arrived at a camping-ground, and went supperless and tentless to bed—too tired to remark, rolled in our blankets, either drenching dew or stony ground, but not so weary as to be unconscious of the absence of shell. Our Last Post for many months had been sounded by bursting shell (for many a man it had been Last Post indeed); the massed buglers of the battalions seemed now a voice from the land of spirits. There were men (they are to be believed) literally wakened by the stillness in the night, restless through the sudden deprivation of the midnight shriek from the flank and of our own roar of discharge from above. For the nocturnal crack and whistle of bullets, here was the distraction of utter quietness. For a week it was disconcerting.

The *réveille* which wakened you at dawn was hard to place in the first few moments of semi-consciousness. "Am I dreaming? Back in camp at Melbourne?" The flood of consciousness sweeps off that sweet delusion—however sweet this island of rest may be. . . . A woman's voice draws you blinking to the tent door—"*Vashung! Vashung!*" It has a Teutonic gerundial flavour. But it's only the Greek ladies soliciting in the mist the soiled garments of

111

soldiers. They move about the camp until the sun is well transmuted from that dull-glowing ball into the mist-dispelling Day's-Eye, stripping the whole landscape down into stony detail and making those volcanic peaks in the north to glow. Before breakfast is well on the women have amassed their huge bundles, and the 'cute Greek boys, in pantaloons and soldiers' cast-off tunics, have sold you a day's store of oranges and chocolate.

The days are easy. We know we shall move to Egypt (or "elsewhere") incontinently, and will take the leisure the war-gods provide us while we may. Only the fatigues necessary to camp cleanliness and to eating mar the day. Most of it is spent lounging, reading, smoking, yarning reminiscently of Anzac, and scrambling. Write letters we may not at this stage. The general order prohibiting letters dealing with the evacuation and with movements of troops either known or surmised has never been revoked; and has been reinforced by a prohibition against correspondence of any sort—except upon field-service cards—those "printed abominations" for which correspondents at home "thank you very much indeed for sending me."

"What'll we do to-day? Go to the village or to Therma or to the stationary hospital?—to the Greek church or the monastery?—or on a voyage of discovery nowhere in particular?—or just have a loaf?—or go and see if there's any mail in?"

The Australian general hospitals claimed a high average of visits from those men who made friends there. They lay across the water. The Greek ferry-men transported passengers in their gaily coloured craft for

as much as they could get. A fare was "laid down,"
but the Greek is as inveterate a bargainer as your
Egyptian, and the Australian's hobby is to elude a
fleecing. So that the burden of the conversation on
the way over lay mostly upon fares, conducted in as
good Grammar-School Greek as could be resurrected :
which was not very good. But the cardinal numerals
were all that was really necessary: gesture and other
physical complementaries did the rest.

The stationary hospital is a township, downright,
with canvas blocks and a main street and side-roads.
Hospital *marquees* of the larger sort always convey
a sense of permanency. But when pitched in such
numbers and with a view to such a lengthy sojourn
as these Lemnian hospitals anticipated, they gave an
impression of stability not ordinarily associated with
even a base. The huts of the Sisters' quarters, dental
huts, canteen shacks, X-ray huts, and so forth, deepened
the impression. And the furnishings took nothing
from it: the matting, the iron beds, the chairs and
lounges, the lockers, tables, medicine-chests. The blue
suits of convalescents were in sympathy, too, though
they smacked rather of the permanence of the peni-
tentiary. And the traffic in the motor-lorries sometimes added the *quasi*-roar of street traffic.

The Sisters entertained friends at tea in their
recreation-tent—a luxurious red and yellow snuggery,
one of the largest *marquees*, furnished in a way quite
adequate to the tone of a vice-regal garden-party.
Distinctions in rank were deleted. Privates, and officers
of the General Staff, hobnobbed as though in mufti.
The recreation-tent was a great leveller; there a sergeant
presumed with impunity to argue the point with a

8

Colonel from Headquarters. It was the most demo-
cratic assembly active-service had yet produced. The
common bond may have been the dainty afternoon-
tea—the fine china; the tiny sandwiches, furnishing
half an active-service mouthful; the fine linen of the
table-cover; the gentle tones of the hostess's voice:
all these were as unaccustomed to the Brigadier-
General as to the Private on the Peninsula. There was
here the sweet half-delusion of a tea-party at home,
which broke down, for a couple of hours, barriers of
rank. You can conceive the exquisite contrast of the
whole thing (you who rail at afternoon-tea conventions
—deliciously absent here, though !) with the enforced
boorish ruggedness of Anzac. And there was the walk
after along the ridge of the Peninsula on which the
hospital lay, commanding the fine harbour both ways:
on the south bulwarked by precipitous hills rising sheer
as from a Scottish lake, and to the north checked by
the gentle slopes of that rich-hued country, volcanic
to the core, from which the afternoon sun drew out
the warm, unnatural colour ; and the purple of the
peaks lay beyond by the seaboard. " Is there a war
on ?" The question recurred again and again, audibly,
and was answered, not by the company, but by the
blue-clothed figures hobbling painfully upon the broad
road or lying helplessly in the warm December sun.

One of the finest churches stands on the border of
Portianus, the village that was nearest to our Sarpi
camp. It is richly decorated with a profusion of
Apostles, Saints, and scenes from Biblical history on
walls and roof. The altar stands beyond a screen as
wide as the building, fairly overcrowded with symbolic
paintings. The sanctuary was filled daily with

soldiers, who placed baksheesh in the plate as they emerged past the old priest, smiling a Benediction at the door. Those who could make anything of it crowded round the fine black-letter vellum Greek Bible at the reading-desk—a treasure indeed. The rest made an attempt at transliteration of the titles daubed beneath the pictures of the Saints. (Most men on Lemnos acquired at least a nodding-acquaintance with the Greek alphabet.) The old priest had little English, but he was very willing to make a shot at exegesis upon the Biblical pictures. There was an enormously large group of them at the door of exit. He liked best to explicate, in his broken English, a painting of the Last Judgment—God, a stout and irascible-looking old gentleman sitting aloft upon the bench, with the Head-Saints about him, suspending above a mortal the scales of Justice; on the right the gaping mouth of hell, belching flame, and Satan uprising from the heat; on the left the golden gate of heaven, with St. Peter graciously admitting one of the approved, and a condemned wretch cowering towards Hell. . . . The realism of it appealed to the priest's powers of exposition. The others he passed over with a mere cursory indication of the subject. He was a genial old man—genial even when he took us out to the sepulchral yard behind the church and showed the vaults of departed parishioners, with the bones deposited upon the slabs.

Christmas came upon us in Lemnos. There was leisure to be unreservedly merry, and that was much. The Billies came a couple of days before. No one who does not remember well the unloading of Christmas stockings can have a notion of the merriment that was

abroad. Santa Claus is not dead. Had the evacuation been timed a little later he would have visited the
trenches. As it was, he came out of the mythological
past as another Greek god to Lemnos. And the
Greeks, in the whole gamut of their worship, never
evolved a deity more beneficent. Psychologists may
debate the point whether Santa Claus, had he visited
Australians in the trenches, would have brought a
keener zest of enjoyment with his gifts than in the
quiet of Lemnos. But the luxury of appreciation of
all things Christmas was upon the Australians at rest
on this beautiful island, and what is certain is that
had the blessed donors seen the distribution and the
opening-up they could have had no more precious
reward. The Peninsula would have offered a sharper
contrast of enjoyment, but less leisure to enjoy. On
the whole, it was probably a good thing that we got
our Billies during a respite.

The letters enclosed mostly assumed the men in the
trenches on Christmas Day. Other assumptions were
made, notably that in the cartoon, on the Billies, of
a conquering kangaroo and the inscription: "This
bit o' the world belongs to us." That hurt.

Soldiers are children the world over—that is to say
the best and the worst of them. In the throes of
Turkish toil and peril they had read in the mailed
newspapers of the initiation of the Billy-can scheme.
Enemy submarines were uncommonly active at the
time. Hypothetical philippics used to be launched
at night against the submarine that might yet sink
the transport conveying the Christmas mail. Men
threatened to desert to the Navy for purposes of
revenge in any such event.

Nothing was lost through the mundane fact that the Billies were a regimental issue—like bacon and jam and cheese. We forgot that. For a half-day (they came in the afternoon) the camp went mad. We masqueraded in fools' caps, swapped delicacies— and swapped (above all) letters. Whatever may have become of the age of chivalry since Edmund Burke mourned it in Europe, the age of sheer kindness-of-heart is vouchsafed to us for ever since reading the letters in our Billies. Those letters stand worthily beside the finest utterances with the indelible pencil from the trenches; for, after all, true heroism resides as much in those who wait and work in quietness at home for their men as in those at war. Some day an anthology of those letters should be made and published to correct selfishness and churlishness on the earth. For that there is no kind of space here. But it may be well to say, in all moderation, that no such fillip had before been given to the men in the war zone as came with those missives which lay beneath the treasures in the Billies. This was not Christmas at home; but it brought us near to it, and proved again unanswerably (if proof were needed) that intrinsic values in the gifts of this life are very little at all.

The revelry of Christmas had hardly subsided when embarkation orders came again. In the mist of a December morning we struck camp and moved out from the stone pier to the waiting transports—wondering, most of us, when embarkation in the service would cease to recur, and how long it would be before embarkation would come for that long voyage across the Pacific to a Christmas under the Southern Cross.

CHAPTER II

MAHSAMAH

"THE ——th and ——th Divisions will move from ——— to —— in flights of —— thousands daily. Two hundred and fifty camels will be allotted to each flight for baggage-transport. Mahsamah will be the end of the first stage. . . . You will proceed to Mahsamah, taking with you —— thousand rations, establish a depôt, and issue rations to the flights for twenty-four hours."

So ran the order. Confound the flights! Why can't they train it? Mahsamah's out of the world. These camps in desert places are ghastly. We shall be enforced hermits. Entraining, they could get the whole thing over in four days; this way it'll take fourteen. The weather's getting midsummer. The battalions have just had a fresh boot-issue. They'll be sore-footed and sick and sun-stricken. What's the game with Headquarters—to harden the men or impress the natives?

What's that to you? You've got to go, whatever garbled motives Headquarters may have. So get your supplies aboard, and your men, and leave in the morning.

So we found ourselves sweeping over the desert at 9 a.m., with tents and camp equipment in the guard's van and half a dozen trucks laden with supplies trailing behind. The sweet-water canal tore beside us, and patches of irrigated land emerged at intervals into the field of vision, and the low sand-dunes standing away towards Ismailia grew higher; and before the canal fir-groves could become more than a blur in the east we halted and got down, and had our trucks detached, and the train moved off canal-wards, and we set about looking for a site on which to build.

And there was no time to waste. The first flight had left Tel-el-Kebir that morning, and any moment their advance-guard might loom up on the heat-hazed horizon and come in soliciting grub.

A permanent camp of Royal Engineers close at hand lent a fatigue. By three o'clock the virgin depôt was well established.

At four, through a cloud of dust, the advance-party (mostly Staff Officers on horseback) rode in very hot and very thirsty. Brigade Majors boast a thirst at any time and in any weather. Aggravated now, it had first to be assuaged. The Battalion of Pioneers who followed us by train had mapped out the plan of camp on paper, and now proceeded to conduct battalions; for they followed close in the heels of their staffs, dusty and sweating under their packs, and dragging a weary way through the yielding sand. Lucky Majors rode, and surveyed their perspiring men from the cool and luxurious height of a horse. The battalions plumped down in the sand and the sun where they stood. The camel-trains followed, plonking along with their flat-spreading feet and aspiring noses and loads of ration, blankets, tents, tables, and general camp *impedimenta*. Their Indian " dravees " led them by the nose. They gurgled with the heat, and foundered on very slight provocation indeed.

By five the whole flight is established in bivouac lines. For a couple of hours there is feverish bustle at the supply depôt. Half the issuing is carried out by lamp-light. The battalions settle down to sleep with the sun, and there is little energy left for horse-play, though there is a good deal of singing, and even concerts improvised.

But the whole camp is quiet by nine; the men are sleeping in the sand under the moon; there are no lights except in the two tents erected for Staff Officers.

You're wakened at four the next morning by the camp astir, to be off at sunrise. But they have their ration, and you don't get up, but thank Heaven you're a part of no flight.

A part of nothing—for the moment. That's the beauty of this mission. You're subject to nobody. You've brought your own supplies, built your own depôt, and can dictate to Staff Captains and Colonels and to all the tin-hats who may approach you for ration. A supply officer is deeply respected, *ex-officio*. Though he be a mere Subaltern, it is known he holds the distribution of fleshly favours. The officer drawing ration who is incivil is in danger of being the worse for it; only the respectful get baksheesh.

The Fortress Company of Anglesey Engineers camped permanently, who had lent an emergency fatigue, turned out to be a boon and a blessing. It took less time than usual to penetrate the admirable English reticence surrounding their companionable qualities. The penetration began with a neighbourly invitation to their regimental sports, held conjointly with those of a detachment of Hyderabad Lancers camped at Mahsamah for patrol purposes.· They united in a half-day's competition in foot-racing, football, jumping, tug-o'-war, cycle-racing, and the rest of the athletics common to Indians and Britishers. Beside, the Hyderabads gave exhibitions in horseback-wrestling, tent-pegging, cleaving the lime at the gallop, and allied exercises, in which Englishmen do not compete. The Captain of the Lancers was a young Indian aristocrat who spoke English faultlessly, and was a regular and interesting member of the Anglesey mess.

The English gentlemen who drew him and the Supply Officer were in no way roughened by a six months' campaign at Suvla Bay. Gordon was an Irishman from Trinity College, Dublin, who had preceded his course in engineering by reclining in Arts three years and browsing richly and refraining resolutely from cram—an engineer balanced ideally between the world of mere mathematical horse-sense and a gentle other-worldliness, and rich in a fitful and whimsical Irish humour that was good to live with; a man devoted to duty (when any was put in his way, which was seldom), otherwise exercising himself genially upon self-appointed surveys, geological rambling, artful shooting, photography, and banter. No tongue in the mess was a match for his; he emerged from argument with ease and credit always, and left his opponents floundering. A fearless, tender-hearted, courteous Irish gentleman, modest to the point of self-effacement and able to the point of genius. His mother was a friend of Edward Dowden and his circle, and Gordon had in store a rich fund of anecdote relating to academical Dublin.

The Medical Officer—"Doc," familiarly—was a Scotchman with a burr and a subtle uncaledonian quality of humour, and a sparkling intellectuality quite out of harmony with the traditional Scotch lumbering cerebration. Doc was lovable; and a butt through his popularity, though not a butt who took it lying down. But he was never a match for Gordon, though he usually routed the Captain—also a Scotchman— whose hobby was the facetious discussion of ways and means to getting a competent M.O. attached. The Doc's duties were purely nominal, the care of any who might fall victims amongst the Angleseys to toothache, boils, vermin, colds, gashes—any ills, in short, to which men in a desert camp might be hable. For the rest, he shot with the mess, dawdled with " films," perused his Scotch newspapers, improvised schemes in sanitation, dabbled in canal parasites and mosquito larvæ, and forged jokes.

Seymour was a highly-intelligent animal (taking seven-and-five-eighths in hats), who argued with a kind of implacable ferocity, and when he sat down to bridge would never stop before two or three. But all his argument was for mental exercise and not from con-viction, and his fiercest encounters were wont to end in a thrust of bathos at which the mess roared. He was a fine intellectual and physical animal, as keen in riding and shooting and bathing as in dialectic.

The Captain was a diminutive, ceremonious Scotch-man, commanding deference out of doors, bullied to death in the mess by his Subalterns. The contrast between out- and indoors was striking. The last letter of the law in discipline and ceremony was ob-served outside the mess, but at table no Australian officers' mess was ever more informal. Barriers of rank were thrown down, and none but surnames tolerated by the least even unto the greatest.

That mess was as luxuriously appointed as a civilian home. Easy-chairs, writing-tables, messing-tables and their appointments, punctilious servants, matted floors, made one forget for a few hours daily that a war was in progress. For the man who makes himself at home on service you are commended to the English officer. And in a permanent camp such as this he excelled himself. Eating was delicate, glass and silver shone and prevailed. Hours for meals were late and irregular: breakfast at 8.30; lunch light, and at any time; dinner at any hour between 8 and 9.30, and long-drawn-out, so that you generally rose from table between 10 and 11, and sat back for pow-wow after.

It was a rare day there was not game in the mess. Adjoining the sweet-water canal was a lagoon, reed-fringed and with reed-islands where you could row a mile and believe yourself in Australia; no sand to be seen. Three times a week we shot. There were duck and snipe and teal. The Sheikh of the village furnished half a dozen shot-guns and as many boats and boatmen, and came himself, carrying a gun (and proud he was of his shooting—and justly so).

One man one skiff was the order. We would set out at 4.30, after tea, and return at 8. The danger was to forget the duck in the still beauty of the evening. As you watched the reddening west over the reeds, the birds coming across the ruddy ground would recall you to business. Shooting was easy, so we got a lot. The place was untrammelled. Except for an occasional General who came up for a day's sport (the Staff had got to know the Mahsamah Lagoon), there was little shooting done, and the water had not yet become a scare-area. The Sheikh did a little on his own account. The underlings he provided knew their work, and would ejaculate and advise in Arabic: *Talihena! Bakasheen kebir!* (snipe — big one!)—in a hoarse, excited whisper, as the birds rose on the breeze. *Aywah*, you mutter, making ready. They would strip and go into the reeds waist-deep for birds fallen there. *Quaiys kiteer!* (fine), greeted a hit; and if you missed, a consolatory *Malish!* (never mind), *Bukrah* (perhaps to-morrow), uttered with a gentle ironical intonation. Rowing back there was always baksheesh in cigarettes or cartridges—or both; and some, with their skins wet and muddied from wading, deserved it. Some did not.

The natives fished the lagoon systematically with nets, at night. You encountered them as you pursued duck. They regularly exported crates of fish to Cairo and Zagazig. When the nets were spread they would " beat-up " the fish with tomtoms in the boats. You might hear their solitary cries and their rhythmic tattoo on the water all night.

They fished with hnes, too—to order. If you gave them an order at the camp for a dozen they would have them back in half an hour, wriggling on a string. They were proud of their craft, and would throw you a triumphant glance, as who should say, " Let's see you do that !"

The Arab village lay on .the banks of the canal. Comely villagers they were, with well-featured women and men with a continent, contented air, living by fishing or growing of crops. The camera they funked, and that distinguished them from the raucous, dissolute denizens of Cairo, who delight to ape attitudes for the photographer. They showed all the best qualities of the fellaheen. There was no obsequiousness in the men, as in the capital. There is no crowd more cowardly and villainous than the Cairene mob. But the men at Mahsamah, when the sojourning Australians attempted to commandeer their canalferry, pushed them incontinently into the stream. This was conduct unprecedented in the Egyptian. A town-and-gown fight ensued. Skulls were cracked, and the Australians had by no means the better of it. There was a dash of the old fighting Bedouin blood in these fellows. There was to be no bullying here; and there was none.

Only the station-master had forfeited his independence of spirit. He alone of the whole village was in habitual contact with " the public." It had wrought in him a fawning plausibility the more contemptible by its contrast with the sturdiness of the surrounding natives. He lied by habit; the fictitious way was more natural with him than the way of truth. In official dealings he lied first, and afterwards modified it into truth. Regardless of consistency, he said invariably what he thought would please. Railway time-tables with him varied with the estimated temper of the inquirer. This seems incredible, but it is true. He was the only village inhabitant who ever invited you to take coffee; and he (the potentially dignified stationmaster) alone, in all the village, was ever known to sohcit baksheesh—an oily, yellow, perennially-smiling, small-bodied, altogether small-souled railway-official,

in him seemed incarnated the slavish spirit of official-
dom in all Egypt.

Bathing in the Canal was forbidden along its whole
length. There lurked a parasite that played Old
Harry with livers. It ravaged the natives in rare cases,
though, having drunk and washed in the canal from
infancy, a sort of immunity was claimed for them.
But there were victims to the parasite to be seen
amongst them—no pretty sight.

A favourite walk at sundown was the canal-bank.
The reed-shot lagoon on the east, traversed by sporadic,
crying duck; the gentle wind, blowing warm off the
Libyan Desert, drifting the silent dhow; a solitary
fellaheen on his ambling beast; an Arab doing his
devotions in the tiny praying-crib on the water's
brink; the west darkening behind the palm-tufts over
the illimitable sand. There was a peace here little
known in our other halting-places in the Delta.

CHAPTER III

CANAL ZONE

AT Serapœum, sprawled upon the Canal-banks just above the Bitter Lakes, you are sufficiently far from Cairo to be delivered from the hankering after the city such as gnaws you intermittently at such a place as Tel el Kebir. From the old battle-ground you may run up in a couple of hours; from the Canal the length of the journey is trebled, and encroaches seriously upon your *feloose*, and that is a consideration which ought not to—which will not—be despised on service. And beside the fact that the rail journey is trebled from the desert camp, there are some miles of dismal sand-plodding between you and the railway-station, and the desert has inspired you with the Sahara lassitude and an unfevered frame. You feel, in this waste of brown sand, the incipiency of the mood of the contemplative Arab, to whom the whirl of the metropolis is anathæma; but only its incipiency, because there is still in your blood the subconscious resentment of eight months' enforced inactivity on Anzac. Compulsory monotony, whatever its form, raises a temperamental hostility: whether the monotony of geographical confinement, limited vision, shell-scream, innutritious food, inescapable dirt and vermin, or that of wide and sand-billowed outlook, delicate messing, tranquil sleeping, luxurious Canal-bathing,

127

heat, and flies. Cairo is Cairo. The Peninsula, as comfortable as this, would have been far less intolerable. But so long as it is something less than the trackless Ægean that divides from the glamour of Egyptian cities, you clamour for leave.

This is unintelligible—this *blasé*, surfeited mind of the Australian soldier, in Cairo. "Never want to see it again! I'm fed up with Cairo!" is a judgment strangely prevalent in the army of occupation. How any land and people so utterly strange to the Australian can become indifferent to him is incomprehensible. Every Cairene alley is a haunt of stinks and filth—but a haunt of wonder, too. Cairene habits that are annoying and· repulsive are at the same time intensely interesting. To get behind the mind of this people and hazard an estimate and a comparison of its attitude towards life is an occupation endlessly amusing.

But you may clamour for leave here with little effect. Divisional orders have minimised it to men. going to Cairo on duty. Duty-leave is a time-honoured slogan that has been accustomed to cover a multitude of one's own ends. But the added stringency of leave regulations which preface a projected move of the division scrutinise very closely all that is connoted by the term "Duty-leave," and lop away a good many of its excrescences. So that, on the whole, you end by settling down in the great sand and feigning a lively response to the call of the desert.

You do respond. You must. Anyone would; but not ardently.

We are on the Sinai side of the Blue Trough which colours richly between its shores of light sand. We

also are colouring richly. It's far too hot for representative uniform clothing. Yet the clothing is uniform—uniform in respect of a discardment of tunic
and cap and a ubiquity of shirt. The broad-brimmed
hat and the gauze shirt and the half-bared thigh for
us; and the daily bathe.

The soldier is very busy indeed—too busy to live—
who cannot get time to trudge over to the blue water,
doff, and disport himself in that cool, tideless limpidity,
which recreates (we are gross, material creatures)
his world. The banks swarm with brown, deep-
chested nudes; the water is strewn thickly with smooth-
haired, colliding Australians, elated by the bodily
change almost beyond belief. Desert livers, desert
lassitude, and desert shortness of temper, cannot persist
in this medium. And the rest of the day is transmuted
by it. The Canal adds to efficiency.

Ships of all nations pass daily, and ships of all classes
at Lloyd's. Those are reckoned A1 which bear
women-passengers. Raucous warning to those men
who are back to nature on the bank is given as the
mail-boat creeps up. Everyone who is wearing his
birthday garment plunges and swims out. The ship
is surrounded by a sea of heads, and greeted with all
the grafted Arabic phrases that Australians have
acquired—no, not all; but with all those suited to
polite society. The facetious cry for baksheesh rises
with a native Arabic insistence (but is responded to
with a freedom not customarily extended to natives):
" *Sai-eeda !—Baksheesh !—Gib it !—Gib it baksheesh
for the baby !—Gib it !—One cigarette !—Gib it tabac !—
Gib it half-piastre !—Enta quies !—Quies kiteer !—
Kattar kairak !*" as the shower descends : tins of

cigarettes and chocolate, and keepsakes that are not edible.

There is as much excitement on deck as in the water. There is monotony of sea-travel as well as of desert life; the same encounter interrupts both. And apart from that, one can believe that these peoples are genuinely glad to see each other. The soldiers have looked in the face of no woman for far too long, and the admiration of the women for the fellows is not necessarily feigned. They throw over greetings with the other baksheesh luxuries, and these are returned in kind. The girls are sports in the Australian sense, offering suggestions to come aboard, and go tripping with rather more freedom than they would probably use were there any possibility of an acceptance of the invitation. Inevitably there is one woman (never a girl) in fifty who spoils it all by a touch of Jingoism—calling them brave and noble fellows to their faces, and screaming ''Are we downhearted ?'' in a way Stalky would have disapproved. This is volubly resented in responses to that oratorical question which have no direct reference to the state of their spirits.

The boat moves on, fluttering with handkerchiefs, to the transport staging, always crowded with men, who are not nude. The shower of baksheesh is flung over again. Women are not notoriously good shots. For the packages that fall short the men leap in, clothes and all, and scramble, and reckon themselves well repaid. One afternoon the largest package for which clothes were wetted proved to be a bundle of *War-Cries* and allied journals, dropped either by some humourist or by one sincerely exercised for the spiritual welfare of the troops. The latter was the inevitable assumption. The donor was greeted by the dripping warriors with a chorus of acknowledgments that could leave no doubt as to their spiritual needs. Soldiers have a religion, but they are not accustomed to make it explicit.

The passing ships lighten the dulness. They bring a whiff of the great British civilian world that is otherwise so unrelentingly far removed, and which Cairo (when one does get there) brings very little nearer.

The Canal is crossed at Serapœum by pontoon ferry, row-boat, and pontoon-bridge. Take your choice. But that is not always possible. Sometimes the bridge is swung open for hours on end to allow liners, tugs, dhows, and launches to pass. It was built for vehicular and animal traffic—for the transport of supplies, in fact, from Egypt to the troops in Sinai.. When open it therefore bears a constant stream of G.S. waggons loaded with army stores. It's one stage of the journey of beef from the plains of Queensland to the cook's " dixies " in the Sinaian desert trenches. Supplies are disembarked at Suez and Port Said, entrained to Egyptian Serapœum, transported by waggon across this bridge to the desert railway terminus on the opposite bank; they are trucked out to railhead beyond the sandy horizon, and thence Canal trains bear them to the desert outposts for final distribution. And that is the chequered career of the Argentine ox, who never dared hope for himself any such distinction as that of contributing to the efficiency of His Majesty's Forces in the Peninsula of Sinai.

The miniature desert railway is no despicable .

contrivance, puffing there and back-firing from its
nuggety petrol engine.   It can make fifteen miles an
hour with fifteen trucks of supplies lumbering behind.
Sometimes it leaves the somewhat flimsy track; sometimes it runs down an unaccustomed Arab in a desert
dust-storm; and sometimes it " sticks " quite as
annoyingly as any petrol-driven vehicle can do.
Whatever the nature of the obstacle—mangled Arab
or jibbing engine—there is lusty swearing; for the
business of the desert railway is of more urgency than
that of most links in the lines of communication.
For instance, it—and it alone—can furnish with anything approaching expedition the daily water-supply
of the advanced trenches in the April Arabian sand.

It was during the first day of the *khamseen* that the
engine-wheels became clogged with the remains of
a man whom the whirling dust prevented from seeing
or hearing anything of engines.   The violence of the
annual April *khamseen* is incredible by those who
haven't suffered it.   The initial days of the *khamseen*
period the Egyptians celebrate in the festival of
Shem el Nessim.   They go out into the fields of the
Delta (of the Delta, mark you) with music and with
dancing.   There's no disputing about taste—if, that
is, the *khamseen* is blowing " up to time."   Nothing
more distressing you'll meet amongst desert scourges.
It's the *khamseen* which kills camels in mid-desert
by suffocation.   That is a fair test of the driving
and dust-raising powers of the storm.

It begins with a zephyr for which the uninitiated
thanks Allah in the first half-hour.   By the end of
an hour he is calling upon Allah for deliverance.   At
the end of a day he speculates upon his chances of

seeing the morning. At the end of the second day he calls upon Allah to take away his life. The *khamseen* this year lasted two days without intermission. It began at dark without further warning than that of a leaden sky and a compression of the atmosphere. But these are indications that are, in Egypt, so often indicative of nothing, that they lose significance altogether. On the 20th of April they proved to have been highly charged with meaning. In forty minutes the gale had reached its height. And there it stayed. Men expected relief momentarily; but it never came that night—nor the next day—nor the night following. " Such violence cannot last," said the Australian. In twenty-four hours he was not sure it might not last for ever. Few tents stood the strain longer than an hour. Men grumbled and turned in with a half-sense of security from the tempest without. They hardly looked for their house to come tumbling about their ears before midnight. But few escaped that; the others spent the night under fallen canvas. Sinaian desert sand cannot be expected to bear an indefinite strain upon tent-guys. Those tents which stood at sunrise (if sunrise it could be called) were kept up only by the frequent periodicity of the mallet's application in the thick night. As soon as one tent-peg left earth, the beginning of the end was come unless the inmate crouched out and replaced it and strengthened the others. He came back with ears and nose and eyes clogged and face stung painfully. At the third attempt to keep his home up he said: " I'll go no more ! Damn it ! Let it come !"—and it came.

The morning showed no sun—showed nothing farther than six yards away. Men showed a face above demolished canvas and drew back hastily, stung and half-choked by the driving grit. In those tents still standing the furniture could not be judged by appearances. Thick dust covered everything as with a garment. Regimental office tents that had fallen before the gale had lost documents that could not be replaced or ' easily recreated. Food in the mess was inedible; no one ate except to satisfy the more urgent demands of hunger. The outdoor work had to proceed. You couldn't see more than in a North Sea fog. Collisions were inescapable. You couldn't smoke; you couldn't speak, without swallowing the gale. Men got disgusted with continuing to live. On the third morning the desert smiled at you as though nothing had happened. The quiet and the purity of the air were like release from pain. Men set to work at cleaning their hair and alleviating a desert throat.

Anzac Day came upon us at Serapœum—the first anniversary of the day of that landing which has seized and fired the imagination of the Empire. No doubt there are other empires than the British which marvelled at the impetuousness of that maiden proving of Australian temperament; for it was temperament that carried us up. The world had no sound ground for being surprised at success on the 25th of April, except in so far as the world was ignorant of Australian temperament. Yet surprise contended with adoration in the newspaper headings which announced our success in planting a foot on Turkish ridges. But inaccuracy in a use of terms is a quality not inseparable from journalistic headlines in times of public excitement. The fact is that, notwithstanding the world's

expectation of the fatal elaborateness of the Turkish
preparation to receive us, there was no call for surprise
at the event in people that knew Australian conditions
of life and resultant Australian character. And,
granting that as known, the fact that we were fleshing
virgin swords was no legitimate further ground for
surprise, though it was commonly published as such.
It should have been anything but that. People
knowing Australians would be due to recognise that,
in all the circumstances, they would fight better,
under the eyes of the world, in a probationary struggle
calculated to establish their reputation than would
experienced soldiers who knew more than they of
what the task exacted and of its possibilities. Ignor-
ance of warfare other than theoretical was in no sense
a handicap to men of Australian temperament: to
such men it was material aid. In a word, Australians
could not help themselves at the Landing. Were it
otherwise, our troops would not have overstepped
requirements to the extent of unorganised and spasmodic pursuit of the routed enemy. Success at the
Landing was the inevitable result of temperament
rather than the contrived result of qualities deliberately summoned up on the occasion. . . .

The supreme charm of the desert resides in her
nights. Long purple shadows spread over the sand-
tracts before evening. This gives to the sand-sea an
appearance of gentle undulation which is virtual only,
but none the less grateful for the delusion. The
distances are shortened; a crushing blow is dealt by
the peace-loving evening to the desert curse of monotony.
The Suez hills transform to rich purple masses, splendid
in the depth of their colour. The Bitter Lakes sleep

in the south. The Canal settles down to gleam
stealthily between its amorphous banks. The fir-
groves on the shore thicken; the dancing daylight
interstices in their meagre ranks are filled by the
on-coming darkness until you feel there are acres of
thick plantation; they moan quietly in the dusk in
relief from the pitilessness of these burning days. The
little rivers of water scooped about their roots are
filled, and the delicious absorption begins.

Down-stream the coolies are chanting together in
response to an improvised wail unerringly consistent
with the rhythm of their chorus. You will hear
nothing more pathetic than this song removed by
distance. The solo comes down the water in the
cadences of desolation. It may be the irregularity
of the cadence that gives the sense of lamentation; it
may be because the enunciation is never full-chested—
nor even full-throated. It is as though extorted by
a depth of desolation of spirit that cannot stoop
beneath the dignity of rhythmic utterance. Near
or far, the coolie choruses bear the same import of
pathos; and, indeed, there is little happiness amongst
the Egyptians: nothing buoyant (their climate forbids
it); nothing approaching French vivacity of spirit.
There is a profound solemnity in the heart of the
Egyptian. It sometimes finds exaggerated vent in
an unnatural but curtailed burst of merriment, which
quickly repasses into the temperamental sombreness.
The folk-songs and chants of a people are a safe index
to temperament: nothing more consistently pathetic
than this will you hear without travelling far.

The chant ceases as the bow searchlight of a vessel
turns out of the Lakes into the Canal channel, and

illuminates it like a walled street. There are ships that pass in the night, and they light their own way with a brilliancy that takes no risk of collision. The tiny wind-ridges in the banks are in relief; for a mile ahead the minutest floating object is discovered. The coolies hail her as she passes. The night-gangs at work on the barges that bear supplies from Suez and Port Said interrogate hilariously, out of harmony with the still glory of the night, but consonantly enough with the brilliant illumination. There is not much dialogue. Most of the hailing is from the shore alone. . . . She moves on. The banks close blackly about her stern. The lanterns swing again about the barges.

CHAPTER IV

ALEXANDRIA THE THIRD TIME

IT'S like returning to visit an old friend—rushing towards the sea of masts behind the sea of white towers glittering beside the sea of Mediterranean blue. At the first glimpse of that multitudinous shipping you lose interest in the sea of green delta through which you are rushing; the mud-walled village-islands rising from it lose charm in anticipation of the big city you know so well. You remember it with a sort of yearning for its nobility. For noble it is. There is no nobility in Cairo, except seen from the fringe of the Mokattam Hills as you stand on the Bey's Leap at the Citadel looking down on the busy expanse under its wealth of minarets. Cairo is more interesting, because more truly Oriental; it has the charm of utter strangeness. Alexandria is better built, more stately, less evil-smelling; it's the charm of a well-ordered European city that holds you; and there is always the loveliness of that Mediterranean outlook from the clean, gener-ously-broad esplanade. The sea about Cairo is true desert-sand, unending, which is not lovely, except at the dawn and sundown, when the colour leaps up about the far horizon.

For three hours, since leaving Cairo, you have been scouring the green plain in a train of the Egyptian State railways, which bears comparison well with most other rolling-stock that a limited knowledge of the travelling world has given you.   The Delta is unnaturally rich and almost unnaturally green.   Many centuries of Old Nile depositing of fat mud have seemed to concentrate, within that Nile Valley all the richness that is in the soil of Egypt.   Nor is it a green that is ultra-rich by contrast with a desert background, for as far as you see either way there is no sand; you're in the heart of the crops.   There's a monotony of level cultivation which tires you in the end, however rich; a monotony broken only by a monotonous succession of out-cropping palm-groves, sleeping canal, white creeping sail, mud-walled village, and dilapidated mosque.   You tire of the regularity of recurrence.   There is a hankering after the quiet stir and variety of the city of Alexandria quite as strong upon you as Johnson's fervent passion for the atmosphere of London.

There is a simple crudity in the man who persists in being an Englishman to the backbone in the land of Egypt.   The Australian enters much more aptly into the spirit of the country—worms his way into the intricacies of the bazaars and markets, and talks much with the Alexandrian denizens, if only in pantomime.   He "does as they do " far more consistently than the restrained Tommy—even to the extent of consuming their curious dishes, riding on their beasts and in their vehicles, tasting their drinks and smoking their pipes.   The Englishman tends to call always for English beer and for roast beef, and sticks tenaciously to his briar.

Alexandria has changed, too, at the quays.   The transports are no longer lading noisily, nor, when they are lading, taking in ammunition. Mostly they are lying out quietly in the harbour, waiting. In March of last year the harbour was alive with barges bearing fodder and supplies and ammunition, and with motor-launches rushing to and fro carrying officers of the General Staff. Now an occasional Arab dhow drifts lazily, bearing nothing in particular, and the quay-sides are noisy only with a sort of civilian bustle.

And the ubiquitous nursing-sister was not ubi-quitous last year; she was rarely to be seen in the streets; then she was hke the motor-car twenty years ago: you turned round and looked until her gharry was swallowed in the traffic. Now she is, in twos and threes, in the cafés, the Oriental shops, the car, the post office, the mosque; on the esplanade, on the out-lying pleasure-roads of Ramleh, the golf-hnks, the race-course; the Rue Cherif Pacha teems with her, shopping or merely doing the afternoon promenade. She is sprinkled among the tea-parties at Groppi's; her striking red and grey adds colour to the Square of Mahomet Ali, the Rue Ramleh, and the Rue Rosette.

Do not infer, gentle reader, that there is nothing to be done in hospital. There is; but less. Gallipoli wounds either are healed or sent to Australia to heal in the fine St. Kilda air. It's mostly sick in hospital now, and sick requiring merely routine attention. And, beside, there are more hospitals than a year ago. Since the Turkish fight began they have been increasing; and now it's over, the Lemnian hospitals of the ad-vanced base have sailed back, and, in cases where they are not yet re-established, their Sisters are running about the capital unchained, revelling in a well-earned respite, with he Ægean roses blowing in their cheeks.

Of hospitals there is no end, in the airy suburbs. The splendid houses of rich Beys fly the Red Cross at unexpected stages of the ride to Ramleh. An amazing number of private houses are in use thus. The convalescents wander over the lawns and through the shrubberies and perch on the balconies. There is evidence of the havoc played by Turkish weapons and Turkish sickness on all hands. The impression is of Alexandria's having been hard put to it to find hospital accommodation.

In these respects Alexandria has changed, but not in itself. It has the same well-bred appearance as a city. There is the same absorption of its regular population in business or in pleasure. The Bourse, the hub of the city, is as animated as ever with bearded, gesticulating French, Italian and Greek financiers taking their coffee on its verandah looking down the Square. The Rue Cherif Pacha is as close-packed as before with the carriages of rich French dowagers and pretty French aristocrats. They have their coachmen in livery, and they know how to dress irresistibly. There are not many finer human sights in this world than is made by a young French mother, gowned and toileted with an art that conceals art, reclining in the barouche with her daughters in the Alexandrian winter afternoon sunshine. The Melbourne " Block " brags of its reputation for beauty, but here is a fine essence of beauty such as Paris at her best would own, which Paris, one suspects, actually does flaunt in the summer. The best beauty of Paris, Milan, and Athens, winters here. So does much of England. At present it is chiefly the wives of officers; and they are no mean stock.

That Place Mahomet Ali is endlessly interesting and endlessly picturesque. The gamut of the city's life is run-over here any afternoon. It's a stately Square: stately in the buildings that surround it— Stein's and the majestic Bourse and St. Mark's and the best hotels. There are the rows of well-kept gharries and well-groomed horses—kept as well as most private carriages. The two well-planted islands stand green and quiet in the midst of the gentle roar and moving colour, and the fine equestrian statue of Mahomet Ali looks with dignity down upon it all. It's perhaps the most cosmopolitan crowd in the world that moves about the Square. The typically Arab quarter is segregated—lies in a labyrinth of bazaars in a well-defined area off the Square. Cairo is flooded with the life and business of the Arab in every quarter. Cairo, too, is compassed about with so much of Ancient Egyptian relics as to distract you from the occupation of first importance: looking upon the living. They are of more import than the dead. In Alexandria the ancient monuments are few, but those few are well preserved and mostly confined within the walls of the Classical Museum. You may watch the life of Alexandria undistracted by any subconscious urging to be out stooping and panting through the Great Pyramid for the fifth time (that nothing be lost), or wandering among the silent Tombs of the Caliphs.

A right good sight in Alexandria is the broad, mansion-skirted promenade of the Rue Rosette on a Sunday morning. The French " quality " of the city seems to reside there, and the best of it all is to watch the dainty little French girls going to Mass in the pleasant sunshine. They promenade that street in groups for two or three hours until all are retired into the residences for the midday meal. There is a delicacy of beauty in these little girls that affects one strangely after eight months from the haunt of woman and child.

The Rue Rosette in the morning, or the Quai Promenade Abbas II., fronting the lovely Crescent of Port Est: this is the place to laze away a morning, hanging over the broad stone wall on the water's edge, or lounging in the open cafés behind the smooth road. There is that generous expanse of glittering sea heaving gently between the horns of the bay. The Fort Kait Bey lies brown on the western lip and Fort Sel Sileh on the east, half embracing the blue. A rich mellow colour they have, and a richer blue it is for that. And the white piles of Alexandria thrust up all about the bay's brink, fringing the clear basin with a sort of stately splendour. It's fine, too, the comfortable laziness of the red-tarbushed fishermen on the wall, smoking and fooling away the morning in the soft landbreeze blowing sweet off the city. The only movement is with the Arab boys racing along the parapet or the quiet motion of the fishing-smacks lying off. An old Russian aristocrat is taking the air in a gharry; the nursemaids are out with the babes; the well-dressed unemployed Egyptians (they throng the city) are sipping their morning coffee in the glass-walled cafés. Alexandria often gives the impression—except in the Square—that there are no livings to be made. There is a luxurious spirit of idleness abroad in the place, which appears on the balconies of the houses, in the cafés, in the carriages of the suburbs. The idle rich—who are largely not the vulgar rich—

are here, whole battalions of them. There is nothing
like the studied idleness of Edinburgh Town or of
Naples—nor of Cairo. There are plutocrats who know
how to dress and how to take their ease without
boredom, and to pursue pleasure without apparent
ennui. All these things (you feel) have they observed
from their youth up; they practise none of them
crudely. They are well schooled in a placid and luxurious enjoyment of life.

The Alexandrian night begins about 9.30. It is
for that hour the opera overture is timed; then cafés
and music-halls begin to be thronged. At one in the
morning it is at its height. The opera may conclude
at two; and after that is the supper, and after that
the drive. Far the best way to see it all is to sit up
in the diggings of your friend overlooking the brilliant
Rue Ramleh from twelve on toward the dawn. There
are sacred pipes and Alexandrian fruits, and other
things; they include the conversation of the man who
has lived in Alexandria a year and looked about him
not casually, and who realises the import of all he
sees in the pulsing street below.

This is the fine side of Alexandrian night life. There
is the sordid aspect, not good—*i.e.*, pleasant—to look
on nor to relate. Alexandria cannot compare with
Cairo in lasciviousness. Perhaps no place on earth
can, nor any under earth. For crude carnality you
are to be commended to the Wazzia of Cairo; there
the flesh-pots of Egypt are seething and steaming.
Apart from the temperately-conducted biological
friendships of the leisured French and Russians and
Italians, the carnal traffic of Alexandria is limited
very closely. It does not clog the alleys, as in Cairo,

on every hand.   Indeed, it is rather the pot-house and the tavern, where the sole business of the waitresses is to bring traffic in beer, that is the scourge of Alexandria.   Their blandishments mostly are content with coquettish inducements to " fill 'em up again "; to achieve that they will perch on the knees of the soldiers and stroke their visages in a fashion not just maidenly, but effective in the eyes of the beer-boss. These taverns are at close intervals in all the poorer streets.   There is always a piano, at least, and an employed performer; sometimes there is an embryonic orchestra—harp and fiddle—whose *répertoire* is Tipperary and another—or perhaps two others.   There is a continuous fierce roaring, which subsides only when a Tommy rises to sing.   The pianist ramps out an improvised accompaniment.   No pianist has ever been known to decline to make an attempt.   Everybody joins in the chorus.   By the time the chorus of the fifth stanza is under way, there is a rare drunken hullabaloo, and spilt beer and broken glasses.   Ogling girls and flushed, embracing Tommies, yells for more beer, and drunken miscalculations of the score and feebly thundering band—all are checked with a parade-ground suddenness when the red-caps appear with their roars of *Nine o'clock !*   And the pot-house, so to speak, closes with a slam.

The picquets are irresistibly strong and numerous. They parade in squads in half-sections, each under an officer.   The Provost-Marshal, with a scrape o' the pen, has placed out of bounds most of the danger-zones which a year ago were open territory to the soldier.

The Arab quarters are at their best at midnight.

They have their music-halls, blatant and raucous and evil-smelling. The star performers are usually confined to one bloated, painted woman who screams an Arab rhythm at intervals under the influence of hasheesh, to the accompaniment of an orchestra of pipes and drums whose performers are elated by the same familiar spirit. Arab music is strident to a degree that sears the nerves. No drunkenness in the audience ever drowns *that*. It soars like a siren above the frantic mirth of the drinkers. Applause breaks forth at unprovoked intervals. The lady is never perturbed. She is reinforced occasionally by the brazen-throated orchestra, which is chorus too. The din is unimaginable when they are working in concert. The Arab sense of rhythm is unerring. Their rhythms are irregular and without consecutiveness in their habits, to the European ear that is not closely attentive; drawn out, as it were, into irregular strands—totally unsystematised, it seems—with the intervals at cross-purposes. They despise the Western mathematical rhythmical " groups " and the regular Western recurrence of stresses and intervals. English rhythm is as much unlike it as the characters of a London morning sheet differ from the gracefully irregular type of the native Egyptian press; the difference is as striking as between the tortuous Eastern mind and the British downrightness; as between an English tweed suit and the Arab flowing robe. Yet in this rhythmical maze no member of the orchestral chorus ever loses his way. There is perfect agreement in the disclosing of the scheme, which, after half an hour's turbulent listening, begins to show its shape through the rhythmical murk. And you know before you leave that though English music may make a sweeter sound than this, the Arab mastery of rhythm is mastery indeed. And that knowledge is, of course, deepened if you'll stop any day and listen to a group of Arab workmen chanting at their job.

So long as you withstand the glad-eye of the serpent of Old Nile (who descends now and then from the boards and collects baksheesh piastres) and keep to coffee, you will find these Egyptian music-halls absorbing enough. There are never women in the audience. The Egyptian woman—at any rate in the lower and middle classes—is never a " theatre-goer," as far as can be judged. She earns most of the living. All the *feloose* would seem to go into her lord's mighty hand, which does the spending—mostly on himself. Night after night he comes there in his red tarbush and sees the evening out with liquor and vociferous talk. Somewhere in the small-hours a gharry comes for the lady, and the hall noisily gets emptied. And as you climb up to your room in the hotel opposite, you can hear the dispersing throng in argument and criticism far along the emptying street. Standing at your balcony door, it merges imperceptibly into the subdued murmur of the city, broken by a belated wailing, street-cry.

In the morning you wake at some hour later than *réveille*, and gloat for a time that is indefinite over the luxury of a spring-mattress and of a day's time-table that is of your own framing—that shall be when you summon up energy sufficient to begin upon it. The city wakens almost as late as you. By the time you have bathed and dressed at exaggerated ease and meandered round to the Italian restaurant it is ten o'clock. Exotic Italian dishes are good for all their strangeness. . . . Across the peopling Square you get a car to Pompey's Pillar, towering above the Arab cemetery. The green mound bearing that granite column is an oasis in the desert of squalor about it. From the crest of the hillock you see Lake Mareotis spread out like a cloud in the morning mist—those shores now waste that grew the wine beloved of Horace.

The old municipal guide totters up the slope and offers you below, through the Catacombs. You have seen the other Catacombs, beside the Lake, which alone are really worth seeing. He shows you the Roman mortuary-chapel in sandstone at the entrance to the galleries, lights up his candle-lamp, and you trapes after him through the labyrinth. The niches in the wall are robbed of their mummies; all epitaphs are long since gone—assuming there ever were any; there is hardly anything to be seen that is even symbolic. The old fellow mutters continually in a lingo quite unintelligible, except in short and isolated fragments. The linguistic accomplishments of many of the official attendants on the ancient monuments of Egypt are deplorably shallow. You notice it far more at places that are of far more historical importance than the Catacombs. The tombs of the Sacred Bulls at Sakkhara afford the most striking instance. A relic so bound up with the ancient religion as is the Serapœum ought to be in charge of an attendant who not only can speak English fluently, but is beside alive to the import of his subject. The old dotard at the Serapœum has no further English (obviously) than: *Sacra' Bool ! Sacra' Bool !* and *Bakshish* and *T'ank you, Sair !*

The Catacombs *par excellence* lie along the Rue Bab-el-Melouk south of Pompey's Pillar; but since we've been there before rather more often than once, they must be passed over.

And so must a great deal else.

The Greek and Roman Museum hard by the Rue Rosette is hard to find, retiring into a side-street with a true classical unobtrusiveness. It is less famed than the Egyptian Museum at Cairo, but more interesting. Most people have at least a nodding acquaintance with the history of the classical occupation of Egypt—and here are the relics of it; whereas Egyptian history is not popularly read, even in a cursory fashion. In any case, for the inveterate Egyptologist there is a small mummified Egyptian section. The Cleopatra relics are well preserved, and especially a magnificent bust of the Siren. Mural and portal decoration of Roman and Greek houses are there in fine fragments, and there is a legion of vases and other ornaments from the living-rooms. Probably the most significant specimens, historically, are the coins; of them there is an enormously large collection. And the priceless papyri lie near at hand. Of sepulchral emblems there are a great many, but none beautiful except the laurel-crowned cinerary urns.

The museum is small but highly charged with meaning. There is a courtyard attached for the preparation (and restoration) of specimens, and it has some Roman monuments and gateways too huge for the interior.

The faithful Soudanese are the janitors and the conductors. Here, again, they are ignorant and English-less, and you sigh for a well-informed, well-paid, and intelligible informant. Only within the last fifteen months has a catalogue been compiled; and that is in French—though in that there is hardly any legitimate ground for complaint.

Most Australians at home will have heard of the Nouzha Gardens lying along the Canal Mahmoudieh: the gardens in whose café their men have sat listening to the band and drinking afternoon beer and watching the youngsters romp—and even joining in the sport; and finding a welcome, too. But few Australians will know of the Jardin Antoniadis, beyond Nouzha, and only half as large; but finer, which is a bold saying. It's the garden of a rich Greek Bey who has attained almost the splendour of the Hanging Gardens. He employs sixty men. In theory, you cannot enter without a pass—to be obtained, Heaven knows where; perhaps "at the warehouse." But five piastres in the palm of the trusty *sa'eda* at the gate passes you through, and you wander amazed for a couple of hours amongst those flowers and lawns, fountains and nymphs, ghouls and fauns and satyrs and dryads, and centre about the master's palace buried in the heart of the garden. It is gardening on a scale of magnificence and ingenuity—so it is said. Any public map of Alexandria will show the Jardin Antoniadis in bold letters. The afternoon we paid a visit we were puzzled to know the motive which could have obliged a dozen stalwart gardeners to stand at intervals of a dozen yards beating tins and howling at the sky. When questioned, they pointed alternately at the heavens and the freshly planted lawn, and we thought they must be calling primevally upon the water-gods for rain. But on consideration the unromantic conclusion prevailed: merely scaring birds or locusts from the springing grass.

The fine drive is from Nouzha round the shore of Lake Mareotis and back to the Square by way of Ramleh—the Toorak of Alexandria. You are defied to conceive a suburb better bred. To drive through it in a gharry is to put yourself in the dress-circle.

If you are back in time—that is, by 6.30—you may perhaps go to the weekly organ-recital at St. Mark's. Nothing will bring Home before you more vividly than the tones of a pipe-organ. But you must close your eyes, for almost everything else in the church tears you back to war. There's more khaki than tweed in the pews, and most of the women present are Sisters from the hospitals. And the organist is a private who plays at an Edinburgh church when peace is on, and the soloist (and well he can sing) is an A.M.C. Sergeant. The " Gyppo " hired servant is even here—as he is everywhere—creeping up and down the aisle in his incongruous colours: none the less incongruous for his brushing against the Cambridge graduate's gown of the Assistant-Chaplain, distributing programmes. Music of Handel and Bach sends you aching back to your hotel. That night you do not want to go into the Arab quarter.

CHAPTER V

THE LAST OF EGYPT

THE map shows Port Said dumped at the end of a lean streak of sand flanking the Canal. For half the distance from Ismailia the train sweeps along this tract. There is the Canal on your right, rich-blue between its walled banks and foiled by the brown heat-hazed world east; and on your left are the interminable shallows exuding the stink of rank salt, and traversed drearily by fishing-craft. Port Said at the approach much resembles Alexandria: the same brown, toppling irregularity, and the multitude of masts protruding.

The Canal at its city mouth is fretted with rectangular berthing-basins crammed with craft, very busy and noisy. A network of railways threads the quays. The green-domed Canal company's offices tower above the smoke and din, redeeming them; they make a noble pile. All the shipping is on the west bank; the east is bare, but for some sombre stone houses and a Red Cross hospital in the sand, and a self-contained Armenian refugee camp south of the city-level. The Canal mouth is stuffed with cruisers and commercial ships anchored between the two stalwart stone sea-walls. They protrude two miles into the Mediterranean, keeping the channel. That on the west is crowned by the de Lesseps monument.

The lean sand-neck that you traversed by rail from Ismailia takes a right-angled turn at the head of the de·Lesseps mole and runs seven miles west into the Mediterranean. It begins with a fine residential quarter standing behind the firm beach and the horde of bathing-boxes; west still, and safely segregated from the decency of the city, is the seething Arab quarter, of enormous dimensions and smelling to heaven; and beyond Arab Town the promontory bears the city's burial-ground, lying desolate in the sand-neck; and then peters out dismally in the shallows.

A new-comer takes in the straightforward geographical scheme of the place at a glance. It's a small city, lying, as it does, midway on the sea-road linking the East and West worlds. Its atmosphere is intensive rather than extensive. It is highly charged with busyness. The little area of the city is thickly peopled with every nationality (excepting German and Austrian), promenading or sitting at the open cafés. The shipping is congested to a degree that is apparently unwieldy. And the period of war has taken nothing from the atmosphere of bustle. This is the main supply base for the whole of the Canal defences and for a good deal of Upper Egypt too. An enormous levy is made daily on railroad and on Canal barges for transport of Army supplies. The supply depôt has commandeered half the Quay space and receives and disgorges day and night without intermission.

For that reason (as well as because shipping is thick in the Canal mouth) the place is good game for hostile aircraft. The morning after our arrival Fritz came

over before breakfast and dropped six bombs and left
two Arabs stretched on the quay. Anti-aircraft guns
let fly, and innumerable rifles. The din of bombs
and guns and musketry took one back for a vivid
twenty minutes to Anzac—for the first time since
leaving that place of unhappy memory. No damage
was done—to the raiders. But the two coolies lay
there, and the rest (seven hundred strong) fled like
one man to Arab Town, and neither threats nor
inducements would bring them back. For forty-
eight hours the work of the depôt would have ceased
had not the Armenian refugees been requisitioned—
a whole battalion of them. They were glad to come,
and they worked well. It was better for them
than being massacred by Turks: and they got paid
for it.

The second raid happened a week later, at three
in the morning, under a pale moon. Four 'planes
came with sixteen missiles. This was more serious.
Our guns could shoot only vaguely, in a direction;
and ten to one the direction was at fault. Four
bombs dropped in the main street. The terror by
night seized the civilians. There was a screaming
panic. The populace poured into the streets in their
night garments and rushed about incontinently. So
a few who would perhaps otherwise have escaped met
their end. A night raid over Anzac when the guns
were speaking without intermission was hardly to be
noticed. But this onslaught upon civilian quietness
in the night watches was heart-shaking. The deadly
whirring of the engine in the upper darkness; the
hoarse, intermittent sobbing of the missile in descent—
none could say how near or far; the roar of explosion

checking the suspense momentarily, but only until the next increasing sob touches the ear; the din of our own wild and random fire and the crackle of the sentries' rifles; the raucousness of the sirens, the piercing screams of the women, and the cries of little children in the extremity of terror; the misdirected warnings and the disorganised directions of the men— these all combined to make an impression of horror of a kind unknown on Anzac.

The visitation lasted half an hour. That half-hour seemed to endure a whole night. Four were killed outright, five died soon of their wounds, seven were wounded who would recover.

Shooting a man from a trench is one thing; this potential and actual murder of women and little children is altogether another. One wishes it could be made to cease. It calls for reprisal, or revenge, or whatever it should be called; but not in kind.

That was a Sunday morning. The Anglican parson at matins later tried lamely to reassure a sparse congregation by preaching futilely from the text: "Thou shalt not be afraid for the terror by night." The latter end of his discourse was drowned in the pitiful *Zaghareet* raised by the Egyptian women next door: they had lost a man in the night. Their shrill, ear-splitting wail submerged the sermon. There was an end of reassurance—even supposing it had ever begun.

The raid had come close on the heels of the Casino dance. The Casino is the best hotel in Port Said, which is to say a good deal. Every Saturday night the Casino "gives" a dance to the quality of the Port. There you will see the best. It's always worth going to. Quite half the European population of the

town is composed of the British Government officials
and their wives and daughters, English visitors from
the mail-boat *en route*, the French Canal Company's
officials and their families, and the wives of British
naval and military officers stationed here. There is
probably as pure a quality of European beauty, well-
breeding, and accomplishment as you'll meet outside
Britain and France. The women and the naval
officers know how to dance. So much cannot be said
of the Army's representatives. They consist chiefly
in stout Colonels and somewhat young and frisky
Subalterns. But apart from that, they may not
carry with them the ballroom gear that a naval officer
can stow in his quasi-permanent home. A valise
or a kit-bag is another thing from a sea-chest, nor is
a moving tent a snug and cupboarded cabin. Especially the French flappers, with their delicate transparent
beauty, dance with an exquisite grace, and the French
dowager-chaperons sit at an end of the room far less
sedately than British duennas. The English Subalterns who can speak French find the flappers rising
easily to the level of their spirits in the intervals on
the dimly-lit piazza; and they probably are not un-
grateful that the fear of a nocturnal bombardment
from the sea has extorted from the authorities an
order obliging the proprietor to subdue his sea-front
lights.

'They're great nights. There's no such stuff in
anybody's thoughts as Taubes. Yet on that Sunday
morning many a girl and many a dowager could
hardly have put head to pillow before the first bomb
crashed. A little earlier timing on the part of Fritz,
and the sound of revelry by night would have been

far more rudely hushed than was that of Brussels
long ago by the distant gun on the eve of Waterloo.
The period of this war is surcharged with dramatic
situations more intense than were held by Belgium's
capital then.   But   there   is   no   Byron   to   limn
them.

The Casino denizens you will find in the surf before
the hotel any morning after eleven.   The girl who
was so charming last night is no less charming now,
as she moves across the sand.   She wears almost as
much this morning.   All that this means (whatever it
may seem to imply) is that her bathing-dress is ultra-
elaborate.   There is a great deal of it; and it includes
stockings; and is so fine in texture and harmonious
in colour that you wonder she has the heart to wet
it.   But there—she's in.   You wait till she comes
out, and marvel that she hardly has suffered a sea-
change.

The surf between eleven and one any day; the
Eastern Exchange open-café from eleven to five on
Sunday; and the de Lesseps Mole from three to six on
a Sunday afternoon: it is there and then you will see
Port Said representatively taking the air—or the waters.
The Eastern is the heart of the City; to sit sipping
there during a pleasant Sabbath afternoon is the
equivalent of doing the " Block " in Melbourne.   The
de Lesseps Pier will reveal the utterly cosmopolitan
character of the populace: all classes promenade it.
And the great bronze engineer towers over them and
points his scroll down the mouth of his handiwork;
and embossed boldly on the pedestal is his own boast:
Aperire terram centibus.   The gigantic de Lesseps is
a landmark of the whole sea-front.   He faces, and points

the way to, every East-bound ship that enters his Canal. There is a sort of pride in his bearing.

The streets are tree-lined and over-arched, and the tables are set out beneath the boughs; and there is singing and dancing in the open air at every café. There is a finely fashioned and adorned Greek church. Nothing expresses the cosmopolitan nature of the floating populace better than the extraordinary notice on the inner wall of the Roman Catholic Cathedral: *Proibito di sputare in terram.*

There are two cabarets—Maxime's and the Kursaal—where wine and fornication is the business, driven unblushingly, as one has come to expect in any part of Egypt. As these things go in the land, Port Said is amazingly clean. It was not ever so. A deliberate campaign was lately organised to purge. The segregation of the Arab quarter did much to effect that. Five years ago the Port was the carnal sink of Egypt. Now Cairo is.

We were hurried back to Serapœum for the move. This had been pending any time the last two months: the Turkish feints beyond railhead had delayed it. But it had come now. We were in the desert a bare thirty-six hours. We entrained in the scorching afternoon. The *khamseen* was whispering potentially, but not menacingly. We moved out in the cool of the afternoon. Nefisha was passed, with its hordes of bints and wales hawking chocolate, fruits, and fizzy drinks—and hawking successfully . . . on through Ismailia cooling off under her fir-groves beside the delicious lake . . . up through Mahsamah, where the flights to the Canal had made their first footsore halt . . . on and on, taking our last look on the soft evening desert, and keeping the placid sweet-water Canal. We felt we were seeing it all for the last time. And we hoped we were, though now it looked inviting enough. But it was not the desert normal, and well we knew it; we had seen too often this seductive evening gentleness turn to relentless blistering heat in the morning. . . . On through Kassassin, always —since reading the Tel-el-Kebir epitaphs—the scene of that " midnight charge " . . . up to Tel-el-Kebir itself, its miles of tents darkening beside the hanging dhow-sails . . . through Zagazig in the late dusk, with its close-packed houses and its semi-nudes in the upper stories . . . and so on into the night, with snatches of sleep, until we were wakened at 2 a.m. by the sudden stop and the bustle at the Alexandrian quays. . . . The three hours' embarking of men and baggage, and so to bunk, and white sheets and yielding mattress and the feeling of a *room* about one—and to sleep.

There were a few hours' leave next day, when we took a last affectionate perambulation about the well-loved, well-bred city. And as we breakfasted next morning we were moving out of the inner harbour. By ten we could look back at the brown towers, and see the place as a whole from the low strip of Mex, away to the eastern sand-dunes at Ramleh. Alexandria had been good to us, and it was hard to leave her, whatever the exaltation of anticipating the new field. Egypt as a whole, despite its stinks, its filth, its crude lasciviousness, its desert sand and flies, heat and fiery, dusty blasts, had charmed and amazed and compensated in a thousand ways. It was our introduction to foreign-ness, and, as such, had made an arresting

impression that could never be deleted. France
may cause us less discomfort, and may hold a glamour
and a brilliance of which Egypt knows nothing; but
the impression left by France can hardly be more
vivid than that of Egypt, our first-love in the world
at large.

BOOK IV
FRANCE

11

SECTION A.—A BASE

CHAPTER I

ENTRÉE

You can conceive the sense of exaltation with which one would enter the South of France in June, after five months in Egypt. You can conceive better than describe it. So can the writer. In a moment it comes back from this distance, with a reality that elates; but it defies description. The universal sand of Egypt: the timbered heights and the flowered valleys of the Riviera; the stinks of the Egyptian cities: the June fragrance breathing down from the hills of Marseilles; the filth and deformity of the Cairene denizens: the fair women of France and the lovely grace of the little children; the searing heat of the desert: the tempered sunniness of this blossoming land. If you can make these things explicit to yourself, you may know something of the high sense of emancipation with which we left the ship. For we had been looking on Marseilles and sniffing the air from the harbour for two days. And in the last hundred miles of the journey by sea we had skirted the Riviera coast, gazing absorbedly on verdure and perching *château*, and nestling, red-topped village and silver sand-strip. Then the cliffs of the harbour mouth—that hide the city—uprose, and we threaded a way beneath them and about the titanic rocks towering in the bay; and a sudden turn to starboard threw all Marseilles into the field of vision in five minutes— red tiles along the water's edge in great congested blotches; thin red patches straggling back in the green up the hills; and in the near, high-reared horizon, grey scarred cliffs overlooking all; and on the main harbour headland Notre Dame de la Garde, dazzling gold in the setting sun, gazing benignly over the city.

We looked and pondered till darkness came on, and in the morning were on deck early to see it all by the eastern sun. But they wouldn't let us land. So we spent two days explicating the detail with glasses.

We moved in suddenly and entrained at once. By the goodness of Heaven we were detailed to proceed by a slow passenger-train, as distinct from a fast troop-train. A troop-train rushes express, and is crowded; ours stopped at every station, and gave room to sleep. At the big towns we stayed as long as four and six hours. For all this we were commiserated by the French: "*Ah! trois jours dans la voiture!*" But we could have wished it would last three weeks.

Think, patient reader! Three days across France from Marseilles to Rouen in the gentle French midsummer; and time to look about you at every village.

Four impressions will always remain: the desecration by war of this beautiful land; the inescapable evidence that the last fit man in France is in the field; the ravages upon these quiet civilian homes by death in the front line; the incontinently affectionate welcome of Australians by the French girls.

It was, above all, pitiful to know that somewhere to the east Teuton shell was ravaging country such as

this. You found yourself saying: Is it such a valley as
that in which the trenches are dug ?   Are German shell
(and French shell, too) changing the whole topography
of a province such as this ?—smudging the sleeping
landscape and tearing up the smiling crop.   Is it in
such a grove that the sacrilege of the guns is perpe-
trating itself ? " Gad !" you would hear, " this
country's worth fighting for !"

In Egypt it's another thing. It is less unnatural
that the godless sand of the desert should be stained
and erupted; but this is different. And the old consolation comes—that has always consecrated the sacri-
fices of Gallipoli—that the ideals in question are more
precious than any land, however fair.

In the fields of the provinces it's women and bent
old men who are working—and boys. They wave
pathetically as the train rushes on. And in the
towns there is not an eligible man to be seen—except
in uniform.

Seven in ten women are in mourning at any stage
of the journey. One attempted at first to be consoled
by the notion that the French temperament would
put on mourning for a second and third cousin. But
conversation with Frenchmen soon corrected that.
Six in ten of these women wear weeds for a son or a
brother or father or lover fallen in the two years that
are past.

It was a welcome and a half that the girls gave.
Apart from all fighting, the deep-lined, barbed-wire
Australian visage attracts in a land where the men
are smooth-faced. And the notion of men fighting for
France from the other end of the earth made no favour
too much. Troop-trains had been passing at regular

intervals for a month, and they were on the lookout for khaki. They swarmed to the stations with favours of fruit and flowers and embraces. They waved as the train came in; they chatted sweetly and unintelligibly at the platform; and they waved long and friendly as we moved away. The little children came with lilies and roses (little French girls are the loveliest things God ever made), and held up their faces to be kissed. And their big sisters not only did not blench at embraces, but invited them; and would get up and ride five miles *pour compagnie.*

We stayed three hours at Avignon—at night. An Englishman we encountered on the station was so glad to see men of his own tongue that he took us about the streets and the cafés to show us the city proper, and missed his train without a pang. This was about midnight, and Avignon was just fairly awake. Trade in the cafés was at its zenith. Amongst other things we saw (for the first time) how tactful, shrewd, and charming a waitress a French provincial girl may be.

Lyons we reached at 2.30 a.m., and had time for a four hours' walk. The inevitable route was over the Rhône, mist-laden, and up the villa-crowned hill in the midst of the city; and, when the sun had overspread the wakening valley, down into the strawberry markets, and away to the station, threading a way amongst the strawberry waggons, bearing in the fruit in voluptuous piles.

Macon, the next long stop, we remember for the provender we put aboard there. This is mere carnality, but the capons and fruits and pies and pastry of Macon were unforgettable.

This lasted us to Dijon. Dijon we shall always

remember as the city where the girls were hungriest for souvenirs. Souvenirs had been demanded (and sometimes given) at any stage of the journey. But at Dijon the houris were infected with a souvenir madness; and since they were the prettiest girls we had yet seen, we departed stripped and deploring we had not brought from Australia each a bushel of badges. For there were bound to be more girls, quite as irresistible.

Then there was Laroche, where more rations had to be got. This was a hungry business—and even a thirsty.

And between Laroche and the great city an unhappy thing occurred. We were due to change at Villeneuve, a Parisian suburb. But at Villeneuve (2 a.m.) no one seemed to be awake; and at 3 we were in Paris, forlorn and regretful (though in a thoroughly half-hearted fashion) of the oversight which had disorganised our movement-order. There was therefore nothing to be done but hastily swallow *café au lait* in a matutinally busy eating-house, and hail a taxi in the Place de la Bastille: this after learning that the Rouen train would not leave before 7.30. " *Vue Générale de Paris —trois heures*," was the order, in crude English-French. And the chauffeur put down the dividing glass window behind him, and in his taxi-jargon showed us everything—Hôtel de Ville, Notre-Dame, the Pantheon, l'Académie de France, Palais du Sénat, the Invalides, the Champs-Elysées, the Eiffel Tower, Place de la Concorde, l'Eglise de la Madeleine, round about the Louvre and the Luxembourg, and the rest of them.

This was vulgar Americanism; but nothing else

was to be done. And so we got back to the Gare
Lyon, and in the half-hour to spare descended and
gaped unsophisticated at the Parisian tube railways
disgorging their freight of men and women (mostly
women) who had found their work.

Then the train began its crawl up to Versailles and
its loveliness, nestling in the thick wooded heights,
and by many blessed stops and shuntings we came by
Juvisy and Achères to Rouen, late in the drizzling
night, took a cup of steaming coffee at the Croix Rouge
Cantine pour Permissionaires, and marched out to
camp; and didn't care much where it might be, so
long as we had where to lay our head.

Three days in Rouen left one with the knowledge
that it is dangerous to transport suddenly a body of
Australians, after eighteen months' residence on Anzac
and in Egypt, to a land where the wine is cheap and
every girl is pretty.

CHAPTER II
BILLETED

THE natural course was to advertise. The *Journal de Rouen* received us tolerantly, even compassionately. No one of us could speak French, but one pretty member of the office staff (more accurately, one member of the pretty office staff) could speak a kind of English. The first demand was for a *petite annonce* in French. And when the lady saw this was out of the question for us, she offered a translation of an English paragraph.

It brought a shoal of responses in French. A kind of horse-sense had led us to get them addressed "to this office," where the fair translator could be requisitioned. They were seductive replies—in the inevitable language of proprietresses. Some offered rooms and meals; some rooms and breakfast; some rooms and no more; others specified a *femme de chambre* of the first quality (and these were looked at twice). None offered a bath. This is the most extraordinary country. It drives you to the conclusion, anyhow, that a bathroom is necessary neither to health nor good looks, and thereby runs counter to a long-established English prejudice. A bathroom is by no means a necessary part of the furniture of a good hotel. Those that have been driven by the English occupation into adding one, brag about it in

their advertisements and charge " a franc a time."
Those that steadily decline to add it are losing custom.

The conclusion of the matter was we yielded to
none of their blandishments, but went to an hotel,
and that for good reasons. They resolve themselves
into a question of feeding—*i.e.*, of meal-hours. You
go into lodgings in a flat, and of necessity there are
more or less definitely limited periods for meals.
This is killing, even when not regarded in the light
of irregular working hours. To be tied to 8 for breakfast, 1 for lunch, and 6 for dinner, is to be in gaol.
The chief beauty of an hotel is that you may have
breakfast from 6.30 to 10, lunch from 12 to 2.30, and
dinner from 6 to 9.30. This leaves you, to some extent, at freedom with the leisure an exacting Headquarters does sometimes throw to you.

Breakfast is altogether French. You'll get no more
than *café au lait* and roll—not even *confiture*, without
paying through the nose for this violation of French
usage. If you order eggs or *omelette* (or both) you not
only wait long for it, but are looked on with disfavour
even in a first-class establishment. But the coffee is
so rich and mellow and the roll so crisp and the butter
so creamy that you can make a large meal of them.
You usually eat and drink far more than it's good form
to consume. He's a barbarian who asks for anything
better.

This you take in the early morning almost alone
in the winter-garden looking on the courtyard. The
matutinal *femme de chambre* is frequent and busy
about the place. The call for hot water and for grub in
the rooms is insistent. If you want to be called early
and to shave, you write up on the blackboard in the

bureau the formula: 31 (*no. de chambre*) — 5$\frac{1}{2}$ — *e.c.*
(*eau chaude*)—*entrez* ; that is, let the damsel enter without knocking. And enter she does with the steaming
jug; and, with a charming frankness, wakens you by
the shoulder, and, if not abnormally busy (and she's
seldom too busy for that), sits on the edge of the bed
with her shining morning face, telling you sweetly
the quality of the weather, and that it's time you were
out, until satisfied you are on the way to uprising,
as distinct from turning over again. And morning
greetings of the most refreshing sort have been known
to be exchanged thus over the edge of the bed. One
of the satisfactions of such an exchange (though not
necessarily the chief) would be that you know the
sweet creature associates nothing sordid with the greeting—even though this is a bedroom and you're in your
'jamas. An English maid in the circumstances would
probably begin with a hostile shriek, and end by relating to the manager how a base and licentious soldier
had made violent overtures to her; and you would suffer
ejection with ignomy.

And so the French (and especially the French women)
score in morality at every turn.

You see nothing of the hotel all morning. But
on returning for lunch your *chambre* is " done " with
a taste and thoroughness that delight, and drive you
to register a vow you'll never more be guilty of un-
tidiness. British officers in France have a reputation
for hoggishly littering their rooms that requires a lot
of redeeming. But the French maid is not dismayed.
She returns to the attack daily, with a pride in her art
which no piggery can dissipate.

Luncheon has the light touch that's the prime charm

of French cooking. There's endless variety without
heaviness or monotony: a whiff of *hors d'œuvre*, a
taste of fish, a couple of " made " dishes (made well),
a scrap of delicious cold-meat, salads, fruits (who shall
do justice to the fruits of Normandy in June ?—her
strawberries, peaches, plums, grapes, melons, and
cherries), *crême*, cheeses, biscuits, *cidre* and coffee. Then
you hear a barbarous Captain beside you blaspheming:
" The first thing I'll do when I get leave is to go to
the Savoy and have a decent English feed. I can't
stick this French grub !" This is the sort of man
that ought to be suppressed by the State and debarred
from going abroad. It's with justice that the French
taunt us with our English " heaviness "—heaviness
in eating, in drinking, thinking, and doing. One of
the privileges of being in France is that of eating what
the French alone know how to prepare.

All the same, one does not immediately get used
to horse. *Cheval,* in some form or other, is served out
every dinner. There's not nearly so much beef as
horse consumed. The French like it better. The
sign of a golden horse's head surmounts the doorway
of most butcher's shops; many a shop displays the
severed head, as the English do those of sheep and pigs.
The Parisian taxi-cabs are ousting the horse-cabs
fast. Proprietors are selling off their beasts. The
newspapers, announcing the result of the sales, will
tell you most of the horses went to butchers, as a
matter of course.

In the medley of French on the menu-card (which
you don't scan very closely) you miss *cheval* until it's
pointed out to you: it's disguised. You then discover
you've been eating horse for weeks, unwittingly, and

enjoying it. It's too late to turn back, even if you
didn't like the beast. So you continue to eat and
relish the faithful defunct friend to man.

Dinner begins about nine. That's the meal for which
people who don't live at the hotel "drop in"—people
from the suburbs and the country: wounded and
base-Colonels, with their wives and daughters; music-
hall artistes, business-men. The place hums and echoes
with high-spirited chatter. Much wine gets drunk—
as much by the women as by the men. At the end of
an hour the place is fairly agog. The proprietor
himself, dressed in his best—as though persisting in
the time-honoured practice of a tavern-host—carves
an enormous joint (a kind of half a pony) in the centre
of the room, under the apex of the dome. This is
very interesting. Only one thing is awry: the women
eat greedily. The prettiest of them (and whether they
take wine or not) masticate with a primitive eagerness
and *abandon* that is disgusting.

The late-sitters remain until eleven over their wine
and cigarettes, and then adjourn to the courtyard and
sit and call for coffee and liqueurs. If they move
before midnight, it's unusual. The courtyard resounds
until the small-hours have crept on. And in those
hours the maids on duty are busy enough answering
the call of the chamber-bells with drinks. You will
see them hurrying up and down the lighted staircases
and in and out the rooms of the brilliantly lit front,
muttering (one imagines) the complaint of the frogs:
" It may be sport to you, but it's death to us !" But
they never let you think so: at two in the morning they
will smile and rap out repartee with a good-humour
that it's hard to believe feigned. And who's to say

that it is ?   These people are unfeignedly light-hearted.
They satirise us for our moods and our livers; and tell
us (not without justice) we don't know how to
live.   By comparison, we're not happy unless we're
miserable. . . .

You will catch the youngsters in the courtyard only
by dining at six.   You can play with them an hour in
the twilight after, and that's a joy not to be lost,
recur as often as it may.   You can talk their language, even if you can't talk French.

CHAPTER III

THE SEINE AT ROUEN

I DON'T know what the Seine at Rouen is like in times of peace-trade. They say war has quadrupled its congestion. I well believe it. The pool is crammed below the Grand Pont—there's nothing above but barge traffic—with ships disgorging at a frenzied rate at the uneven cobbled quays.

One can imagine the port lazing along before the War in the informal and leisurely way that is French. The French enjoy living. They are industrious enough for that. But they don't take their work hardly nor continuously. They take it in chunks. It gets done. But there is no sort of inflexible determination in their method. The Egyptians, too, have not continuity, but with them the work does *not* get done. Both peoples work sporadically. But the Egyptian takes his chunk of work because he has to; the Frenchman because he likes it. That is the difference. The Egyptian is not industrious. The French like work, and therefore take it in tastes, never hogging it. They like to get the flavour of work. The Englishman who eats it down misses all that, and is commiserated by the French for the desecrating greed with which he attacks his task.

So you can envisage the quay in peace-time: the unsystematic and picturesque dumping of merchandise in the open quays, and the hum of leisured talk; the additions to the acres of wine-barrels under the elms beyond, and the subtractions from them; and the rich fruitiness of the *bon arome* soaking out of those casks. You get it now if you walk amongst them : walk through the shadowed wine-store on a hot day, and the odour hanging beneath the trees is a refreshment in itself. But in these days the lading and the discharge of the wine-ships is done feverishly and raucously, and too hurriedly for any attempt at arranging them on shore. The wine-ship lies there with the stuff piled monstrously on every yard of her deck, and it's being slung off as fast as may be. It's the only drink of the French soldier; there's as much urgency for its transit as for the off-loading of English supplies. Huge tanks stand as waggons on the adjoining railway and they wait to be filled, and so the *vin ordinaire* goes up in bulk that exceeds the content of many score of barrels.

The same urgency hurries off supplies from the ships. The Admiralty is shouting continuously for the completion of discharge. No ship, at this time, lies there at her ease. She fairly groans and creeks in travail of discharge. It proceeds as vigorously at night, under the flares, as by day. Hordes of labour battalions are handling it into the store-hangars, or into the waiting supply-trams, or into lorries. The parti-coloured French are trundling the wine-barrels hither and thither for store or for despatch. The rattle of cranes, the panting of lorries, the scream and rumble of trains, the shouting of orders, are deafening and incessant. Supply-ships, timber-ships, coal-ships, wine-ships, ammunition-ships, petrol-ships, are strung down-stream in a deafening queue. The base is a distractingly busy place.

Over against all that is the quiet domesticity of the barges. War doesn't hurry them, nor sap at the foundations of their family life. They'll sleep along the river, happen what may. General Joffre's professed aspiration *après la guerre* is to retire tò a Seine barge, and finish there. He could choose nothing in sharper contrast with the turmoil of war. The reaction from Generalship could not well be borne in more complementary circumstances. The comfortable somnolence of a Seine barge is invincible. They are not yet requisitioned for the base purposes of war. They are a thing apart, and therefore have no call for busyness.

They are enormously long, and have a grace of outline unexampled in the world of barges. A Thames barge is stumpy and crude beside them. There is scope in their length for grace of line. Look down on them from the heights of Bonsecours, packed òrderly amongst the Seine islands. Look at them in queue dreaming along in the wake of some fussy tug; either way ỳou'll get their nobility of contour.

Each is a microcosm. They are · self-contained as to family, burden, poultry, pony, cat and dog, rabbit-pen, and garden. The mother and daughter and the small boys all take a hand in pushing on the business of *le père*. In fact, it is they who do the thing: he lounges and smokes and directs the policy. In the waist of the ship is the stable, with a pony that usually is white, and perhaps a cow, and the pens of hens, and the basketed rabbit-hutch. The boys pursue the dog round the potted plants when there's no work.

In the same circumstances the mother and daughters
sun themselves on the hatches. Children are born
there to a lifelong sojourn in the craft. There they get
their schooling, and there, until adolescence, they
acquire their knowledge of the world. There probably
is scope for a science of barge-psychology. Can one
in reason expect a world war to intrude far into the
life of a Seine barge ? Hardly that.

They hold as much as a small ship; the journey to
Paris is far and slow. They are cut off from the world
almost as effectually as a marooned Swiss Family
Robinson.

Hospital ships berth below the bridge, and are filled
from the motor ambulances with an awful celerity.
You may always know when an ambulance train is
at the Rive Gauche Gare by the long procession of
Red Cross motors streaming from the station over the
Grand Pont to the hospital berth, and by the wide-
eyed crowd making a slow-swaying cordon round the
military police to watch the procession of stretchers
ascending the gangways. The Red Cross ship may get
her complement in two or three hours. Then she
turns business-like and heads down-stream for *le
Havre*. And then !—*Blighty*, for comfort and fitting
alimentation, and *home* for the tortured.

The Seine is a tragic stream at Rouen. Corpses are
fished up daily. Parisian suicides float down and are
intercepted, and dogs and other beasts seem to get
drowned in plenty. This is hard on so fair and happy
a city. Why can't Paris look after her own weary-of-
breath ?

The Ile la Croix stands at the heart of the city.
The Pont Corneille rests across it. The island is a

town in itself, with theatres, churches, factories, baths, and thick residential quarters, and groves, and well-defined streets. Here is another little world in itself, consistent with the barges that lie about it.

All over the island—and, still more ubiquitously, all over the quay-sides—are girls and women hawking fruit and cakes and chocolate. The girls are pretty. They better custom by fooling English Tommies to the top of their bent by that French-Arcadian inter-sexual frankness of discourse and gesture of which English girls know so little, and which Tommy adores so ardently and furtively. This gives the right to put up the price. Tommy, in this land of vines, and in the season—finds himself paying her two francs a pound for grapes. " *Très cher aujourd'hui, Monsieur !* "—" *Mais oui, m'selle—voulez-vous m'embrasser ?* "—" *Nothin'doin', ole shap !* " . . . These girls are quick-brained, as alertful in mind as you could expect by their well-moulded features and their lithe, straight bodies. There is no insistence, in France, upon the ugly vulgarism of rotundity in women and girls. The girls of France spell, in their bodies, anything but sombreness in spirit or clumsiness in brain. They have never been out of Rouen, but they fling repartee in Arabic at Australians as though they had lived in Cairo. Their only source of such an accomplishment is the Australian soldier himself, and the persistence of Arabic with him. And he does not go out of his way to teach anyone. He learns French with halting slowness, even when some Rouennaise is making efforts to teach him. But these girls take up his English and his incidental Arabic in their swift and light mental stride.

CHAPTER IV

ROUEN *REVUE*

EXCEPT when Lena Ashwell comes with her English concert-party, evening entertainments—that is, public entertainments—in Rouen are limited by some cinemas and two theatres that stage *revue*. The cinemas are like all other cinemas, except that the humour is broader and sexual intrigue is shown in a more fleshly and passionate form. The audience differs from an English, not in that flirtation is more fierce, but in the running fire of comment directed at the film, and from the way in which crises in the plot are hailed. Everyone smokes who has the habit. The women who do not, masticate noisily at sweets. The girls in the front row of stalls playfully pull the hair of the orchestra, specialising in the 'cello: his deep, detached notes amuse them. This is their way of showing he attracts their attention. The conductor is the pianist too. In his dual capacity he displays astounding resource and agility. The combination of these functions is diverting, even in an Englishman. The films present a preponderance of carnal domestic problems.

Revue is another story. An Englishman has no right to attend French *revue* without being prepared to discount it at a rate governed by the difference between the national temperaments. Where English *revue* suggests and insinuates, French explicates the detail. French insinuates too, on occasion, but with the motive of subtlety as distinct from that of English furtiveness: the difference between cleverness and morbidity. All this applies to *amours*, chiefly between the already-married. French *revue* goes further, and deals disgustingly in physiological detail which the English stage declines to handle even by implication. And the ladies on the stage are obviously amused by the cruder passages to an unprofessional degree. They giggle outright. The work on the stage, in fact, is curiously informal. Dialogue *sotto voce* in the corners is not make-believe—nor rehearsed. They carry on a genuine conversation, much of which is criticism of their colleagues at work, much personal comment on the advanced rows of the audience. A French company is never afraid to let you know that, after all, it's only acting you're looking at. English downrightness would maintain the delusion at all costs.

A lot of improvisation goes on—some by choice, some of necessity. French versatility flashes out brilliantly here and there with something that's not in the book; and when a fellow's memory fails he improvises with convincing readiness. There's no such thing as a breakdown; though *revue* here runs for so long a season that actors might easily be forgiven for growing too stale to improvise. But that they avert by the habit of improvisation from choice.

When, therefore, there comes a "turn" which purports to be classical poses, the effect is blasphemous rather than ludicrous. The spectacle of thick-painted whores clutching clumsily at the spirit of Greek motion and Greek suspension-of-motion, with their lewd simperings and vulgar disproportion of bust, is repellent. At the critical moment someone giggles in the wings and the goddess baulks. The orchestra swells to cover the gaping *hiatus* which no improvisation can bridge. The Salome-dance and the *ballet* are quite other things. They perform them here to perfection. Their temperament provides the *abandon* without which such turns fall stodgy. But classical poses ? No !—hardly that !

A French audience in war-time clamours for a military turn or two; and gets them. There's a scene from the trenches presented with a convincing sort of realism— from the death of a comrade to the exchange of fornicatory ribaldries and the pursuit of vermin. Asphyxiation is effected, not by the enemy, but by the corporal's removing his boots. The humour is broad and killing. Shrieking applause drowns half the repartee. Judged by the accompanying gesture, some obviously good things are missed. The delivery of the mail under the parapet, and its perusal, leave little doubt as to the proper function of *la bonne marraine*— the fair unknown correspondent acquired by advertisement.

Then there is a turn military which discloses the nature of the friendly encounters between the *Poilu* and the girls of the village through which he is passing.

There is some really good singing. And there is always a song in English, delivered with a naïve crudity of pronunciation, to which the English soldiers respond at the chorus with allied fervour. " The Only Girl," " Who were you with Last Night ?" " Here we are Again," are the favourites.

The ushers are girls. They know how to keep in order the crowd of lewd French youths in spirited attire who affect the pit, who, without restraint, would make the place unbearable. Mostly the ushers do it with their tongues; where these weapons fail they cuff them, and cuff them hard—no mere show of violence. The French termagant is a fearsome creature. She's here, and she's conducting on the tram-cars. There she is a match for any man. No lout is free to dispute her authority. She always emerges from a battle of words master of the situation. *Master* is the word. The conductors are the only girls (though mostly women) in Rouen who are not pretty as a class. Individuals are, but the class is unsexed, growing moustaches which are often more than incipient. The only womanly thing about them is their black dress and perky, red-edged cap. They give the impression that they would do well in the trenches. The theatre ushers—who are " chuckers-out " too—are less masculine and less plain-featured. The management chooses them with half an eye to feature, with a regard chiefly to physical strength. The tramways manager lays no store by looks. Why should he ? Good looks don't draw custom on the cars. But he does ensure that they shall be able to take care of themselves, and " boss " the vehicle.

CHAPTER V

LA BOUILLE

THE steamer leaves the Quai de Paris every afternoon at two. Most days it is crowded. The War does not hinder women and the ineligible and *les blessés* from taking their pleasure down the lovely Seine. Why should it ? People should in war-time look to the efficiency of civilians as well as of soldiers. It is as profitable, to this end, that the Seine pleasure-boats should run as that the London theatres should keep open under the darkened anti-Zeppelin sky.

It's women who crowd the boat, with their sons and their younger brothers. There's also a leavening of handsome women who go down for purposes not considered virtuous by the British. There are many soldiers—*en permission*, with powers of enjoyment equal to those of the Tommy who shouts to the lift-maid in the Tube: "Hurry up, miss ! I've only got ten days !" These fellows from the trenches, with their women hanging upon them, are prepared to compress much into their leave. There are a few wanting limbs, who are not on leave.

The boat races down the pool of Rouen through the gauntlet of colliers, timber-ships, supply-ships, multitudinous barges, and swinging cranes. Once past the island, the commercial river-side is done with, and the journey proceeds through some of the most exquisitely beautiful hill-country in Normandy. Rouennaise merchants have grown fat on the trade of decades of peace, and have built their *maisons* on the grand scale on the slopes of the Dieppedale and Roumare Forêts. The forests clothing this Seine Valley are famed through all Europe for growth and colour. The *maisons* lie buried in their depths, thrusting up their towers and high gables. The slim Seine Islands are thick with groves, and mansions stand in the midst of them too. And for many miles down the right bank under the chalk ridge the houses stand trim in their orchards on the river's brink. Their little summer-houses overlook the road, seated and cushioned; and the old people sit there looking on the river, watching the youngsters play and the old men and the soldiers fishing from the wall.

These banks are castled, too, like the Rhine. The potentates of Normandy chose the heights of this river basin from all the rest of Normandy, for reasons that are obvious. Apart from the elevation of these hills, the beauty of the sites is something to aspire to live in the midst of. Many of these old seats are crumbling. Some are so strongly built they will last for ever. All were built by men with some force of personality. Famous amongst them is the fine old castle of Robert le Diable, the rough parent of William the Conqueror. It's the oldest, and half decayed, but its strong points are still reared up there on the hill-brow.

You move on under these noble hills, broken rarely by a timbered valley. There is nothing sombre aboard. Whatever the French can or cannot do, they can talk — gratefully and incessantly. The Norman tongue, however unintelligible, is incredibly pleasing in the mouths of its women. It is as free from harshness as the landscape. And the prattle of the children is music which a river orchestra would defile.

The beautiful La Bouille is the objective of most passengers. *Untrammelled* is the word for this little town. The women are fresh; the men are simple; the houses straggle quaintly and cleanly along the front; and the white walls and the gables climb in an unsophisticated fashion up the wooded hills beside the white, winding road. There is a *Place* set out by the landing-stage, lined with cafés under the trees. The river-men in their wide *pantalons* and loose corduroy blouses sip wine with their women; their children romp in the centre of the square. You will be nobly entertained if you do no more than sit there and call for refreshment to the red-cheeked waitress. But you will probably not be content without wandering up the hill-road after an hour at the tables. And if you do not grow envious of the youths who sit on the bank with company by that roadside, you are more than human. In Normandy love-making there is nothing embarrassed, but an unforced give and take that is not traditionally reputed to lie along the path of true love. Whether this is true love or not (and it probably isn't), it looks quite as delicious, and it sufficeth them. One wonders whether, after all, they are due to demand much more. The girl looks at you frankly from the midst of it, as who should say: "And why do not you, in this land of sweet sunlight, fulfil, too, the law of your existence ?"

From almost every house, as you ascend, some houri smiles a half-welcome at you and would not be greatly confused or displeased if you took it for a whole, and, entering, made yourself at home.

At the hilltop you'll come on the old *Maison brûlée*, with a café in the recess, and much merry company. If you stay there as long as you want to, you'll miss the last boat to Rouen. So you quit drinking-in the Seine beauty revelling below you up and down the river basin, and saunter back to the steamer. All the town is there to see her leave. Everyone smiles and " waves " and says *Come again* in no uncertain panto- mime. And all the journey back in the soft evening you say you will.

SECTION B.—PICARDY AND THE SOMME

CHAPTER I

BEHIND THE LINES—I

THE road between —— and —— is a fearful and wonderful place in the swift-closing winter evening. The early winter rains are drifting gustily across it. The last of the autumn leaves are whirling away. The far western valley is a gulf of mist; the rain-squalls wash about its slopes.

The road beneath you, between its low flanks, is a channel of mobile black slush, too far churned for striation. Ever since the rains began, two weeks ago, there has been a traffic on it that is continuous— a traffic that has had to be directed and disentangled at innumerable stages along its length. So the road surface (it washes over a solid foundation) is a squirting slime.

The motor-lorry is the vehicle *par excellence*. The wonder is how it is supplied and maintained at this rate. In most villages is a tyre-press where its wheels are re-rubbered as often as need be—and begad! that's often enough to keep a large and noble army of mechanics hard-worked. Any day you can see the old tyre being prised off and the new, smooth, full, blue one pushed on. The old is like nothing so much as a rim of Gruyère cheese, with the perforations clean

188

through to the rim, everywhere. The question that always occurs is: Did the lorry run to the last on a tyre like that ? The answer is: Yes—had to.

The motor-lorry it is, then, that monopolises the road. There is a stream of them passing either way which is not quite constant, but is nearly so. Lorries are almost as thick as the trees that line every road in France.

Between these honking, rumbling streams, and in the gaps of them, other traffic goes as it can—that is, Colonel's cars, motor-cycles (there are almost as many cycles as lorries; but they can pant an intermittent course through any maze), motor-ambulances, tractors. There are French Colonels, English Colonels, mere Majors, and even Generals, threading impatiently through the maze. It is obviously aggravating to them, this snail's pace. A Colonel likes to tear along, because he is a Colonel. One is speaking now of a main road between railheads. Put them on a side-road, where there is nothing in sight but a few ambulances, a lorry or two, and some cows and women, and they move at a pace that inspires an adequate respect in all who have to stand aside for their necks' sake.

But in this horde of beastly lorries what can a Colonel do, more than glare and gnaw a rain-dewed moustache ? There are supply lorries, ammunition lorries, Flying Corps lorries, road-repairing lorries, lorries bearing working-parties, freights of German prisoners, lorries returning empty. Beside, there are always a few 'buses moving troops, and sometimes, participating in the general *mêlée*, is a troop of cavalry or a half-mile of artillery limbers or a divisional

train of horse transport—or all three—making an
adequate contribution to the ' creaking, rattling,
lumbering, panting, honking, shouting, cursing, squelch-
ing, bobbing, swaying, dodging throng. A military
highroad in France behind the line, any time in the
day or night, baffles description—especially if it's
raining.

Conceive (if you can) what this becomes at ten
o'clock at night in an advanced section of the road
where lights would be suicidal. But I doubt if you
can—no, not unless you've been in the whirl of it.

Far the pleasanter journey you'll have by boarding
your motor-lorry on a fine summer morning. The
country smiles all about you. *Smile* is the only word.
You catch the infection of green bank, green plain
flecked with brown and gold stubble and streaked with
groves of elm and beech, poplar and plane: you get
infected and rejoice. If you climb the crest of one of
the slopes less gentle than most slopes here, you may
look down on it all—on the double line of trees setting-
off here and there across the plains, up the slopes,
down the valleys, marking the roads, of which trees
are the invariable index; at the winding stream,
banked with hop and willow, flowing through a belt
of richer greenness: that's how you know a stream
from a height—not by the water, of which you see
nothing for the groves that border it, but by the
irregularity of these plantations (the roads are planted
with a deliberate symmetry) and the deepening in
the colour of the lush grasses of the basin.

You'll look down, too, on the villages dropped
irregularly along its course. There's the low roof,
the gable, the amorphous mass of greys and yellows

topped by the pyramidal church spire rising grey slate to its summit. The number of villages you may see in thirty square miles of the Somme district is amazing. The whole Somme Valley is a mazed network of roads and streams, with groves and harvest-fields in the crowding interstices, the whole teeming with grey villages. This is the character of the country; and very lovely it is.

From your hilltop you'll see, perhaps, a bombing-school at play in the valley—the line of murderous, irregular bursts in their white, vapourish smoke, all forced into the extremity of unnaturalness by the deep colour of the wood behind.

In June the depth of the colour in this French country gave the sky itself a depth of colour not known in Australia. The cumulus resting on the sky-line would be arresting in its contrast with wood and pasture, and the blue of the gaps above it heightened too. Sometimes the days were clouded in the vault, but with a clear horizon; then you would get a kind of rich opalescence, the sunlight shut out above deflected and concentrated in the glowing horizon, its streaks of colour intensified fourfold by the depth of green in the landscape. Some such middle afternoons I never shall forget.

Upon the less frequented roads civilian traffic is frequent. It's mostly country-women in carts with pigs or oxen behind or with produce (or merchandise) for a village market. The village markets for a whole district are conducted by a sort of mobile column of vendors. They move (under a pass issued from the *gendarmerie*) from village to village in a species of caravan. Every village has a set market-day; the

vendors move in agreement with it. They sell under
booths on the pavements—sell fabrics, fruit, vegetables,
fish, drapery, and clothing; and at some corner agreed
upon they have the cattle market, with all the beasts
tethered by a rope from horns to knee.

Approaching a village which is "holding" its
market, you'll meet these beasts being driven in gangs,
united in sixes and sevens by a rope connecting their
horns. They are almost all conducted by women and
boys. The boys are incredibly cruel to them, not only
en route, but at the market-place.

It's not the women and girls conducting the market
cattle who abuse them. They (and those in the market
wagons) give you a smile and "*Bon jour, m'sieur*."
There is a charm about this French usage of looking
you in the eye and giving you a frank smile and a cheerful *Good-day* without ever having met you before.

You cannot go far without traversing some part of
a military highroad—such is the frequency and the
height of mobility. Especially is this so about those
railheads adjacent to the line. Troops of cavalry,
infantry, and artillery and horsed transport crowd
French routes, even to the exclusion of the motor-
lorry. For miles you may see nothing but a sea of
yellow, bobbing, wash-basin trench-helmets. Unlovely
they are, but useful. In such parts, too, the motor-
'buses for rushing up reinforcements prevail. They
come in long, swaying processions, filled with grinning
warriors, who exchange repartee between themselves
and the freight of other 'buses, and spend a lot of time
in gnawing biscuit and jam. They gesticulate with
these morsels.

The 'buses are just such as you see in the Strand,

except for colour, which here is, of course, a dingy khaki. Above and within, when they are stuffed, they have an enormously useful carrying capacity.

At some stages of a route (and at very frequent stages) you pass a lorry-park, in the vicinity of which you are ordered to reduce the pace. There are whole battalions of lorries laagered and parked—miles of them—lining the main roads, lining the side-roads, lined in the fields; hordes of them radiating from the H.Q. at the main road. They are splashed and streaked and pied with colour, like Jacob's ewes, to baffle aircraft. They resemble, indeed, the streaked cruisers off Anzac. Some columns have other decorations. You'll pass, for instance, a Dickens convoy: the lorries are named from the novels—Sarah Gamp preceding Mr. Pickwick, with Little Nell panting in the rear; Bill Sykes, Scrooge, and the rest of them—with (in rare cases) crude attempts at illustration by portraiture.

The fleets of lorries give a sense of efficiency and mobility—even of dignity—as they stand ranked there.

Casualty clearing stations are very frequent indeed in these advanced posts. With a curious appearance of contradictoriness, their marquees are streaked and splashed against aircraft, but here and there bear an enormous Red Cross glaring an appeal at the heavens. The language of all this is: " We're hospital, and you know it from these outward and visible signs. But if you're going to be frightful, we'll make it as hard as we can for you to hit." . . . Over the road is the burial-ground, significantly full.

Mostly these hospitals are on a railway-line. Some

13

are not. From the latter the stream of motor-ambulances is continuous at certain seasons. There are Sisters in these advanced stations; they are little more than dressing stations, and more than seldom they are shelled. It's no joke for women; they do not blench. There have been " honours and rewards " made them for continuing to dress cases when suffering wounds themselves.

And who shall describe the strafings suffered by some of the advanced railheads ? Shelling of clearing stations may be more or less accidental, but railheads are good game and are shelled very deliberately and very thoroughly. I visited one afternoon a railhead supply depôt that had been shelled from five to nine that morning. The havoc was good ground for self-congratulation by the enemy batteries that caused it. Nine-inch shell for four hours, if well observed by those who deliver it, can do great things. There were shell-holes all over the station yard—lines ripped up, trucks blown to splinters, supply stacks scattered to the fields, petrol dump smouldering, station-house battered. This is horribly disorganising. Only one thing is worse, of that kind: the strafing of a railway junction by bombs. This is obstructive, and isolating almost beyond retrieve.

The villages about such stations suffer seriously. They bear the marks about the house walls. Villages adjacent to batteries—apart from railheads—get it even worse. Generally they lie behind a wood which conceals our heavy artillery.

At any junction along a military road you are impressed by the usefulness of the military police. They stand there directing the traffic by pantomime, just as in London. Their word is law from which there is no appeal. If a driver grows argumentative it is always the worse for him. District A.P.M.'s will allow no dispute of the directions of their minions. You must wait for their instructions and obey them very exactly. If they tell you to wait you dare not budge; if you do, there's your number glaring on your bonnet, and your goose is cooked. The military police are all-powerful on the road, and proportionately autocratic. A sergeant will step into a stretch of clear rural road and address the driver: " What limit is on your speed ?"—" Six miles."—" My instructions to you are to go much slower."—" Why " (irritably), " what am I going now ?"—" Never mind that " (with a conclusive gesture); " I've timed you from the last post, and you're too fast. I'm not making a case of it, but you go slower. Hear ?" And this monument of British administrative exactitude walks off, after saluting perfunctorily (he gives you no loop-hole), and throws you permission to go on and behave.

You proceed, with the guns belching over the ridge, the observation balloons overhanging the slope silently spotting and sending down cool and deadly mathematical messages. The 'planes drone above; the multitudinous machinery of war creaks and rumbles down the road; the landscape lies around you incongruously quiet and lovely.

CHAPTER II

BEHIND THE LINES—II

THE lines of communication one can expect to be trailed with interest. There the strings are being pulled—though that is a pitiable figure. It is more than a rehearsal for the soul-shaking drama enacting on the Front; but it is as full of interest as orchestral rehearsal is more interesting than the performance *coram publico*. Rehearsal in orchestra shows the final performance in the making: here you see the Somme Battle in the making. A French town that is within seven miles of the guns, and is also the Headquarters of the ——th Army, unites the ordered busyness of the base with the fevered activity of the second line. It slumbers not nor sleeps. The stream and the screech and roar of trains is intense and incessant. There is no more appreciable interval between troop-trains, supply-trains, ammunition-trains, rumbling through than there is between the decipherable belchings of the guns over the north-east ridge. The buzz of 'planes is as unintermittent as either. The Army Head-quarters in the Hôtel de Ville is as strident a centre by night as by day. "The sea is in the broad, the narrow, streets, ebbing and flowing." These words recur by suggestion with a peculiar insistence. It is the flood military; and to this peaceful pastoral town it is as foreign and as ubiquitous as an encroaching sea. The Hôtel de Ville is the centre of a wide area of civil buildings commandeered for its purposes by Headquarters. This sometime produce-store is now " Reports Office "; that hotel is " Signals "; a private *maison* adjoining is for " Despatch-Riders." All civilian and pedestrian traffic stands aside for the horde of despatch-riders and their motor-cycles. The cars of the Staff whirl through the crowded streets with a licence which takes account of nothing but their objective. Mounted officers are trooping day and night.

More significant than all this is the unending stream of motor-ambulances. They transport from the dressing stations behind the line to the colony of casualty clearing-stations here; they transfer from them to the ambulance-trains; and what these cannot take they pant away with gently to the nearest base. You may stand on the upreared Citadelle ramparts any night and watch these long processions of pain throbbing quietly down the sloping road from —— into the town. And simultaneously you will see another column climbing the road to —— at the other side. The head-lights make a long concurrent brilliance, like the ray of a searchlight.

An advanced C.C.S. behind the line sees a constant ebb and flow. Jaded Sisters will hear with a sense of relief the order to evacuate, glimpsing a respite, however brief. But before the evacuation is completed a causal connection is evident between the order and an attack at dawn on the —st instant, and all its ghastly fruits. And whilst the last of the old maimed are being put gently aboard, the new-comers, stained with mud and blood, are being laid in the still warm beds. There is no time for orderliness here. Life for the Sisters is one fevered and sporadic attempt at alleviation—more than an attempt: the relief is accomplished, but at a cost to the workers which leaves its index on feature and figure.

All this is in piteous contrast with the healing peacefulness of the country-side. If you climb the low ridge behind the town any evening you can see the flap-flap of the gun-flashes like a disorganised Aurora. And if you stay till midnight you'll see it intensify into a glowing wall. So gentle is the landscape immediately about you that you can conceive what it would be without that murderous wall of fire and that portentous heart-shaking thunder. This is war, relentless and insatiable.

The days open dewy and crisp with the first touch of winter's severity, before his tooth is keen. The first breath of a French September morning is elating. The harvest is just reaped and cocked, and stands in its brown and yellow stubble. The head of a slope will give you the landscape gently undulating under its succession of woods and streams and gathered harvest, with frequent villages scattered down the valleys and straggling up the slopes. Over all this you look away to the captive balloons depending over the line spotting for the belching guns; and the song of the little birds that the distant guns cannot quench is swallowed in the buzz of the aircraft engines of a flight of scouters setting off on patrol; to-morrow it will be the whirr of a squadron of battle-'planes tearing through the upper distance on a raid. And any morning the air above you is flecked with the puffs of missiles sent hurtling after a Fokker out of its proper territory. As the peaceful evening settles down you will see a whole school of our craft coming home to roost at ——: eighteen to twenty, like a flock of rooks settling at the end of the day. The *Angelus* ringing in the belfry of the village *Église* is drowned in the hum.

The little wayside Calvaries are daily smothered in the dust of motor-lorries. Peaceful French domesticity makes an attempt to live its life in the welter of trains and 'planes, tractors and lorries, cars and cycles, horse and foot. It will get it lived *après la guerre*—not before. The children of the villages do not play much; they gaze open-mouthed and wide-eyed at the incessant train of troops and strident vehicles. Unless the War finishes soon, they will have forgotten how to play. The village estaminet is no longer the haunt of the lighthearted, light-speaking, wine-sipping French *paysan ;* it is overcrowded with noisy, sweaty Tommies who have no abiding city, demanding drink. The air of it reeks. The girls are too busy for repartee; they have time only for feverish serving.

Passenger trains are rarely to be seen—traffic *militaire* by day and by night. Rural domestic journeys on the *chemin de fer* are over and gone. It is supplies or troops or guns; a frantic railway staff and a frenzied *chef de gare* who has forgotten what smooth and intermittent traffic on his line is like.

CHAPTER III

C.C.S.

THE ——th C.C.S. claims to be the hospital farthest advanced on the Somme. The claim is justified. Its grounds are lit at night by the gun-flashes. The discharge of our own heavies rattles the bottles in its dispensary and makes its canvas tremble. Sleep is sometimes driven from the eyes of its patients, not by pain, but by the thunder of bombardment. Convoys from the dressing stations have but a short run. The wounded arrive with the trench-mud wet upon them. Clearing them up is quick, if filthy, work, and in clearing them up is engaged a small battalion of orderlies.

The whole hospital is under canvas, except the operating-theatre, which is a hut, hermetically sealed, as it were, and heated to a working temperature—and, incidentally, an even temperature—by some ingenious device. Surgery cannot get done with numbed hands. Yes—and the officers' ward is a hut, to deepen the great gulf fixed between Tommy and his officer, even when they both are in mortal pain. The difference in the degrees of comfort between a marquee and a hut, in the Somme winter, is incredible. Unhappily, too, in these winter months there is a horrible shortage of coal and paraffin. This tells again in favour of the hut. The officers' hut is as warm as your civilian sitting-room, and wellnigh as comfortably furnished. No ingenuity could make it possible to say this of a marquee.

But it is only the wounded officers who are comfortable. The Medical Officers freeze and soak in bell-tents. You'll see the batmen drying their blankets nightly at the mess-fire before their " bosses " go to rest. No artificial heating is possible in these tents, because there is no fuel available for those who are well. M.O.'s retire after an all-night bout in the theatre to their clammy beds, and sleep from exhaustion; and for no other reason. They wake, and shiver into dewy clothes. They shiver through their meals in the biting mess-tent, and they plod through the sea of slush that surrounds the wards incessantly, now that the winter has set in. For the ground is never dry. When it's not raining (which is seldom) it's snowing—and snowing good and hard, as a rule, in fat flakes as big as carnations.

But they're a cheerful mess, with work enough to save them from dwelling overmuch on the discomforts of the Somme winter. There are twenty of them. The Colonel is a Regular, with long years of Indian service behind him, whose favourite table topics are big-game and economic problems—particularly those hypothetical economic difficulties which are likely to confront us after this war. His customary opponent is Padré Thomas, the Roman Catholic Chaplain, who took a double-first at Oxford and was one time an Eton master. He receives weekly from a favourite nephew, reading for matriculation, Latin prose exercises, the merits of which he discusses with those members of the mess whose classical scholarship war has not quite obliterated.

There is Wallace, the X-ray expert, whose chief topic is the shortage of paraffin, lacking which his apparatus cannot carry-on. He's a Scotchman who once graduated in Arts. He is chief consulting specialist with the Chaplain on the merits of his nephew's prose composition.

The Anglican padré is a raw-boned Scot (six-feet four) who has lived mostly in Russia and Germany. He talks a great deal of vodka and the hoggishness of German manners. "What a treat it would be," he says, " to march into Berlin with the pipes playing, go through to meet the Russians on the other side, and have a foregathering ! That night I should cast away *all* my ecclesiastical badges !"

He preaches to the camp of German prisoners close by with a grace that is not altogether good. He cannot abide Germans. One envisages him as delivering them fire-and-brimstone discourses and calling them weekly to repentance.

The quietest members of the mess are the surgical specialists, P—— and R——. They are also the hardest worked and the most irregular at meals. It is rarely that they are taking their soup before the others have finished. This is perhaps a good thing, in the light of their frank physiological discussion at table of cases just disposed of in the theatre. On taking-in day they frequently do not come to table at all. I doubt whether they eat; if they do, it is a snack between cases in the *abattoir*. The hospital takes in and evacuates on alternate days. Theatre cases must be done at once, for it may be necessary to evacuate them to the base on the following day; it. is, in fact, necessary, unless they are unable to bear transportation, and many are too critical for that—head cases, spinal cases, and the like. Cases that suffer greatly are visited with the merciful hypodermic before they start on their jolting journey in the ambulance-train. Not that A.T.'s are rough: they're amazingly smooth. But however smooth, they are agonising to the man whose nerves are lacerated and exposed, or into whose tissue the scalpel has cut deep.

The A.T. draws into an improvised siding adjacent to the wards. There is no question of mechanical transport to the train. It is the practice to establish C.C.S.'s beside a railway, where evacuation during a push can be facile and expeditious.

P—— and R——, the men of few words, but of great and bloody deeds, have operated in some degree or other on wellnigh every case that boards the ambulance-train.

Added to the shortages in fuel which hit the wounded so hard is that other present hardship: the congestion on railways. As soon as an A.T. is wired as having left the Army garage at ——, such preparations must be made as will ensure that the wounded will be ready to board her immediately on her arrival. They must be waiting in the evacuation tents by the siding before the minimum time of her arrival. But notwithstanding regulations which provide that A.T.'s shall take precedence over all other railway-traffic whatsoever, that requisitioned is frequently four or five hours late—such is the present state of the roads. That means four hours of frozen agony in the evacuation tents. Fuel cannot be spared for warming them, when it is more than the wards can do to get warmed. A shivering padré moves round amongst them administering comfort which makes no pretence at being spiritual, except in a punning sense. That's one thing very few padrés in the war-zone have been obtuse enough not to learn: that attempts at spiritual consolation may sometimes be inopportune. Every padré knows the full war-value of creature-comforts—even for his spiritual ends. So he moves about the evacuation tent ministering to the body rather than to the soul.

The surgical specialists have long since ceased to have connection with this stage of their patients' movements basewards. They are in the theatre making ready more for the journey down.

The mess harbours the O.C. of a mobile laboratory. He moves between the hospitals within the Army testing serums. He wears the peering aspect of a man accustomed to microscopic examination. All his table conversation is of an inquiring nature—better, an investigatory nature—into matters that are quite impersonal. During a whole meal he will talk of nothing but the Northern Territory of Australia or the structure of the Great Barrier Reef on the Queensland coast. If he's talking of the Reef he deals in a series of questions and in an examination of your answers thereto, until he has built up for himself—with the aid of diagrams contrived with table implements and slabs of bread—an accurate notion of the surface structure. He's as much interested in modern history as in science. One evening he edified the mess, by arrangement, with an hour's discourse on the causes leading up to the American Civil War. For this he prepared with academic care. It was curious to see how he could, for an hour, sustain the interest of the mess in so remote and comparatively insignificant a struggle, when that mess was stationed in the heart of the Somme at the height of the push. . . . His laboratory walls were decorated with pictures by no means scientific, and yet physiological. They are extracted from *La Vie Parisienne*, a French weekly illustrated journal of extraordinary frankness. But in this man there is nothing lewd. But he has an unusual appreciation of French cleverness; and that is a faculty alarmingly wanting in the normal English officer. French drawings. which the English call lewd are by no means lewd: merely intensely clever. They convey no notion of lewdness to the French mind. But.the English, except in the case of isolated representatives of that race, will never understand the French—in other matters than that of art. So great is the gulf of miscomprehension fixed between the French and English that it becomes a daily deepening mystery how they could ever have found themselves Allies. Still more mysterious is it that they should continue so. . . .

These are the men who impress you most in the mess. There's Wallace, the Scotchman who never says more than he's obliged, but has the tender heart with his patients. He always trembles when giving the anæsthetic in critical cases. He calls himself weak-kneed for it, and reviles himself unmercifully for a womanish fellow (he's intensely masculine); but he can't help it.

There's Thompson, another Scotchman (the mess is fairly infested with Scots) who is dental surgeon. His gift is disconcerting repartee, with which he occasionally routs the C.O.

These are the officers. But what of the Sisters?
There are eight of them. When you have said they
are entirely unselfish, you have included most at-
tributes. That includes an irrepressible spirit that
no continuity of labour can break. It includes gentleness which familiarity with pain in others does not
quench. And it includes a contempt of personal
comfort that must sometimes amaze even themselves
if they ever find time to grow either introspective or
retrospective. They sleep in tents; they lack fuel;
they shiver by the hour in damp beds unless exhaustion
drives them to sleep; and they rise in the murky
morning to don sodden garments. They work hard
and without intermission for twelve to sixteen hours
—and indefinitely when a "stunt" has brought the
convoys from the line. But none of these things
beats them down.

The theatre Sisters deserve immortalisation. All the
qualities of patience and gentleness, endurance and
cheerfulness, seem intensified in them. They have not
the smallest objection to your watching them work
in the theatre; nor have the surgeons. Rather, they
encourage you, and get you to help in a minor way
when the place is busy.

It is rarely on receiving-day that four "tables" are not
in use simultaneously. This makes it inevitable that
the victims, as they are brought in and laid out for
the anæsthetic, see within six feet sights not calculated
to fortify them. Some smile in hardy fashion; some
smile in a fashion that is not hardy. The abject terror
of those wretches out of whom pain has long since
beaten all the fortitude is horrible to see. What must
be the state of that man, made helpless by unassuaged

suffering, who sees the scalpel at work upon a fellow beside him—the gaping incision; the merciless pruning of the shattered limb; the hideous bloodiness of the steaming stump at amputation—and hears the stertorous breathing of the subject and his agonised subconscious moaning, which has all the infection of terror that actual suffering would convey ?

Yes; this is inevitable. There can be no privacy. Despatch is everything. Nowhere is rapidity so urgent as in the theatre of a C.C.S. It means lives. The hideous gas-gangrene forms and suppurates in a single hour. This is the worst enemy of the field hospital surgeon. Half an hour's postponement of operation— even less—may mean death. And in other cases, if the preliminary operation is not performed in time for the case to move by A.T. for finishing at the base, it may cost a life equally. The surgeon has not time to fortify his victim by explanation or exhortation. He is lifted from stretcher to table; the anæsthetist takes his seat at the head, sprinkles the mask and applies it; the surgeon moves up (he has already seen the case in ward); the stertorous breathing begins; the Sister attends and places ready to his hands what the surgeon requires in swabs and implements; and with the impressive directness of long and varied experience the incision is made and the table is in a moment stained. But let there be no confounding of rapidity with haste, despatch with carelessness. As much time as is necessary, so much will be given; but not more. Most striking feature of all is the curiously impersonal and scientific thoroughness of the surgeon here: this, and the providential faculty of humour in both surgeons and Sisters in the throes of it all, without which the tragedy of the place would be overwhelming. The case is treated with the impersonality (and the persistence) due to a scientific problem, and as such is wrestled with. Three hours will be given, if necessary; and sometimes they are. It is a grim and continuous fight with death, without intermission. But, like any successful warrior, the surgeon jokes in the midst of it. A smile—even a gentle guffaw—comes with a strange effect in this place of blood, but it " saves the situation." This, with the marked impersonality of the surgeon, can be nothing but reassuring to the potential victim, waiting his turn on the adjacent table.

One does not realise until he sees it what hard physical labour an amputation involves, with scalpel and saw; nor how bloodless it can be; nor how revolting is the warm stink of steaming human flesh suddenly exposed; nor how interest swamps repulsion as you watch a skull trephined; nor how utterly strange, for the first time, is the sight of a man lying there with his intestines drawn forth reposing upon his navel.

A man can suffer many wounds and still live— one man with multiple bomb and shell wounds; not a limb untouched; an arm and a leg gone; a skull trephined; fragments extracted from thigh and chest and shoulder; the other hand shattered; to say nothing of wounds and bruises and putrefying sores innumerable. Human endurance and survival can become incredible.

There are sessions in the theatre at which an orderly is kept almost busy passing between the M.O.'s, registering, for purposes of record, the nature of the operation.

" What shall I enter, sir ?"

" Appendicitis, acute—abdomen closed," says P——.

" If you had not added *abdomen closed*," says R——, " would one be at liberty to infer it had been left open ?"

" Get your head read !" says P——. . . . . The orderly passes on.

" What's this, sir ?"

" Damn you ! Can't you see I'm busy ?" K—— is boring, with all the strength of his massive shoulders, into the skull of his case. Trephining is, literally, hard work; but not that alone. L—— is cutting, cutting, cutting, at the buttock of the wretch, paring the hideous gas gangrene as one would pare the rottenness from an apple. A third surgeon is probing for bomb splinters in rear of the thigh; and getting them. The man is splintered all over. For one horrible moment you conceive him as suddenly and treacherously deprived of unconsciousness, with —— boring here to the brain membrane, —— slicing generously at his buttock, and —— probing relentlessly to the bone in the gaping incision.

" Well, it certainly looks as though we are doing what we like," says ——. " It *is* rather bloody; yet the C.O. says the most revolting operation to watch is that of the removal of a finger-nail."

" If we go much further, he'll drop his subconscious ire upon us," says ——.

" Yes, I suppose his subconsciousness is protesting in blasphemous silence: '*Pourquoi* ?'"

" Stitches, Sister," says ——, at the head. The blood-clot has flowed; and in a twinkling the triangular exposure of skull is covered by the stitched scalp.

" He'll be easier," says ——.

And then begins the tabulation of his multiple wounds.
They cover half a page. It's a miracle of symbolism
which can suggest all that man has suffered (and has
yet to suffer) in the handwriting of half a page. . . .

" Clear, thank God !" says ——, as Multiple Wounds
is borne out insensible half an hour later. " It's
eleven, and I've been here since the middle of the
morning; and I could almost sleep. Good-night,
Sister ! I'm off."

So they go to the freezing dampness of their camp
stretchers. The orderlies set about " cleaning up."

But at one they're all called. The railhead, three
kilometres off, has been shelled. A convoy has
brought forty casualties. Half of them must pass
through the theatre without delay. So the nerve-
jangling work recommences, and goes on past the murky
dawn, beyond the breakfast hour. It is snowing hard.
They are hard-pressed to keep the theatre warm
enough for delicate surgery. To equalise the temperature has become impossible. But things are as they
are, and cannot be bettered; and there will come an
end to this spurt, though how long will be the respite,
who can say ? It would be longer if the surgeons were
not so dangerously understaffed. There's —— on a
long-deferred and necessary leave; there are —— and
—— who have fallen ill: one through the overstrain
of incessant surgery; the other a victim to his sopping,
inclement tent. The watchword is *Carry on*. There
may be assistance by importation to the staff; on the
other hand, there may not. There will be, if possible;
but the pressure is severe all over the Somme Hospitals
during the offensive, and the bases are drained.

The hospital railhead was shelled one afternoon. One may have the charity to surmise the Hun was shooting at the aerodrome; which stands seven hundred yards from the hospital; for the shell fell about the aerodrome rather than in the C.C.S. However that may be, shell did burst in the hospital, either by accident or design.

The order was to evacuate immediately. The Colonel ordered the Sisters to enter a car and be transported beyond range. They declined. The Colonel, a bachelor, not skilled in negotiation with the long-haired sex, commanded the matron to command them. Matron ordered them to their tents to prepare to flit. She went to them in ten minutes' time. "Are you ready?"—"No, Matron; there's a small mutiny brewing here. If the patients are to go, we're going with them."—"I'm not going; I was just in the middle of my dressings; I'm going to finish the others."—"They shan't go without us, Matron!" . . . So with a splendid indignation they disobeyed. The Matron is accustomed to obedience, but she didn't get it. She went to the Colonel and explained. "Well, damn 'em! the witches! Let 'em have their way!" The Matron broke into a run. "Take your flasks and your hypodermics; you can go!"

So they superintended all the removings, attending here and there with the merciful preliminary syringe; and, when the preliminaries to the journey were over, jumped up with the car-drivers, and the evacuation began into a field on the —— road. Those that could walk, walked; and some that couldn't well walk had to do so. . . .

They laid them out in rows, by wards. Some were

dying. Some died on the way. Some died in the grass, cut by the bitter wind as they lay there gazing into the unkindly heaven. The rain came in frozen gusts. Those still hovering on the border-line were blown and soaked into death. The groaning of the wounded was hideous. Shattered limbs are hard to bear in the complete comfort of a civilian hospital. What is a wounded man to do but die, exposed to the pelting rain of the Somme winter? Brandy and hot tea and cigarettes brought a transient consolation: most men were insensible to aid from such fragmentary comfort. It began to be plain that the risk from shell-fire was not more dangerous than this from exposure; a return was ordered. Sisters, doctors, patients, concurred with equal fervour. And so they were taken back.

The shelling had ceased.

Next morning came the ambulance-train.

CHAPTER IV

THE FOUGHTEN FIELD

I VISITED the fields of Beaumont-Hamel and Miraumont and Bapaume soon after they had been abandoned, in the pleasant sunshine of an April Sabbath
afternoon. It was the abomination of desolation I
saw—and felt. Of Beaumont-Hamel there was not
a stone left standing, it was not until I had been told
that a village once stood there that I began to distin-
guish the powdered rubble from its surroundings.
There was difficulty in doing that, for not only were
the buildings demolished, but their bricks crunched
and crumbled.

As we approached the old line from ——, the degrees
of demolition in the villages showed clearly how near
they had stood to the field of fire, and how systematic had been the German bombardment. The remoter
villages showed merely sporadic gaps in the walls—
which might have been the result of accident rather
than of purpose—or a church spire tottering. Nearer
villages showed large areas containing not more than
the skeletons of houses. The villages which had been
in occupation—such as Beaumont-Hamel itself—
had not one stone left upon another. The twisted
wire straggled through them; the battered trenches
wormed about.

We left the car at Miraumont and walked up the old road overlooking the village and Grandcourt Wood. They call it a road for the sake of topography. But did you ever see ring-barked trees standing in a morass ?—that is it, with this difference: that these trees are branchless. You can conceive nothing more gaunt and desolate than that colony of splintered trunks standing down in the grassless valley of pools. The pools are shell-holes, so frequent that they have the aspect of a morass striated by thin ridges of black mud. The ridges are the lips of shell-holes.

Miraumont stands down the slope above the wood. It is less completely ruined than Beaumont-Hamel, but by that the more pathetic to look on. You can see what it has been: you cannot judge what Beaumont-Hamel may have been.

As far as you can see in any direction there is no blade of grass, though the spring has begun, and all the earth untouched by war is greening. Between —— and —— the loveliness of the early spring is upon the land; the primrose and the violet are starring the grass in the woods, and all the terraced slopes of the valleys are fair with the young crop. Here you see nothing but brown clay pocked by shell, the graceless grey zigzag of the ruined trench, the litter of deserted arms and equipment and smashed shelter, battered frames of village dwellings, and the limbless deformity of the splintered woods.

We walked up the ruined road beyond Miraumont. Both sides were thick with dug-outs. The road had been a kind of shelter between its low banks. I thought what the traffic on this road must have been when it was ours and the Germans were entrenched beyond it;

how it would be shelled because it was low and naturally congested with British traffic; how the dug-outs would be peopled continuously by passers-by flinging themselves in for a momentary respite when the bursts were accurate. . . . The dug-outs were deep and littered with cast-off great-coats, tunics, scarves, boots; with jam-tins, beef-tins, rusted bayonets, clips of unused cartridge, battered rifles. It had been a road for the supply of ammunition to the front line. Its corners were choked with bombs, shell-case, and small-arm ammunition. In its excavations were dumps of barbed wire unused. You could infer all the busyness and congestion, the problem and the cursing of harassed and supercrowded transport in this road.

We reached the crest of the hill and struck to the left across the old field. This brought us upon a plateau. There had been more intense fighting here than on the slopes. There had been rain incessantly, too. The shell-holes were filled, and they were so frequent that the landscape resembled nothing so much as a coral reef at low tide. It was with the risk of slipping in that one made a way along the field at all. To have fallen in and taken a mouthful of that green liquid would have meant death. Those pools that were not green were red. Either colour implied only the degree of putrefaction of the corpses that lay beneath; but not always beneath. Here protruded a head, there a knee or a shoulder or a buttock; sometimes a gaunt hand alone outstretched from the stinking pool. The pools stunk; the ground stunk; the whole land-scape smelt to heaven. My friend had brought, in his wisdom, some black Burmah cheroots. They were as strong as could be got, but they could not overwhelm the revolting stink of human putrefaction that rose all round. One asks what will it be when the spring is advanced and the pools are dry. One asks, too, when and how this land will be re-farmed. It is sown with live bomb and " dud " shell. One foresees the ploughing peasant having the soul blown out of him one spring morning. It will be long before the sword becomes the ploughshare. In the making of the *via sacra*, too, will there be many casualties.

Fighting on this plateau must have been hellishly intense and deadly. The only conceivable cover was the trench and dug-out: no natural mound nor sheltering bank. The dug-outs were correspondingly deep, burrowing down into the bowels of the earth. Like pimples on the broad face of the plateau were machine-gun and artillery emplacements. These had plainly been built extraordinarily strong, but not strong enough to stand the direct fire to which they had been exposed inevitably. How any structure—or any excavation, indeed—withstands the intensity of modern artillery fire is inconceivable.

The tangles of wire that traversed this high ground were gapped and contorted. A rifle was wrapped about in the murderous mesh; it had been grasped by a human hand; beyond was the man to whom it may have belonged, caught in the same gentle embrace. The steel helmet beneath the network, the rag of tunic flapping in the breeze from the jags, were all-expressive. You needed not to be told explicitly of what they were the symbols.

Near the edge of the plateau was the crater of an exploded mine. It had been sapped from beneath the brow of the rise. Now it was a pond. The hideous deep green hue of the water betrayed the full meaning of that formula: " We exploded a mine and occupied the lip of the crater." Some of them were still occupying it: others were lying in the foul mouth of it.

To look on the whole of it—mottled acres, pimples of emplacements, streak of trench, wall of wire—was to know something of the hellishness of life here when this area was the field of battle.

We stumbled off the tableland into ground which had been German. Immediately beneath the crest they had had their howitzer emplacements. There were battered guns of theirs still there. We nosed down into their dug-outs, built well, and to a depth that was safe. They had been artillery dug-outs; the telephone-wires still crept down the wooden wall beyond the entrance. Below we found hideous dead, some shattered, as though bombed by an invader; heaps of beer-bottles, too, and many German novels. You could visualise these fellows having nights of revelry down there, drinking themselves oblivious to the roar of the guns above. It was possibly in the height of mirth that we broke through and bombed them where they reeled below in festivity. One does not know. This may be maligning them. Possibly they were a temperate lot, filled with zeal for the Fatherland. These bottles may have been the moderate collection of months. They may have been bombed beneath because they had decided to die hard. The facile assumption is far too common that the German is a drunken brute whose hobby is debauchery.

The area about the gun emplacements was littered with scores of tons of ammunition, which will probably never be salved. Littered with bombs it is too, and

with trench helmets, and the leather and brass and iron
of equipment.   We got many souvenirs here, creeping
about like ghouls among the dead and the heaps of
material.

We returned to the main road past the groups of
irregular graves, past the French labour-parties at
work upon fresh roads and upon salvage, back to the
skeleton of Miraumont.   Then the car swept down
behind   Beaumont-Hamel,   through   the   woods   to
Albert, which we skirted by the putty factory.   The
Virgin with her Child looked down, hideously maimed,
from the cathedral spire.   We came home through the
ridges and the avenues of Acheux, down the valley
of the Authie.

CHAPTER V

AN ADVANCED RAILHEAD

AT an advanced railhead one has to contend with other difficulties than that of the congestion of railway traffic, which is inevitable near the line. There are the French, who control all the traction. This includes the shunting: you must not forget the shunting. It's the shunting that kills. Your pack (*pack* is the technical term for supply-train) may arrive at railhead at 5 p.m.; but it may not be in position for clearance by divisions until midnight. This plays the devil with divisional transport. You advise them by telephone that their pack will arrive at railhead at 5: let them get their transport down. Transport arrives at 4.30, to be " on the safe side "; but it waits impatiently six and eight and ten hours to clear. Very hard on horses, this; almost as hard on lorry-drivers, if the division is clearing by mechancial transport. There is language used by drivers waiting thus for hours in the snow or the bitter wind. The language of a horse-transport driver is a very expressive thing; it has a directness that is admirable.

At —— the transport—and especially the horse transport—got tired of this system, if system it could be called. They got to the stage at which they posted an orderly at railhead to watch the shunting of packs with his own eyes. That orderly was not to move off until he not only saw the train arrive, but saw it in position too. Not until he returned to Headquarters with this doubtfully welcome news were the horses taken from their lines.

It's urgently necessary that packs should be "placed" early, for more reasons than one. But one is that the men in the line are depending on a prompt delivery of rations by the divisional transport. If, therefore, the pack arrives twenty-four hours late (as frequently it does), it is manifestly undesirable that thé French should delay its clearance ten hours more. Another reason is that if you have four packs arriving in the day—as many railheads have—your *cour de gare* will not accommodate them all for clearance simultaneously; usually it will not accommodate more than two at once. For yours are not the only trains whose clearance is urgent: there are ammunition-trains, stone-trains for road-making, trains of guns and horses for disembarkation, trains stuffed with ordnance stores and canteen stores, trains of timber for the R.E.'s. The clearance of any is needed urgently at any railhead. The term " railhead," by the way, is interpreted somewhat foggily by the popular mind. There used to be a notion abroad that it connoted a railway terminus. That is, of course, not so. It does connote a point in the line convenient for clearance by divisions. There may be five railheads in eighty miles of line, and the last of them not a terminus. A railhead, therefore, because it is a point convenient, is inevitably busy.

If tardiness in despatch from the base or railroad congestion -*en route* should congest your railhead suddenly, it may be necessary to indent for fatigue from the corps whose railhead yours is. Usually it is a night fatigue that must be requisitioned. Conceive the attitude of the fatigue that marches to railhead at 9 p.m. through the snow-slush, for eight hours' work. Conceive, also, the ingenuity with which, during operations, they secrete themselves in the nooks and crannies of supply-stacks, out of the bitter blast, until the rum issue is made. Half the energy of the N.C.O.'s is dissipated in keeping their disgusted mob up to strength. Conceive, too, the appropriation of "grub" that goes on in the bowels of these supply-stacks, and the cases of jam and veal-loaf dropped and burst by accident in transit. All-night fatigues that are borrowed are the very deuce.

The winter-night clearance at railhead goes on in the face of much difficulty and hardship. The congestion of transport in the yard is almost impossibly unwieldy: it moves in six-inch mud and in pitch darkness, except for the flares of the issuers, and except when there is neither rain nor snow, which is seldom. The cold is bitter and penetrating, so is the wind. Horses plunge in the darkness; drivers, loaders, and issuers curse; and to the laymen, who cannot be expected to see the system which does lie beneath this apparent chaos, it is miraculous that the clearance gets done at all.

The mistakes occur which are inevitable in the circumstances. The divisions clear by brigades. One brigade sometimes gets off with the rum or the fresh vegetable of another. Sometimes this is accidental; sometimes not. In any case it is a matter for internal adjustment by the division itself.

The adjustment of packs is a matter of extreme
difficulty at the railhead of a corps whose troops are
mobile. Any corps railhead in the Arras sector in
March, 1917, furnished a good example of that. We
were to push at Arras. This meant that reinforcements whose arrival it was difficult, if not impossible,
to forecast, were constantly coming in and raising
the strength of the divisions drawing. It takes three
days for orders on the base increasing the packs to
take effect at railhead. An increase of five thousand
in ration strength may be effected at half a day's
notice only. They must be fed. The pack is inadequate to this extent. The division must be sent to
another railhead to complete, or to a field supply
depôt, or to a reserve supply depôt. It may take them
a day to collect their full ration. You immediately
wire the base for an increase in pack. By the time
the wire has taken effect at railhead, the reinforcements
(in these mobile days of an advance) may have moved
on beyond Arras; you have all your increase as surplus
on your hands. They must be dumped, and the
increase in pack cancelled. It's not impossible that,
the day after you have cancelled it, you will have need
of it for fresh unadvised arrivals.

The thaw restrictions in traffic hit very hard the
clearance at railheads. For seven days during the
thaw, such was the parlous softness of the roads, it
was out of the question to permit general traffic in
lorries. All the clearance must be done by horse
transport, which, by comparison with M.T., is damnably
slow. It delayed the clearance of trains by half-days.
Divisions which had to trek by G.S. waggon to other
railheads to complete were hard put to it to get their
men in the line fed.

Units which had no horse transport available had been instructed beforehand to draw thaw and reserve rations to tide them over the period. They stuck to their quarters, and ate tinned beef and biscuit.

But special dispensations had to be granted for traffic by lorries. When a coal-train arrived at railhead it was unthinkable to clear it by H.T. General Service waggons would take a week to clear four hundred tons of coal. Dispensations had to be granted for other urgent reasons. The cumulative effect was that of lorry traffic to a dangerous extent—dangerous because the frost bites so deep that when the thaw is at its height ruts are two feet deep. It bites down at the soft foundation beneath the cobble-stones of the village streets; and on the country roads the subsoil has no such protection as cobbles from the oppression of loaded lorries. But it was curious to see, in the villages, the cobbles rising *en masse* like jelly either flank of the lorry, or rising like a wave in the wake of the lumbering thing. Lorries got ditched in the country roads beyond immediate deliverance by other lorries. Nothing less than a steam tractor could move them. A convoy of tractors was set aside in each road-area for no other purpose than to obey calls to the rescue of ditched lorries. Certain roads were so badly cut that they had to be closed to traffic of any kind: motor-cycle with side-car that ventured on was bogged. The personnel of the road-control was increased twenty-fold to check speeds and to indicate prohibited roads. The worst tracts of the roads in use were so bad as to be paved with double rows of railway sleepers until the frost had worked out. Some roads will never recover; they will have to be closed until remade.

This advanced railhead was so near the line as to be full of interest on the eve of the April push. It was here you could see the immediate preparations and the immediate results of the preparatory activity. The local casualty clearing stations gave good evidence; you could tell, by watching their convoys, and talking with the wounded, and observing in the operating-theatre, what was going on. Such significant events as the growth of fresh C.C.S.'s and the kind of reserves they were putting-in, were eloquent. Talk with the legion of Flying-Corps observers who were about railhead was enlightening; so was the nature of the reserves they were laying up. The bulk and description of the supply-reserves dumped at railhead for pushing up by lorry-convoy to Arras told their tale also. Every night a convoy of lorries would load and move up under cover of the darkness. There was no mistaking the meaning of such commodities in their freight as chewing-gum and solidified alcohol. Do not suppose, reader, that chewing-gum is for mere distraction in the trenches. Neither is solidified alcohol for consumption by the addicted, but for fuel for Tommies' cookers when coal and wood are impossible of transport. Commodities such as these make one visualise a sudden and overwhelming advance. —— tons of baled straw were dumped at railhead. This was not for forage, but to strew the floors of empty returning supply-trains for wounded. Each C.C.S. in the area had to be prepared to improvise one such ambulance-train per day when the push was at its height. The handling of these things makes one abnormally busy; if he gets four-hours' sleep in twenty-four he is doing famously. But one is never so jaded as not to be interested in these portentous signs.

Once I went up to Arras on a night lorry. The convoy crept up into the lip of the salient. The guns flashed close on either flank; the star-shells lit the road from either side. The reserve dump was in an old factory in the Rue ——. An enormous dump it was. The Supply Officer lived next it on a ground-floor. His men burrowed in an adjacent cellar. He had laid on the floor of the attic above him eight layers of oats. A direct hit would have asphyxiated him with oats. His dump was unhappily placed. There were two batteries adjacent. Whenever there was a raid and the batteries let fly, they were immediately searched for. In the search his dump was found, on more than one occasion. There were ugly and recent shell-holes about it. The off-loading convoy was hit many nights at one point or another. He took me to the bottom of the road after dark. The scream of shell was so incessant that it rose to a melancholy intermittent moan.

Next day he took me about the town. Civilians were moving furtively. They were not used to emerge before night. In any case such shops and *estaminets* as remained were prohibited from opening before 7.30 in the evening. Wonderful!—how the civilians hang on. They have their property; also, they have the money they can always make from the herds of troops who make a fleeting sojourn in the place. Apart from the proprietors of cafés and *estaminets*, they are mostly caretakers who stay on: caretakers and rich old men with much property who prefer the chance of being hit to leaving what their industry has amassed over thirty years of labour. . . .

15

The German fatigue on the railway was useful, if slow. It was supplied from the prisoners of war camp near the station. When the thaw was in progress we lost them, so heavy were the demands upon the camp for road labour. The O.C. the camp sometimes visited to see what manner of work they did. He threw light on their domestic behaviour in camp: " The greediest ——s on earth !" he would say. " If one of them leaves table for two minutes, his friends have pinched and swallowed his grub. They steal each other's food daily—and they're fed well enough. They're a sanctimonious crew, too; most of their post-cards from home are scriptural, laden with texts and pictorial demonstration of the way the Lord is with them. The camp is half-filled with religious fanatics; they sing psalms and hymns and spiritual songs when they're free. But there's not much of the New Testament notion of the brotherhood of man amongst 'em; they do each other down most damnably ! . . .

When the Arras advance was imminent their camp was moved farther back from the line, and we lost them. The Deputy-Assistant-Director of Labour sent a fatigue of 125 of the halt and the maimed—the P.B.'s; altogether inadequate.

A Permanent-base man may be incapable of lumping. And even if he is not incapable, he is usually in a position to say he is—none daring to make him afraid. P.B. fatigues are highly undesirable.

" Pinching " supplies was by no means unheard of amongst them. (Amongst whom at all is it unheard-of ? Australians themselves are the arch-appro-priators of Army supplies.) But P.B. men do not pinch with that faculty of vulpine cunning which is clear of detection. One morning, after an all-night clearance, the A.P.M. found one of the P.B.'s sneaking back to billet in the cold grey dawn with three tins of pork and beans, two loaves of bread, six candles, imperfectly concealed. He promptly put him in the clink. There was a court-martial. The unhappy fellow got three months. Pinching in the Army should be done judiciously. It is not a moral crime. Getting caught is. At any rate, that is an intellectual, if not a moral crime.

I messed with a C.C.S. Most messes of medical officers are interesting and varied. The Colonel was a Regular—an accessible and companionable Regular. An Irishman he was, kind of heart and quick of temper; and so able that it was never dangerous for him to allow his Captains to argue with him on questions of administration, because he could always rout them: he was always right. A less able man would have taken risks in permitting argument on the subject of his administration.

He was the fiercest smoker and the ablest bridge-player I have ever known. He used to complain bitterly of the standard of bridge played by the mess in general. He put out his pipe chiefly to eat—to eat rather than to sleep. He was a hearty, but not a voluptuous, eater. His appetite was the consequence of genuine cerebration and of hard walking. He walked, unless hindered by the most inevitable obstacles, five miles a day—hard, with his two dogs and the Major. He was very deaf, and very fond of his dogs. They slept in his room, usually (one or other) on his bed. He slept little. He read and smoked in bed regularly until about two; was wakened at six;

took a pipe (or two) with his tea before getting up;
and sometimes—though rarely—resumed his reading
in bed until eight, or spent a happy hour in earnest
conversation with the dogs before rising.

His officers liked him; the Sisters loved him. To
them he was indulgent. The day before the push
began a Sister approached him in his office. She said
that although it was her afternoon off, the Matron
had advised her against tramping, lest a convoy of
wounded should come in suddenly. He said: " My
dear, you go."—" And how long may I be away ?"—
" Well, you don't go on duty until eight in the morning;
as long as you're back by then, it's good enough.
But mind—don't come reeling in at 8.30 with your hair
down your back ! That's all I ask." She left,
adoring.

The Major was a mid-Victorian gentleman, with the
gentlest manners and language, except when it came
to talk of Germans. He got an acute attack of
Wanderlust soon after I came—felt the call of Arras—
and got command of a field ambulance up in the thick
of it. The last I heard of him was that he was hurrying about the city under a steel helmet, succouring
with his own hand those stricken down in the streets.

A French interpreter was attached to the hospital.
He was a man of forty-five, with the heart of a boy of
fifteen. He would sit at the gramaphone by the hour,
playing his favourite music and staring into vacancy.
His favourites were: a minuet of Haydn, Beethoven's
Minuet in G, selections from the 1812 Overture, the
Overture to *Mignon*, and the Dance of the Sugar-
Plum Fairy. Everyone " pulled his leg "; everyone
liked him—he was so gentle of heart, but so baffling

in repartee. They called him the *Pawkie Duke*, a name that came to him through his comments when the facetious song of that title in the " St. Andrew's Song-Book " was being sung. He lived in a hut in hospital. Part of his duty consisted in mediation between the civilian sick and the English M.O.'s; for by international agreement they were due to treat any civilian sick who needed it. I first met Pawkie waiting in the anteroom of the operating-theatre with a distracted mother whose child was within under operation for appendicitis. She was a lovely girl of ten. The mother was weeping anxiously. Pawkie was almost in sympathetic tears himself. He made excursions of high frequency into the theatre to report progress to the mother. I went in. He came after, fumbling nervously with his hands and regarding the surgeons with a gaze of appeal. He would whisper to the Colonel, who reassured him. He tore out, colliding with the orderlies who were bearing in another " case." Seizing madame by the hands, he cried: " *Bien, madame ! Elle va bien ! La pauvre petite fille fait de bon progrès. Les chirurgiens-major sont très adroits. Le Capitaine est le chirurgien-spécialiste. Le Colonel assiste aussi. Ça ne fait rien, madame !*" And he left madame with the conviction that nothing could go wrong.

But it was pathetic to see that beautiful child, her fair face smothered under the mask. At the end, when the wound was stitched, the surgeon took her up as gently as though she were his own offspring and carried her to her mother, and so on to the ward. There she stayed two weeks, tended by him with the affection of an elder brother.

On the eve of the push, during the preparatory and

retaliatory bombardment, the theatre was a ghastly
chamber. An abbatoir it was, five hours after the
arrival of the convoys, when the preparation of the
cases for operation had been completed. Five "tables"
were in continuous use. On "taking-in" night the
surgeons invariably worked through to daylight.
This is very exhausting, so exhausting that they never
worked continuously. At about two o'clock they
adjourned to the mess for a rest and a meal—a solid
meal of bacon and eggs and coffee. For the push
there came reinforcements—*teams*, as they were called.
They amounted to eight fresh surgeons, ten Sisters,
and fifty additional orderlies.

The Colonel called his M.O.'s together in the ante-
room the Sabbath before the attack, and gave them
plain words of warning and advice. In a push they
were not to be too elaborate; it would lead to injustice.
Better twelve "abdominals" done roughly but safely
than four exquisitely finished operations. In the
former case all twelve would be rendered safe as far as
the base; in the latter, the remaining eight would
probably die on their hands. . . . The examining
officers in the reception-room must come to a complete
agreement with the surgeons as to what manner of
"case" it was imperative to operate upon before
evacuation to the base. There must be waste of
neither surgical time nor surgical energy in operating
upon "cases" that would carry to the base without
it—and so on. . . .

Anything one might say of Nursing-Sisters in France
must seem inadequate. The wounded Tommy who
has fallen into their hands is making their qualities
known. They work harder than any M.O., and

M.O.'s are hard-worked. Indeed, I defy a man to bear indefinitely the kind of work they do indefinitely —its nervous strain and its long hours. The M.O.'s do their examinations and their dressings and pass on; they are the merest visitors. The Sisters stay on and fight for the man without cessation, and then see him die. Five and six deaths in the ward in a night is horribly hard on the Sister in charge of it. No one but a Sister could do the work she does, in a ward or in the operating-theatre. It is nonsense to speak of abolishing women from the medical service; it would be inadequate without them. But their work will leave its mark upon them for ever. They have not a man's faculty of detachment.

Because they are so absorbed by their work—as well as for other feminine reasons—they see the ethics of the struggle less clearly than a man.

Sisters on service are more prone to depression out of working hours than are men; which is not amazing. They are more the subjects of their moods, which is but temperamental too. But in the reaction of elation after depression they are more gay than any man—even in his most festive mood after evening mess. They smoke a good deal (and they deserve it), but not as heavily as their civilian sisters in general, though in isolated cases they smoke more heavily than any civilian woman. But no one blames the fair fiends, however false this form of consolation may be.

ARRAS AFTER THE PUSH

THE traffic on the cobbled road to Arras raises a dust
—although it is cobbled. The spring green of the
elms that line it is overcast with the pallor of a man
under the anæsthetic. The fresh breeze raises a dust
that sometimes stops a motor cyclist; sometimes it is
the multiplicity of traffic that stops him. His face
and hair are as dust-pallid as the trees.

The push is over. The traffic in and out is as
heavy as it could be. There is no intermission in it.
It files past the road control in a procession in which
there are no intervals.

The ingoing traffic is not all military. Incongruously among the lorries lumber civilian carts stuffed
with all the chattels of returning refugees. One knows
not whether it is more pathetic to see these forlorn
French families returning to the desolation of their
homes or flying from it. They will lumber down the
flagged streets lined with houses, rent and torn and
overthrown, that were once the homes of their friends
and the shops of their dealers. Here at one time
they promenaded in the quiet Sabbath afternoon
sunshine. Now the pavement is torn with shell-
holes and the street is ditched with them and defaced
with half-wrecked barriers. The Grand Place, where
once they congregated for chat in the summer twilight,

or sunned themselves in the winter, is choked with supplies and sweating troops. The troops are billeted in the half-wrecked houses of every street. The refugees will drive through to the place of their old homes and see the spring greening the trenches which zigzag through their old gardens, and clothing the splintered trees in their old orchards. This is worse than fleeing from the wrath of shell to come. But they love their town so intensely that they rattle through the city gate with an aspect of melancholy satisfaction.

The push has left its mark all over Arras. There was desolation before it. But such was its punishment when it was the centre from which we pushed, that destruction has spread into every street. Intensity is the quality of the destruction. And it is still going on. Shell are still screaming in.

The splendid cathedral is, an amorphous heap of stone; there are infrequent pillars and girders that have escaped, and stand gaunt among the ruins. The Hôtel de Ville retains but a few arches of its beautiful carved front. Splendid *maisons* are in ruins. In the streets there are the stone barricades and entaglements of barbed wire. The *gare*, as busy as the Amiens *gare* before the war, and as fine, is rent and crumbling. The network of lines under its glass roof is grassgrown. The fine *Place* before it, where you can envisage the peace traffic in taxi's and pedestrians, is torn by shell, or by fatigues which have uprooted the stone for street barricades.

Most people who see for the first time the desolation of such buildings as the cathedral cry out angrily upon German vandalism, with the implication that it is because they were fine and stately that the cathedral and the Hôtel de Ville were battered. This is not only unjust, but nonsensical. The German has other things to think of than the deliberate destruction of beautiful buildings because they are beautiful. What he has to consider is their height and their potential usefulness as observation-posts. And this is what he does consider, as we would and do consider such features too. Had we been bombarding Arras, it is the tall and beautiful cathedral that we would have shattered first. You may as logically rail against the Germans for smashing down these potential observation-posts as object to the prosecution of the War on Sunday. . . .

The old warning notices persist, and have been put up more plain and frequent: *Assembly-Point*, indicating the cellars of refuge; warnings against touching un-exploded shell; and so forth.

The Town Major, the Railhead Ordnance Officer, the Railway Transport Officer, the Railhead Supply Officer, the Railhead Salvage Officer—all are intensely busy, and all well sandbagged. The Salvage officer is beset by his friends for souvenirs. The R.O.O. is beset by the quartermasters of battered battalions for fresh equipment. The R.S.O. is hunted by the hungry. The R.T.O. is at his wits' end to entrain and detrain men and guns—especially men. The town teems with troops.

The returning refugees trouble none of these officials. They go to the French Mission for directions as to resettling.

As soon as you emerge on the eastern side of Arras you see the line from the rising ground. The captive balloons mark it well; they are so frequent—huge hovering inflations with the tiny observer's basket dangling, and the streaming pennon halfway down the cable to avert collision with the patrolling aircraft. For they must be patrolled well. The Hun has lately the trick of pouncing on them from aloft, shooting the tracer bullet as he dives. The tracer will put the thing in flames in the twinkling of an eye. The observer does not wait if he sees a Hun coming for him. He leaps for it. His parachute harness is always about his shoulders, and his parachute tucked beneath the balloon. But even with the Hun making for him, this leap into space is a fearsome thing. He falls sheer for some seconds before the parachute is wrenched from its place. Then there is that second of horrible uncertainty as to whether she will open. And if there is a hitch, his dive to earth becomes a flash and his breathless body thuds into pulp below. So ended the man who " made " the song " Gilbert the Filbert." So end others, failed by their parachute. . . . Sometimes combustion is so rapid that the parachute is burnt with the balloon; then he leaps from the death by fire to death of another sort. Nor does a well-released parachute always let you down lightly. If the wind is strong and contrary, you may drift five miles and land 'midst Huns. If the wind is strong and favourable, your pendulic swing beneath the parachute may land you roughly with wounds and bruises. You may be smashed against chimneys, torn by trees, dragged through canals, and haled bleeding up the bank. But if the Lord is with you, you will swing slowly down in the still air and be landed tenderly in a field of clover.

Sometimes balloons get set afire by lightning. If then the parachute is saved, the observer is fortunate indeed. Lightning gives rather less warning to leap than does the flying Hun.

All the country from Arras to the line bears the scars of recent fighting. A great deal of it bears the marks of German occupation; you see this in German *Verboten* signs and in German canteen notices.

The dwellings of the eastern suburbs lie in ruined heaps of brick; there may be the ground-plan indicated by the low, rugged remnant of wall. A jagged house-end may still lean there forlornly, with the branches of the springing trees thrusting through its cracks and the spring vines trailing through its shell-rents. With the spring upon it, the whole landscape is more pathetic than in the bareness of winter. This ruination sorted better with leafless boughs and frozen ground. The sweet lush grass smiling in the interstices of ruin is hard to look on. The slender poplar aspiring with tapering grace above the red and grey wreckage is the more beautiful thereby, but the wreckage is more hideously pathetic. It would break your heart to see the pear-tree blossoming blithely in the rubble-strewn area that was once its orchard. The refugee who returns will know (or perhaps he will not) that in place of this *débris* of crunched brick, splintered beam, twisted iron, convulsed barbed wire, strewn about the trenches and shell-holes of his property, was once the ordered quietness of orchard and garden—his ranks of pear and apple, trim paths, shrubberies, the gay splashes of flower-colour and carpeted softness of lawn. This will wring his heart more than the loss of furniture. Though much of his furniture was heir-

loom, this little orchard and garden were the fruit of
his own twenty years of loving nurture. This little
area he idealised as his farmed estate, his stately
parc. Here on Sabbath evenings he walked down the
shrubbed paths with his wife and children, after returning from the weekly promenade of the streets of Arras.
His children romped on the lawn since they could
crawl. Now not only is it gone, but its associations
too—torn by shell, defiled by trenches, desecrated
by the cruel contortions of rusting wire. The zig-
zagged clay parapet winds about his well-beloved
plots; the ruins of a machine-gun emplacement lie
about the remnant of his summer-house; beef-tins,
jam-tins, and undischarged hand-grenades, are strewn
beneath his splintered shade-trees. The old sweet
orchard air is defiled by the sickening, indefinable
stink of a deserted trench; the broken sandbags lie
greening about the turf.

This is all ruin of a sort more or less inevitable.
Follow the road winding down the valley beyond the
suburb, and you will see the foul, deliberate ruin of
whole avenues of trees that once lined the route.
You know how these stately elm and beech met overhead for leagues along the pleasant roads of France;
there they lie now naked in the turf by the roadside,
untimely cut down by the steam-saw of the Hun.
He traversed the whole length of this road with that
admirable German thoroughness of his and felled them
all across it to bar our progress. The shattering
of Arras Cathedral was necessary; this is mere ex-
pediency, and near to wantonness. Forty years of
stately growth lie there gaunt and sapless. Soon you
will see the tender tufts of green spring from the smooth-

cut stump. They have been beautifully cut: German machinery is unimpeachably efficient. McAndrew's song of steam is the noble celebration of the triumph of human mechanical genius; these bleeding stumps are the monument that will testify for half a century to the blasphemous misapplication of German mechanical skill. The steam-saw must have worked beautifully. You can conceive the German N.C.O. in charge of it standing by emitting approval as the stately beech crashed across the road from the fine, smooth cut—" *Schön!* . . . *Schön!*" . . .

This will hurt the French more than other peoples think; they are so proud of their forestry; they plant with such considerate foresight into the pleasure that posterity will have in their trees—with such prevision as to the arrangement of plantations and as to the *tout ensemble* of the avenue and the *forêt* when the trees shall be mature. A tree is nothing until you have personified it: the French personify the trees of their private plantations; they are like members of the *famille*. And such is the State care of forestry that you almost believe it has personified the State plantations in a collective sort of way, regarding them almost as a branch of society or of the nation. The national care of trees is with them a thing analogous to the administration of orphanages. The German will have reckonings to make after the War for maimed and murdered trees and for annihilated orchards, as well as for fallen and deformed Frenchmen. . . .

After the trenches of Anzac, you are overwhelmed in France with the pathos of the contiguity of trench with dwelling. It is less unnatural that the un-peopled wilderness of Anzac should be torn by shell and scarred by trench-line. In France there is a piteous incongruity in the intimacy of warfare with domesticity. The village that has been the stronghold is shattered beyond all reviving; and inevitably the villages of the fighting area have been used as a fleeting shelter from the fierceness of the tempest of shell. *L'Église* is a roofless ruin. *L'Hôtel de Ville* and *la Marie* are amorphous masses of jagged and crumpled wall. The trenches traverse the street and the garden and the *cour de maison*. The tiny rivulet on the outskirts of the village has been hailed as a sort of ready-made trench and hastily squared and fire-stepped. The farm is pocked with shell-holes; the farmhouse is notoriously open to the heavens and gaping about the estate through its rent walls. On Anzac only the chalk ridges were scored and the stunted, uncertain growth uprooted; there were not even trees to maim. Here the cellars are natural dug-outs in the trench-wall; the *maison* is the billet for the reserve battalion; the communication trench ploughs rudely through the quiet cobbled street. The desecrating contrast cries from the ground at every turn. The village that used to sleep in the sun with its pleasant crops about it now sleeps in ashes and ruination for ever. The battle-lines of Turkey will be effaced and overgrown by the seasons, but that which was a village in France will never more know the voices of little children again in its streets, because it has no streets, and because new villages will be built rather than this hideousness overturned and effaced and built-upon afresh.

If you walk east an hour from Arras you'll get near enough to Tilloy to see the shelling of our line. Again

Anzac is superseded. Anzac never saw shell of this size (except from the monitors that bombarded from the sea); nor did Anzac know bombardment of this intensity, except in isolated spurts. Here the normal bombardment is intense. This is mere routine; but it's as fierce as preceded any attack on Gallipoli. What chance has the individual when modern artillery is at work ? Yet the chance of death cannot be greater than say, one in four; otherwise there would be no men left. The rank of balloons is spotting; the 'planes are patrolling them; other 'planes are circling over our batteries—spotting; others are going in squadron over the line—" on some stunt," as Tommy puts it. Our own guns are speaking all about, so loud that the noise of crowding transport is altogether drowned: by them, and by the crack of the German bursts and by the shell-scream. The transport on this road is not mechanical; we are too near the line for that.

A German 'plane is being " archied " to the north, and there is a barrage of " archies " being put up behind it to give our 'planes time to rise to attack it. Two of them are climbing up to it now over our heads. They climb very steep. They are very fast 'planes. They are on the level of the Hun very quickly: they are above it. The barrage has ceased, because the Hun is trying to risk running through rather than waiting to fight two Nieuports. But one has intercepted him and is coming for him in the direction of the line. The other is diving on him from above. There is the spasmodic rattle of Lewis guns. The Hun is firing thick on the man rushing him. He has done it, too; for suddenly our man swerves and banks in a way that is plainly involuntary, and then begins to fall, banking irregularly. Suddenly the flames begin to spurt from her body. As suddenly she seems to regain control and dives steep for earth, flames streaming from the wings and in a comet-tail behind. She tears down at a horrible angle. Then you know in a moment that this is not steering, but a nose-dive to death, and that it is controlled by no pilot. We can hear the roar of flame. She is nearer to us, making for us. She crashes horribly a hundred yards away and roars and crackles. The delicate wings and body are gone long before we reach her; there is only a quiet smouldering amongst the cracked and twisted frame, and the sickening smell of burnt flesh and of oil-fumes.

The Hun has escaped—at least, we fear he will escape. He and our other man are small specks in the blue above the German line. They cannot "archie" them together. Our man turns, and grows. Then he gets it—the deadly white puffs on every hand of him. But he comes through, and proceeds to patrol.

SECTION C.—FRENCH PROVINCIAL LIFE

CHAPTER I

A MORNING IN PICARDY

THE beginning of spring in Northern France is elating above the month of May in the Rhône Valley—not because spring in Southern France is not more beautiful, but because it is less welcome. It is by comparison that the loveliness of the Picardy spring takes hold upon you: by comparison with the bitterness of the Picardy winter. You may walk about Marseilles or Lyon in January without a great-coat; in Arras this would be the death of you. The frozen mud, the sleet, the snow, the freezing wind, the lowering sky, and the gaunt woods of Pas de Calais, are ever with you, from September to April. But by the beginning of May the leaves are sprouting and the greening of the earth is begun. There is rain—much of it. But there are sunny days without the bitterness of wind. There is singing of birds in the early morning. The children no longer creep along the frozen street to school; they race, and fill the street with their laughter. The 'planes whose hum fills the air look less forbidding than they seemed a month ago. In February, in the darkening heaven, they showed a relentless aspect; they seem to fly now as though at sport. The old *citadelle* has lost its grimness; the ramparts are green-

242

ing; the shade of blackness taken on by its grey slate-roofs when the trees were leafless is gone now; the moat that was a pool of mud is flowering.

The Authie flows below it, full-tided. The margin now is not snow. It has been snow for long, and half the stream was murky snow-slush. Now it is clear. The ducks from the château that looks up at the Citadelle are sporting in it again.

Saint-Pol Road, Amiens Road, Arras Road, are beginning to stand grey again. In the winter there was nothing but their bare trees to mark them; they were the colour of the fields. Now both trees and fields foil them, setting out over the slopes.

It is a joy to walk down the Authie on a spring morning. The Citadelle towers above you on the left. You are conscious of its graceful immensity long after you have passed it. The little French cottages straggle down-stream from the Citadelle base. They are white and grey, red and white— French in construction from their tiny dormer windows to the neat little gardens with their bricked-up margins flushed by the stream. Long tree-lined boulevardes start away from the road which skirts the river; you can see for many kilometres along their length. The wine-barrels are piled beneath the plane-trees. The children play about them. You will come upon a château standing stately in its low ground fronting the river. And beyond the château, which marks the border of the town, you are in the richness of the river fields and the river slopes. Here are the elm-groves, and the clumps of soaring poplar, and the long lines of stubby willow clipped yearly by the hand of industry; they sprout long and delicate from the head.

Groseille and hop tangle about the bank. Far off on the ridges the white road traverses under its elms, picking a way among the hedged terraces. You see no denizens here other than the old men and the girls who are at work in the fields. From them you will have a cheery " *Bonjour* " and some shrewd remarks on the weather: " *Ah, oui!—toujours le travail, m'sieur—toujours! Mais ça ne fait rien : nous sommes contents—oui.*" And so they are.

Then you come to Gezaincourt. That fine old château in its *parc*. The *parc* is of many acres, and there are deer in the woods of it, and a lake where the wild-fowl are.

To return we left the river and struck up into the ridge. We came to Bretel, midway between Gezaincourt and the Citadelle. We entered a private *maison* standing back in its garden; it was, none the less, marked *café*. Madame received us unprofessionally, inviting into the kitchen to drink. There she was preparing the dinner. *Je ne sais pas pourquoi*—but the French are deliciously friendly with the Australians. They take us into their homes with a readiness that is elating. They will not do it with the English. But, after all, they are frank, and we approach them frankly. We are given to domesticity, and they are intensely domestic. Indeed, the Australian temperament is far nearer to the French than is the English. The Australian tendency to the spirit of democracy finds sympathy in the provinces of this splendid Republic. The national spirit of democracy has its counterpart (may even have its roots) in the local trend towards communism which, in France, makes you welcome to enter the *maison*, chatting easily about its domestic affairs, and, in Australia, makes you welcome in the house of the country stranger, where you drink and eat without embarrassment at the hospitable table for the first and last time. The Australian is guiltless of the habitual industry of the French—of their intense interest in the detail of their lives and work; but he has their unconventionality and their lightness of heart and their hospitality. He understands their communistic way of life in the provinces. And when a French girl on a country road looks him directly in the eye for the first time, and with the smile of friendly frankness gives him a " *Bonjour, m'sieur,*" he is no more embarrassed than she. He meets and returns the greeting with an understanding of which an Englishman knows nothing. The French and the Australians are allies by nature. There is nothing amazing in their immediate understanding of each other. How, on the other hand, the English and the French continue to do anything in conjunction is a source of continual wonder. Between their temperaments there is a great gulf fixed.

So Madame takes us direct to the kitchen, where she is basting. She makes exhaustive inquiries into the Australian methods of cooking. We explain that the foods are largely the same—but in the mode, *quelle différence!* She thinks the Australian practice of the hearty breakfast an extraordinary beginning to the day. The drinking of tea she cannot away with: wine and *cidre* are the only fluids to be taken with food—or without it. She prefers beef to horse; it is in Normandy they eat so much horse. We express approval of the French universal usage of butter in cooking: they fry their eggs in butter, roast their meat with it, fry potatoes in it. She asks what is our substitute for it. Lard and dripping. " O, la la ! Quel goût !" And so it is; Australians know little of the blessings of butter in cookery. She asks if we are fond of salads. " Up to a point, yes; but not as you are." " En France, toujours la salade, m'sieur ! Regardez le jardin." She takes us to the window and indicates the vegetable-garden with a proud fore-finger: " Voulez-vous vous promener ?"—" Oui, madame, avec plaisir."

" Madeleine !" She calls her daughter. Madeleine is a comely girl who has been at work in the next room. She shakes hands as though she had known us as boys, and fills up the glasses again before we go out, and takes one herself with the grace of a lady. For high-bred ease and graciousness of manner, in fact, you are to go to the demoiselles of the provinces. " A votre santé, m'sieur." She raises her glass and smiles—as well as enunciates—the toast. " A votre santé, madé-moiselle !" " A la paix, madame !" " Bonne santé !" —" Oui, à la paix, messieurs !—nécessaire, la paix !" . . .

Madeleine leads the way into the garden. It is clear at once to what degree the French are addicted to salads: canals of water-cress, fields of lettuce and radish and celery. Most of the plants in that garden are potentially plants for a salad. But there are some fine beds of asparagus, and of these le père is proud. He is obviously pleased to meet anyone who is interested by his handiwork. It's politic even to feign an exaggerated interest in every plot; you are rewarded by the old man's enthusiastic pride: " Ah, messieurs, le printemps s'est éveillé ! Bon pour le jardin !" We finish by the rivers of water where the cress grows. "*Regardez la source*," says Madeleine. She points to it oozing from the hill-side. They have diverted it and irrigated a dozen canals each thirty yards long and two wide. There is more cress there than the whole village could make into salads, you say. But three housewives come with their bags, buying, and each takes such a generous load of the *cresson* that you know the old man has not misjudged his cultivation.

"*Voulez-vous une botte de cresson, messieurs?*"— "*Oui, s'il vous plaît, m'sieur : merci bien!*" The old fellow places his little bridge across the canal, cuts a bundle, and binds it from the sheaf of dried grass at his waist. "*Voilà, messieurs!*"

The purchasers stop far longer than is necessary to talk about the War and the price of sugar and the scarcity of *charbon*. Conversation is the provincial hobby, as it is the national hobby. Yet I have never seen the French mutually bored by conversation— never. Nor are there, in French conversation, those stodgy gaps which are to be expected in the conversation of the English, and, still more, of the Australians. French conversation flows on; *ebbs and flows* expresses better not only the knack of apt rejoinder which gives it perfect naturalness, but also the rhythmic rise and fall of it which makes it pleasant to hear, even when you don't understand a word. That, and its perfect harmony of gesture, make it a living thing, with all the interest of a thing that lives.

We (unnecessarily, again) wander about the garden with Madeleine. She gives the history of each plot. What interests us is to her a matter of course: the extraordinary neatness of the garden, the uniformity of plot, the assiduous exclusion of weeds, the careful demarcation of paths, the neatness of the all-surrounding hedge. The French genius for detail and for industry shows itself nowhere so clearly as in a garden. They are gardeners born.

On returning to the house, madame insists that we stay to dinner. We accept without hesitation. *Le père* comes in and brings the dogs. Soon we know their history from puppyhood. *Finu* is morose and jealous; she has a litter of pups that make her unfriendly. *Koko* is a happy chap—always a friend to soldiers, as the old man puts it. He is a *souvenir* left by a Captain of artillery. All this is, in itself, rather uninteresting, but in the way in which it is put it is absorbing. That, in fact, is the secret of the charm of most French conversation. In the mouth of an Englishman—such is its trifling detail—it would be deadly-boring. The French aptness and vividness of description dresses into beauty the most uninteresting detail.

It soon appears that the whole family are refugees from Arras; have lived here two years. I told them I had recently visited Arras. This flooded me with questions. I wish I had known the detailed geography of Arras better. The narrative of a recent Arras bombardment moved them to tears. They love their town: they love more than their home. This is the spirit of the Republic. The Frenchman's affection for his town is as strong as the Scotchman's for his native heath.

They had brought from Arras all their worldly goods. They took us to the sitting-room and to the bedroom. Much of the furniture was heirlooms.

Each piece had its age and history. The carved
oak wardrobe was extremely fine; it had belonged to
madame's great-grandmother. Chairs, table-covers,
pictures—all were treasured. Here was more evidence
to expose the fallacy that French family life is decay-
ing. Gentle reader, never believe it. Family history
is as sacred in the provinces as natural affection is
strong: which is to say much.

But the typical French family heirloom is antique
plate. This takes the form of china and porcelain em-
bellished with biological and botanical design. Some of
it is very crude and ugly, but dear to the possessor.
Every French *salle à manger* has a wall-full; they are
in the place of pictures.

The dinner was elaborate and delicious. No French
famille is so poor that it does not dine well: soup, fish
with *salade*, veal with *pommes de terre frites,* fried
macaroni with onions, prunes with custard, coffee and
cigars. This—except for the cigars, perhaps—was
presumably a normal meal. And between each course
Madeleine descended the *cave* and brought forth a
fresh bottle of *cidre*. And Madeleine's glass was filled
by her parent, with a charming absence of discrimination, as often as ours—or as her mother's. The colour
mounted in her cheeks; but she did not talk drivel.
To generous draughts of wine and *cidre* had she been
accustomed from her youth up. And the youngest
French child will always get as much as Madeleine to
drink at table. So the French are not drunkards.

After lunch came two visitors to talk. They were
sisters, friends of Madeleine. For two years and a
half they had been prisoners in a French town held
by the Germans, near Albert, and had been liberated

only a month before by the German evacuation. They told pitiful tales of German ill-usage, though not of a physiological nature. But constantly the Boches demanded food and never paid, so that they themselves went hungry daily. Also, they worked for Germans under compulsion, and never were paid; and worked very hard. The German soldiers they described as not unkind, though discourteous, but the officers were invariably brutal. *Maintenant vous êtes chez nous* was the German officers' formula, with its implied threat of violation; which was never executed, however.

We rose to go, and made to pay. This was smiled at indulgently. "*Au revoir, messieurs! Bonne chance!*" cried *le père*. "*Quand vous voudrez*," said Madame. "*Quand vous voudrez*," echoed Madeleine. So we went —like Christian—on our way rejoicing.

CHAPTER II

THÉRÈSE

I was sitting on a log at the crest of the splendidly high La Bouille ridge gloating over the Seine Valley. Here, from the grounds of *La Maison Brûlée* (now raucous with revellers in the late afternoon) you have a generous sweep of the basin and of its flanking forest slopes. A Frenchman and his wife sauntered past with their daughter and took a seat beyond. The daughter was beautiful, with an air of breeding that sorted well with the distinguished bearing of the old man and the well-sustained good looks of her mother. They sat for half an hour, and as they repassed on the return mademoiselle said: " How do you like the view ?" in excellent English. This was justification enough for inviting them to share my log. We talked a long time, mademoiselle and I; the old people hadn't a word of English. She had had a two years' sojourn in Birmingham about the age of sixteen, and had acquired good English ineradicably. She had got caught into Joseph Chamberlain's circle; he used to call her Sunny Jim. The name sat well upon her: the facetious aptness of it was striking. She was of the " fire and dew " that make up the admirable French feminine lightness of spirit-vivacity, frankness, sunniness, whimsicality, good looks, and litheness of body.

The end of it all was that I was to come down to Sahurs (over the river) the next Sunday and see their home and get taught some French in an incidental fashion. There was no manner of doubt of every need of that.

And there was no manner of hesitancy in accepting such an invitation. She flashed a smile behind as they left, and I resumed the log, wishing to-morrow were Sunday, as distinct from Monday. This was a damnable interval of waiting. As I was repeating this indictment over and over, watching them disappear into the forest, she waved. I lapsed into a profane silence, and brooded on the flight of time, and reviewed in turn all the false allegations of its swiftness I could call to mind.

It was obviously wise to leave the margin of this darkling wood and get down to the boat. It would never do to miss it, and be driven to crossing to Sahurs to tell them so. No! that wouldn't do: better catch the thing and be done with it. So I did; and had a journey of easy contemplation up to Rouen.

Next Sunday I got a " bike ": it can be made to leave earlier than the boat. And the river-bank is more interesting than the middle-stream.

From Rouen to Sahurs the right bank of the Seine is bulwarked by a traversing limestone ridge, clothed with forest. But the river-side is escarped and precipitous, thrusting out its whiteness beneath the forest crest and, as a foil, casting up the châteaux and splendid *maisons* on the river level, with their embracing gardens and orchards.

This rich accumulation of colour—deep, forest, gleaming cliff-side, red roof, grey mellow wall, and blooming garden and orchard, and white river road—is unforgettable, and perhaps unexcelled. Nothing finer you'll see in the whole Rhône Valley; and that is a bold saying.

The especial charm of a cycle is that you can stop and look. You can gaze as long as you like (as long as is consistent with the fact that Sunny Jim is at the other end of the journey) at this quaint half-timbered, gable-crowded *maison* standing in its graceful poplar-grove; at the sweet provincial youngsters playing on the road. You can lay up your machine and enter the rambling Normandy café squatting on the river-bank, with its groups of blue-clad soldiers *en permission* making · the most of things with the bloused and pantalooned civilians and with their cider (*cidre* is the national drink of Normandy, as wine is of most other provinces) and you are greeted, in such a house, with the delicious open French friendliness which is so entrancing (by contrast) to most Englishmen. After their own national reticence, this is pleasant beyond description. Of some it is the undoing. The soldiers greet you, and you are adamantine if you don't sit at their table rather than alone. The girl who serves welcomes you like a brother. Quite sorry you are, at rising, you never came here before. . . . You push on with your wheel. On the slopes of the other bank they are getting in the harvest on the edge of the wood—some old men and many women and a handful of soldiers on leave who have forgotten the trenches.

There are soldiers with their families fishing on the bank beside you at intervals. You stop to talk to these. You can't resist sitting with them for a spell and kissing the little girls who nestle up. The basket that contains other things than bait and the catch is opened; you're a villain if you don't sip from that yellow bottle and take some bread and a handful of cherries. . . .

Halfway to Sahurs, opposite the timbered island, you pass the German prisoners' camp, patrolled, beneath the barbed wire topping the wall, by those quaint, informal French sentries. They're in red- and-blue cap, red-and-blue tunic, red-and-blue breeches. They lounge and chat and dawdle, with their rifles slung across their backs, and their prodigiously long bayonets poking into the upper air. They appear casual enough, but they detest the generic German sufficiently to leave you confident that, however casual they may seem, he will not escape.

Farther down, you'll meet a gang of Boches road-making—fine, brawny, light-haired, blue-eyed, cheerful beggars they are. Obviously they don't aspire above their present lot so long as wars endure.

Four kilometres above Sahurs is the Napoleonic column marking the spot where the ashes of Bonaparte were landed between their transfer from the boat which brought them up the river to that which bore them to Paris. As I approached this column from above, Sunny Jim, on her wheel, approached it from Sahurs. Her friend Yvonne was with her (wonderful, in this land, is the celerity with which the barriers surrounding Christian names are thrown down !), and the dog.

The ride on to Sahurs is on a road that deflects from the river. It is overarched with elms continuously. Thérèse (that's her name) calls it *la Cathédrale* :

and the roof of branches aloft is like the groined roof of a cathedral.

M. Duthois and madame come out to meet you. It's a welcome and a half they give—none of your English polite formulas and set courtesy. A warm, human, thoroughgoing sincerity sweeps you into the hall, and there you stand in a hubbub of greeting and interrogation (of which less than half is intelligible: but no matter!) for ten minutes, everyone too busy talking to move on, until Thérèse suggests we go round the garden and the orchard.

Everyone goes.

Thérèse gives us the French for every flower and shrub to be seen, and the old man makes valiant, clumsy attempts at English, and you make shamelessly clumsy attempts at French. One evidence of the thoroughgoing courtesy of the French is that they will never laugh at your attempts at their language. We smile at them: somehow their English is amusing. Possibly the reason they do not smile at us attempting French is that there is nothing at all amusing in our flounderings—more likely to irritate than amuse. The old man is accommodating in his choice of topics that will interest you and be intelligible—accommodating to the point of embarrassment. He talks quite fifteen minutes about the shape and coloration of your pipe, certain that this will interest the selfish brute. Madame doesn't say a word—carries on a sort of conversation with smiles and other pantomime.

Somehow, in the garden (I don't know how) Yvonne got named *Mme. la Comtesse* by M. Duthois. This for the time being embarrassed her into complete and blushing silence because we all took it up. All manner of difficulties were referred to the superior wisdom of *la Comtesse.* It was she who must decide as to the markings of the aeroplane humming up in the blue; the month when the red currants would be ripened; the relationship of the two crows croaking in the next field; the term of the War's duration.

But an authority on this last subject now emerged from the wicket-gate which opened from the neighbouring house. Madame —— had taken Thérèse to Alsace after her return from Birmingham, and had taught her to speak German there. Madame had lived in Alsace three years before, and spoke German very well indeed. She related in German her dream-message of the night before, that fixed the duration of the War unquestionably at three months more. This subconscious conviction was so conclusive for her that she would take bets all round. Thérèse staked all her ready cash. No doubt she will collect about Christmas-tide.

We all went on to tea spread in the orchard, and spread with an unerring French sense of fitness: such a meal, that is, as would be spread in the orchard but not in the house—French rolls and dairy butter, and *confiture de groseille* made from the red currants of the last season, fruit and cream, Normandy cake, cherries, wafers, and *cidre* sparkling like champagne, bearing no relationship whatever to the flat, insipid green-and-yellow fluid of the Rouennaise hotels.

There was no dulness at table. French conversation flows easily and unintermittently. There were tussles to decide whether Thérèse should or should not help herself first. The English custom of " ladies first " is looked on as rather stupid, with its implied inferiority of women: "But you will not beat me! *Mais oui!* but you are very obstinate!" And she would not be beaten; for she said she didn't like Normandy cake (though she adored it), and helped herself generously when it had been round, and proclaimed her victory over English convention with a little ripple of triumph. *Après vous* became a mirth-provoking password.

All the pets came round the table—the fowls (to whom I was introduced singly; they all have their names); *Mistigri* the cat, *Henri* the goose, the pigeons, the pug, the terrier. All these you are expected to make remarks to, on introduction, as to regular members of the family—which they are, in effect: "*Bon jour, Henri! Comment allez-vous? Parlez-vous anglais? Voulez-vous vous asseoir?*" When these introductions are over, M. Duthois brings forth his tiny bottle of 1875—the cognac he delights in.

Thérèse proposes a walk. Shall it be down by the river or through the village? "*Both,*" you say. So we go by the river and return by the hamlet.

Setting out, Thérèse pledges me to the French tongue alone, all the way. If I don't undertake to speak no English, I cannot go walking, but must sit with her in the summer-house behind the orchard and learn French with a grammar. I at once decline so to undertake. She varies the alternative: she will not reply if I speak in English. Well, no matter: that's no hardship. She forgets the embargo when she squelches a frog in the grass. English is resumed at once. She is led on to a dissertation in English upon frogs as a table-dish. This leads to talk of other French table abnormalities—horse as preferred to ox, the boast of French superiority in salads and coffee, the outlandish French practice of serving your *pommes de terre* after meat; and such carnal topics.

Pappa wanders ahead at an unreasonable pace with *Mme. la Comtesse.* Thérèse and I set about gathering daisies and poppies, with which the green is starred. The dogs come out from the neighbouring farmhouse; and Thérèse, who fears dogs horribly, has to be adequately protected.

We come up with pappa on the river-bank. We all set off dawdling single-file along the brush-hemmed river-path. . . . The Normandy twilight has settled down; but it will last till ten. La Bouille lies on the other shore under the cliffs that gleam through their foliage. The river gleams beneath them. There is a long track of light leading to the' ridge at the bend where the tottering battlements of the castle of Robert le Diable stand against the sky-line. A hospital ship, now faintly luminous, lies under the shadow of the la Bouille ridge. The village lights have begun to twinkle on the other shore. The soft cries of playing children creep over the water. The cry of the ferryman ready to leave is thrown back from the cliffs with startling clearness. The groves that fringe the cliff are cut out branch by branch against the ruddy sky.

We don't want to talk much after coming on the river: neither do we. . . .

It has darkened palpably when we turn to enter the village, an hour after. The hedged lanes are dark under the poplar-groves. The latticed windows of the cottages are brilliant patchwork of light. The glow-worms are in the road-side grass and in the hedges. We pluck them to put them in our hats. Thérèse weaves all manner of wistful fancies about them. We pass under the Henry VIII. *église* to the house, and enter quietly.

Thérèse sits at the piano without stupid invitation, and sings some of the lovely French folk-songs, and (by a special dispensation) some German, that are almost as haunting. The old man watches his daughter with a sort of fearful adoration, as though this creature, whose spirit gleams through the fair flesh of her, were too fine a thing for him to be father of.

Between the songs we talk. There is cake and wine— that and the common-sensed sallies of *Mme. la Comtesse* to restrain the romance and the sensuousness of the warm June Normandy night.

I left at midnight. We said an *au revoir* under the porch; and far down the road came floating after the dawdling wheel a faint "*Au 'voir . . . à Dimanche*" —full of a sweet and friendly re-invitation to all this. I registered an acceptance with gratitude for the blessings of Heaven, and wandered on along the white night road for Rouen. Why hasten through such a night? Rouen would have been pardoned for being *twice* ten miles distant. The silent river, the gleaming road, the faintly rustling trees, and the warm night filled with the scents of the Forêt de Roumare, forbade fatigue and all reckoning of hours. . . . And that was the blessed conclusion of most Sabbath evenings for three months.

CHAPTER III

LEAVES FROM A VILLAGE DIARY

Sunday, —*th.*—This morning a Taube came over our village, dropping bombs. They all fell in the neighbouring wood. Our aircraft defences made a fervent response, but ineffectual.

At 6.30 this evening I counted eighteen of our 'planes flying home. They have a facetious trick of shutting off their engines high and far from home and floating down on resistance. It's curious watching a 'plane suddenly dissociated from the raucous buzz of its engine.

To-night the whole eastern sky is illuminated as though by summer lightning in which there are no intervals—an unintermittent flap-flap. The din is tremendous and heart-shaking. This is war—" and no error." Anzac was hard. The country was rough and untenable—a hell, in our strip, of lice, stinks, flies, mal-nutrition and sudden death. Food was repulsive, and even so you did not get as much as you desired. You got clean in the Ægean at peril of your life. Here, on the other hand, is fighting-space gentle and smiling —a world of pastures, orchards, streams, groves, and white winding roads, with room to sanitate and restrain plagues. There is an over-generous ration of food that tempts you to surfeit; Expeditionary Force canteens, as well stocked as a London grocer's, as far up as the riskiest railhead; snug farmhouse billets, with un-infested straw; hot baths behind the lines; cinemas for resting battalions. But Anzac never knew the relentlessness of this offensive fighting. There we faced an enemy with whom fighting was a hobby, taken sportingly, if earnestly. Here we wrestle at sweaty and relentless grips with a foe to whom the spirit of sport is strange and repulsive, and who never had a sense of humour; who fights hating blindly and intensely. Most days you could not jab a pin between the gun-belches. You feel the whole world is being shaken, and, if this goes on for long, will crumble in a welter of blood and hate. It cannot last at this rate: that's the assurance that rises day by day and hour by hour within you. But the assurance is melancholy: how much of either side is going to survive the intensity of it ? What will be the state, when all is over, of the hardly-victorious ?

Monday, —th.—To-day, in nine hours, three divisions were rushed through this town for the —— sector. They came in motor-'buses. At twelve miles an hour they tore through the astonished streets, which got themselves cleared quickly enough. The military police tried to restrain the pace. They were French 'buses driven by Frenchmen who had got a fever of excited speed in their blood. They cleared the military police off the route with impatient gestures, as one waves aside an impertinence. . . . This is mobility.

Feverish processions of this kind are altogether apart from battalions marching, cavalry clattering, engineers lumbering. A fifteen-inch gun, distributed over five steam 'tractors, goes through at midnight

with flares and clamour.   One trusts that such engines
offer compensation for their unwieldiness, for that is
incredible: five gigantic tractors *with* trailers, to move
one of them at this strident snail's pace.   The nine-
point-two's are accommodated each on one tractor.
The field-guns, tossed on to waggons, hurry through,
toys by comparison.

Tuesday, —th.—I was on the —— Road this morning
in the gusty drizzle.   A column of artillery was moving
towards ——.   It was miserable weather for horsed-
transport.   All the men had wry-necks, with the list
against the wind.   The flanks of the officers' horses
were overspread by the voluminous waterproof cape.
At —— there was a horse column encamped.   Nothing
could appear more miserable than the dejected horse
lines in the sea of mud—manes and draggle-tails
blown about in the murk.

A party of ineligible Frenchmen were road-patching
near ——.   The main roads have them at work
always.   They fill the holes and minute valleys that
military traffic makes continuously.   Lorry-holes are
insidious things.   They magnify at an astonishing
rate if left for two days.   They must be treated at
once.   The gangs move up and down the roads with
mobile loads of earth and gravel, treating all the
depressions and maintaining a surface tolerable for
Colonels' cars.   (You can judge the freight of a car
by its speed; the pace of Majors is slightly less fierce
than that of Colonels.   Brigadiers make it killing.)
The road-menders get in where they can between the
flights.   It's a disjointed business, and a mucky one,
this weather.   A Colonel's car-wheels spurt into the
green fields.   The gangers get mottled with the thin

brown fluid. They are a pathetically decrepit folk—
men too old or infirm for the trenches and boys who
are too young. But this work, in this weather, carries
a test almost as severe as that of trench-warfare.

The road-signs—admonitory, hortatory, prohibitive
—are raised at very frequent intervals. Military
routes behind the lines are in a state of continual flux—
to such a degree that road-maps are not only useless,
but misleading, to drivers of vehicles. Their best
course is to ignore the map, watch the road-directions
as they are approached, and use their horse-sense.
Signs are quite explicit: " Closed to lorries and ambulances "; " Closed to traffic in this direction " (arrow-
head). The distance and direction of every village,
however small, is put up with a clearness that ex-
cludes the possibility of error. The location of every
ammunition-dump, supply-dump, railhead, camping-
ground, billeting area, watering-place, intelligence
Headquarters, motor-tyre press (an institution much
in demand), is indicated very exactly. Most other signs
are designed to regulate speed: " Maximum speed
through village —— for lorries and ambulances, ——
for light tractors, —— for cars "; " Danger: cross-
roads "; " Lorry-park; slow down "; " Go slow past
aerodrome to avoid injuring engines through dust."
(Can you conceive British administration in the Army
giving the reason, thus, for an order ?)

Some French signs persist: *Attention aux trains.*

Some signs are not official: " Level crossing ahead:
keep your blood-shot eyes open."

The village streets show signs that have no reference
to speed. Most estaminets publish " English Stout ";
" Good beer 3d., best beer 4d."; " Officers' horses, 10 ";

" Cellar, 50 "—*i.e.*, we have a cellar that will billet fifty men. The villages are very quiet and old-time— grey and yellow walls abutting directly on the roads (footpaths are unknown); thatch or slate roofs; low windows from which, sitting, your feet would touch road; tortuous streets; plentiful girl and women denizens; a wayside Calvary on the outskirts; a church spire rising somewhere from the roofs; a pre- ponderance of taverns, estaminets, cafés, and sweet- shops in the chief street.

Wednesday, —th.—I got some notion this morning of life on the ambulance trains. They move between railhead and the bases with the ebb and flow of the offensive tide. After their load is discharged to a base they garage at a siding erected in this station for the purpose, and await orders. They may rest three days or three hours. Sisters and M.O.'s have lived on the same train—some of them—for twelve or fifteen months, but are too busy to be mutually bored. At the garage you will see them dismounted from the train taking their lunch among the hay-ricks in the harvested field beside the line. An orderly will alight from the train and race across the field, and you'll see the party rise, hastily pitch their utensils incon- tinently into a rug, and climb aboard as the train steams out. The order has come to move up again and " take on." . . . This is one aspect of the state of flux in which the world behind the lines stands day and night, month after month.

At the *gare* here is a canteen for *voyageurs* exclusively. A blatant and prohibitory notice says so with no uncertainty. This is English. An English girl is in charge of it. She gets as little respite as the *chef de gare.* Who can say when she sleeps ? She is supplying tea and cakes and cigarettes to troops every day and every night. No one is refused at any hour, however unhallowed. French railway-stations on the lines of communication all carry such an English girl for such a purpose; and usually they are in the front rank of English aristocracy. The English nobility have not spared themselves for "the Cause." Their men have fallen thick; their women have resigned the luxury of their homes to minister to the pain and the hunger of the force in France. And they do it with a thoroughness apparently incompatible (though only apparently so) with the thoroughgoing luxury and splendour of their civilian way of life.

Thursday, —th.—This afternoon I walked down the river that winds through the town and goes south. It is a comfortable, easy-flowing trout-stream. Beyond the town bridge it turns into pastures and orchards and cultivated fields, nosing a way through stretches of brown stubble, apple-groves, and plantations of beet. Groves of elm and beech overspread the high grass on its brink. The hop clusters with the wild-strawberry and the red currant: a solitary trouter stands beyond the tangle. The fields slope gently away from the stream—very gently—up to the tree-lined road on the ridge. The brown-and-gold stubble rises, acre beyond acre, to the sky-line; and in the evening light takes on a rich investiture of colour that is bold for stubble, but not the less lovely because it is virtual only. As the evening wears on, this settles into a softness of hue that you cannot describe.

Such is the Somme country: such is the land of war.

At nine to-night all the station lights were switched

off. Advice had come from —— of enemy aircraft approaching this junction. They did not come—not to our knowledge. But the *chef de gare* waddled over to his private house and bundled wife and children down into the cellar—and *cave*, as they call it—and when he had seen them safely stowed, returned to his station to await orders. The French girls and women inhabit the cellar with alacrity at such times. Every house has its funk-hole, for there is hardly a dwelling so small as to neglect a vault for *cidre* and *vin ordinaire*. " In the season " they lay up a year's store; as a rule, the *cidre* is home-brewed, too. At table the jug goes round, filling the glass of the *enfant* and the *père* without discrimination. By the end of the meal the colour has mounted in the cheeks of the little girls, and they are garrulous and the boys noisy. Amongst the *cidre* barrels there is good and secure cover from Taubes.

When the lights got switched on again, the detraining of the ——th Division resumed. . . .

Friday —*th.*—I was wakened at two o'clock this morning by the hum of their collective conversation. Sergeants-major were roaring commands in the moonlight; some of them were supplemented by remarks not polite. Many English sergeants-major speak in dialect: most of them do. There is something repellent about words of command issued in dialect. Why can't England cut-out dialect ? It's time it went. Dialect is a very rank form of Conservatism. Why can't a uniform pronunciation of vowels be taught in English schools ? Active-service over a term of years will perhaps help to bring about a standardising of English speech. One hopes so. . . .

I got up and looked out. As far as could be seen along any street, and all over the square, was a faintly mobile sea of black on which danced the glow of the cigarette (damnable, how the cigarette has put out the pipe !). Detachments were still marching from the train to the halting-places, and detachments were moving out momentarily on the night march.

> " Hark, I hear the tramp of thousands,
> And of arméd men the hum."

They moved off—some to drum and fife band; some to the regimental song; some to the regimental whistle; some to the unrhythmic accompaniment of random conversation. The general impression they gave, at two in the morning, was of an abnormal cheerfulness.

A French ambulance-train came in this afternoon crowded with slightly wounded—sitting cases. They were immensely cheerful, though there was not by any means sitting accommodation for all. These were all nice light " Blighty " wounds; they meant respite from the dam'd trenches without dishonour. The fellows were immensely cheered by this. They were more like a train-load of excursionists than a body of wounded warriors from a hell like the Somme. They had hundredweights of German souvenirs. Most of it was being worn—helmets, tunics, arms, and the like. I bought several pieces. They were not expensive. A French Poilu's pay is *cinq sous* (twopence ha'penny) per day: fifteen or twenty francs means about three months' pay for him. He'll part with a lot of souvenir for that. And he has such a bulk of it that a few casques, trench daggers, rifles, and telescopic sights, more or less, are neither here nor there.

The English girls who administer the *gare* canteen move up and down with jugs of coffee. They are thanked (embraced, if they'd stand it) with embarrassing profusion.

Saturday, —st.—Bombs were dropped in the Citadelle moat to-day. The Citadelle is now a casualty clearing station. This is not incongruous with its history. It was besieged in the fifteenth century. No doubt there were casualties within it then—though, judging its defensive properties at this distance of time, there were more without: many more. It's tremendously strong still—an incredible depth of dry moat, thickness of wall, and height of rampart surmounting it: outer ramparts on three sides from which the defenders retired across the bridges—still standing—after they had done their worst. And there are bowels in the place from which galleries set out to neighbouring villages whence reinforcements used to be brought up. You can walk miles in these galleries beneath the Citadelle itself, without journeying beneath the surrounding country; for the ground-plan of the Citadelle is not small. A walk round the walls will lead you a mile and a half, traversing buttresses and all: the buttresses bulge hugely into the moat-bed.

The whole area is terraced, originally for strategic purposes. The buildings are many and strong and roomy.

A fine hospital it happens to have made. The multiplicity of buildings offers all a C.O. could ask in the way of distribution of wards and facilities for segregation, and isolated buildings for stores, messes, Sisters' quarters, officers' quarters, operating-theatres, laboratories.

His convalescents can bask and promenade on the ramparts in the winter sunshine, and stroll healthfully through the groves and about the paths of the area. In the wide level, grassy, moat-basin the orderlies play their football matches and the C.O. takes his revolver practice.

The ghastliness of the wards is all out of harmony with this. There is a gas-ward, hideously filled—blackened faces above the ever-restless coverlets. The surgical wards in a station so near the line hold the grimmest cases—cases too critical for movement down to a base: head wounds, abdominal wounds, spinal cases that can bear transport no farther, and that have almost no hope of recovery as it is. Men plead piteously here for the limbs that a cruelly-kind surgeon can do nothing with but amputate. "Doctor, I've lost the arm; that won't be so bad if you'll only leave the leg." The plea is usually put in this form, which implies the power of choice in the M.O. between alternatives; whereas the gangrenous limb leaves him no room for debate.

In a station so close, too, the operating-theatre cannot afford to be either small or idle—no mere cubicle with two tables; but two large wards with six tables each, and (when a push has been made in the line) with every table in use late in the night: a bloody commentary on the righteousness of war.

CHAPTER IV

THE CAFÉ DU PROGRÈS

THE Café de Progrès stands in the Rue de —— half-way down to the river. It's the place where merchants most do congregate. The manager of the Banque de —— leads them. · The place that the first bank manager in the town frequents daily is thereby given a tone which no other café in D—— can have. So it is the first among the lounging-places only. That leads to a rough division of all the cafés in the town into two great classes: those you lounge and drink in, and those to which you go for a meal. In the one you will see the French relaxing (there are some rich "retired" gentlemen who do nothing *but* relax); in the other you will see the English officer satisfying his hunger more or less incontinently. Need I say which is the place of interest ?

Our favourite seat used to be upon a small dais in recess overlooking the billiard-table immediately and the whole room generally. Its only disadvantage was that it did not overlook that other recess—separated from it by a partition—in which Thérèse mixed the drinks and brewed the coffee.

The billiard-table occupied one-half the room; the other half centred round the stove. The tables were arranged in concentric circles about it. The regular denizens of the place—the men who lived there—

would, during the snow, come early, occupy the innermost circle of tables, and omit to move out until sundown. And sometimes they would stay far into the night. The retired business-man is more amenable to a sense of cosiness than any other mortal of his age. He would get Thérèse to bring him snacks—they were not meals—at intervals during the day. And there he would settle himself, with his boon companions, for twelve hours on end.

Cards is the diversion: cards and dominoes. The habitual inner circle there is made up by the proprietor, the ex-Mayor of the town, *le directeur de la Banque de* ——, and the manager of the *Usine de* ——. The last named used to have inscrutable spells of absence—inscrutable until it was explained that the occasion was the visit of M. —— the elder, himself, from Paris—a man of iron and the proprietor of the *Usine*. He it was who quelled with his own hand and voice an ugly strike of his *ouvriers* who dared ask for more money.

The ex-Mayor was never absent. He was a well preserved old dog whom no severity of weather was allowed to keep from the post of duty by the stove. The whole room was obsequious to him by force of habit. He was the presiding genius over the café: he, rather than the proprietor himself. He would come rolling in, and fairly rattle the glasses with his " *Bonjour, messieurs!* " He usually walked over to the buffet before seating himself, and, if so minded, greeted Thérèse with a fatherly kiss, which she—poor girl!—thought dignified her; whereas Thérèse, to be accurate, was worth far more than the embraces of this pompous old aristocrat. With his intimates he shook hands noisily, and slapped them on the back.

The herd half-rose in its seat throughout the room in traditional deference. I suspect it was the general obsequiousness, rather than the interest of the game, or of the company, which brought the old egoist here daily.

The *directeur* of the bank is not worth considering. He was the incarnation of obsequiousness. It was plain that he had habitually sold his soul to patrons. And since it is likely that at one time the ex-Mayor was his chief patron (and perhaps was so still), you will believe that he was more slavish toward him than the humblest townsman sipping his cognac. You almost looked for him to lick his master's mighty hand.

The proprietor was a sinewy fellow who had been a soldier. It was wounds he had had; which had not, however, incapacitated him for vigorous action. Also, he had been a prisoner of war in Germany. These German experiences he would recount to you with much wealth of gesture, and a wealth of exaggeration too, if by chance—or by design—he were drunk enough. He was in a state of perennial intoxication; at any hour of any day or night it was only a question of degree.

In the game of cards in a French café the stake is superfluous. Englishmen profess they require the stake to hold their interest. Usually the French play with counters only. The interest of the game is enough. It is a very voluble game with them. They excite themselves seemingly beyond all reason. You might imagine them a nest of pirates, inflamed with liquor, playing in some den of the sea with fair captives for stakes. These French enthusiasts upset the drink by thumping down their cards. They have rare disputes; but they are not quarrels.

Thérèse is the girl who carries drinks. She has dimples and a happy smile. French girls are either very free or super-continent; there is no middle course. Thérèse is of the latter class, but not puritanical. Subalterns have been seen attempting to kiss her in the seclusion of a recess. They have been routed. The only occasion on which Thérèse allowed herself to be kissed was New Year's Day. Then it was general. Everyone was doing it—in the street—the merest acquaintances. That day Thérèse submits as a matter of course. That day, too, the ex-Mayor gallantly embraced that old hag, her aunt, to the diversion of the populace.

The aunt brews and dispenses behind the buffet. She objects to Thérèse's loitering when she serves, even though loitering may be good for trade. Thérèse describes her as a very sober-minded woman.

The billiard-table attracts a lot of attention—from onlookers as well as from players. There the *directeur* of the *banque* plays his chief accountant and drinks champagne and *grenadine* between the shots—a poisonous combination, that, but a popular. The French like things sweet, and they like them definitely coloured. The *directeur* is a handsome fellow, with a perfectly balanced head and a curiously pleasing harmony of nose and chin in profile. His accountant is a loose-looking youth.

The billiard-table is a favourite resort of officers' batmen. They have nothing else to do, and they can play half a day for almost nothing at all. I always remember an acute-looking Scotch batman in kilts (servant to the Rents-Officer). He was proud of his calves and of his French—and (justly) of his billiards.

18

He could bring discomfiture upon any Frenchman who would play with him. He is the sort of officer's servant (and there are many of them, the voluptuous dogs!) who could carry a commission with ease and credit. But they prefer the whole days of idleness on which they are free to follow their own devices.

The *facteurs* drop in for a drink on their rounds. They hobnob here a great part of the day, seemingly. And there is poor Marcelle at the pork-shop pining for the letter from her *garçon* in the line which this gossiping dog has in his *serviette* beside the cognac. All *facteurs* are discharged soldiers, and should know better. There is, I fear, but a belated delivery of letters in this easy-going old town.

On market-day the café is filled with *les paysans*, who have come in to vend their pigs and cattle, rabbits, eggs, butter, and vegetables. The elderly ladies from the farms, with their generous growth of moustache, sit and drink neat cognac with a masculinity that is but fitting. The young girls sip white wine. The old men gossip, between draughts, with their pipes trembling in their toothless gums. There are no young men.

CHAPTER V

L'HÔTEL DES BONS ENFANTS

It stands facing the Place de l'Église, with its back to the Route de ——. There is something medieval in its name; so is there in its surroundings and in its appearance. The gargoyles of the Église frown down upon its southern door. There is an old Flemish house facing it in the *Place*. It is Flemish and rambling in design itself. Its stables are low and capacious, like those of a Chaucerian inn. The rooms of the hotel are low-roofed, and each is large enough for an assembly ball. There is an air of generosity about the place. You have the feeling, as you enter, that these people enjoy living; they would have a love of life which is Italian in its deliberateness. They would taste life with a relish.

If you see madame you will be confirmed in this. She is rotund and high-coloured. The placidity of her feature is infectious. As soon as you see her (and it is not long before you will) you want to bask about the place. The pleasantness of her smile will tell you that her first concern is not lucre, but life. She must work to live. But neither work nor the money it brings are ends in themselves for her.

In her day she must have been very well featured. She is still. But rotundity is clouding the lines of her beauty in face and figure. She has a daughter

275

of eight playing in the ante-room. She will be as handsome as her mother has been. She is pretty, with a regularity of feature uncommon in a child so young. A placid nurse-girl has the care of her. She is reading at one of the small round drinking-tables. In fact, it is the domesticity of the place which charms you as much as its quaint architecture. English officers in groups and French officers with their lady friends are entering and taking seats. But madame talks audibly and ·naturally of nursery matters with the nurse; the child herself is engaged upon her *leçon de l'école* beside the buffet, and her nursemaid is at work upon a garment at the same table as two highly-finished Subalterns are taking their aristocratic ease and their Médoc.

But however homely the hotel may be in France, it is rarely free from the blemish of the *upper room*. Officers may dine gaily with their lady friends with as little obstruction from the management as is offered to the payment of the bill.

We had our Christmas dinner at the Bons Enfants. It was not home, but it was very jolly. Jolly is the word rather than happy. At home the grub would not have been French. There would have been sisters (and others) with whom to make merry afterwards. And we would (we hope) have been served by someone less unlovely than the well-meaning middle-aged woman whom madame detailed to wait upon our table. But we sang long and loud in chorus; and afterwards went into the hall and took possession of the piano and danced with each other; and those who couldn't dance improvised some sort of rhythmic evolutions about the room. At any rate, we were gay. We were determined that absence from home was not going to seem to make us sad. And perhaps some of us forced the merriment rather obviously. But madame, I believe, thought we were completely happy. She came and shook us all by the hand at parting, and gave us good wishes, and was happy she should have helped us so far to Christmas jollity in " a furrin clime." Someone reproached her with the plebeian features of our waitress when we had got out into the shelter of the street, and someone—I forget who—kissed her (*i.e.*, madame) in the shadow of the porch; and she gave a gentle little scream of delight, retrospective of the days of her blooming youth when she was more prone to thoroughgoing reciprocity.

We returned some weeks later. Someone of the mess had a birthday, and went down in the morning to madame and in the sunny courtyard talked to her intimately of pullets, and *poisson*, and *boisson*, and *omelettes*, and wafers, and cheeses, and fruits; returned to the mess before lunch, furtively countermanded the standing orders amongst the servants for the evening meal, and at lunch flung out a general invitation to the Bons Enfants at eight. We lived again through the Christmas festivities—with the difference that madame detailed a less unhandsome wench to wait on table; and that we left earlier.

PROVINCIAL SHOPS

ALL *magasins* of any standing are served by pretty girls. This is a point of policy. Proprietors of French shops in the towns of the War area have come to know that the man to whom they sell is largely the English officer in rest about the town or on his way through it. He also knows enough of the psychology of the English officer to be sure that if his shop is known to be served by pretty girls, the officer who has been segregated from women for three months will enter, ostensibly to purchase, actually to talk with the girls; also that every time he wishes to see pretty girls he will make a purchase the pretext, and will not be dismayed by the frequency of his purchases nor by their price. To the officer from the line feminine intercourse is reckoned cheap at the price of socks and ties.

They know the temper of the man in rest from the trenches; he will have what he likes, and hang the price. So they ask what they like, and get it. This is, of course, hard on the man permanently stationed in the town; but it is not for him they cater. And even should he refuse to buy at all, it is nothing to them. They can batten on the traveller and the man in rest, and they do.

The best-remembered shops in D—— are the provision shop (agent for Félix Potin), the newspaper shop opposite the Hôtel de Ville, the boot shop in the Rue ——, the pipe shop in the Rue ——.

Félix Potin's agency is proprieted by a masterful woman, extremely handsome and well-figured. She is consciously proud of this as she sits at the receipt of custom and directs the policy. She is a very able business woman. She is never baffled by the smallest detail referred to her by an underling. She knows the price of the smallest bottle of perfume (though there she may, of course, be improvising—and with safety). If stock has been exhausted in any commodity she knows when its reinforcements will arrive from Paris. She herself does the Parisian buying. The whole town knows when she has been to Paris, and when she will be going next. She makes a knowledge of these buying-excursions intimate to all her considerable patrons. Her periodical trips are parochial events. You will hear one officer say to another in an English mess: " Oh, Madame —— is off to Paris on Sunday;" or, " Madame —— will be back to-morrow." This is very flattering, and very good for business.

But she purchases well. There is the finest array of perfumes and soaps, champagne and liqueurs, cakes and biscuits, chocolates, Stilton and Gruyère, eggs and butter, almonds and chestnuts. It is Félix Potin in little, with all the richness of Félixian variety and quality. If it's wine you are buying, she'll take you below to the cellars; that's a rich and vivifying spectacle. The whole shop is shelved, desked, and finished with an appearance of distinction; the windows are dressed with a taste and an avoidance of super-crowding that would grace the Rue de la Paix. The whole *magasin* is in a class beyond compare with any other shop in D——. It puts one in the dress-circle to purchase a box of chocolates there. But in the interests of finance he had far better make the purchase at the Expeditionary Force Canteen. At the canteen you pay neither for the atmosphere of the place nor for the expense of importation from Paris.

The stationer's shop opposite the Hôtel de Ville gets the English newspaper daily. Towards evening there is an incessant stream of privates, N.C.O's, and Staff-Officers asking for the daily sheet from England. "' Delly Mell,' m'sieur ?—pas encore arrivée." (The voyageur arrives late in these parts.) It's with difficulty you can elbow your way about this shop at most hours of the afternoon. Soldiers who call for the paper loiter, attracted by the post-cards or the range of English novels. The post-cards are spread out in an inciting array. They are Parisian in their frankness.

Everyone knows the boot shop. There are four boot shops in D——. But when you speak of the boot shop there is no doubt in the mind of the company which is the shop referred to, because the prettiest girl in D—— is there. When an officer appears in the street with new boots (though he guilelessly bought them at Ordnance) his friends will say: " Ha ! did she try them on for you ? Was she long about it ? It's a pretty pair of shoulders, n'est-ce pas ?" It is but fitting that the shop with the prettiest girl in D—— should be the most expensive. So it is. Better go barefooted unless you have " private means " or can get access to an Ordnance clothing store—or (better still) get an " issue."

But who can avoid the tobacconist's in the Rue —— ? One must have a well-finished pipe now and then, and the widow's daughter is handsome and speaks a kind of English. In accordance with the French usage, madame, as a widow, has been given this tobacco shop by the State. Had she been daughterless, or had her daughter been unlovely, she would have imported some *jolie demoiselle*. But she had no need. Marie Thérèse fills the rôle. And Marie Thérèse is kept busy by a genuine queue of purchasers. For this is the shop where small purchases are most excusable, and in any case it is an easy matter to ask for an impossible brand of tobacco and listen with feigned amazement to Marie Thérèse's pretty, well-gestured regrets that she has it not. But she has other. But you explain how you are a purist, and none other will do. And if the shop is not busy—which is seldom indeed—such explanations can be made elaborate and prolonged, and Marie Thérèse can be made intelligently interested in the inscrutable whims of thoroughgoing smokers. But the damsel is not all guileless. If it is your ill-fortune that she has what you ask, you pay well and truly. And Marie Thérèse knows as well as you (though neither says so) that you have paid for the repartee.

BILLING AND SONS, LTD., PRINTERS, GUILDFORD, ENGLAND

Lightning Source UK Ltd.
Milton Keynes UK
UKHW032011280119
336360UK00013B/1603/P